THE DRAGON SOLDIER'S
GOOD FORTUNE

The Dragon Soldier's Good Fortune

Robert Goswitz

OPEN ROAD

INTEGRATED MEDIA
NEW YORK

Copyright © 2018 by Robert Goswitz

ISBN: 978-1-5040-8871-8

This edition published in 2024 by Open Road Integrated Media, Inc.
180 Maiden Lane
New York, NY 10038
www.openroadmedia.com

This book is dedicated to my lovely wife Jody, my first reader and best listener—she who knows my thoughts before I think them.

THE DRAGON SOLDIER'S GOOD FORTUNE

Dulce bellum inexpertis.
"War is sweet to those who have not tried it."

—Erasmus

The mouths of the righteous utter wisdom,
And their tongues speak what is just.
The law of their God is in their hearts;
Their feet do not slip.

—Psalm 37

PROLOGUE

Quang Nam Province, Republic of South Vietnam,
August 9, 1972

The muzzle flash of the Degtyaryov fifty-one-caliber heavy machine gun lit the air like a small lightning strike, piercing the green screen of banana trees separating the gun from two GIs crawling toward it.

Ed Lansky and Israel Nunez rested at the edge of the trees listening to the fifty-one's hot brass ping the dirt during the uncommon wrath of each thunderous volley. Nunez pointed at Lansky's watch, held up two fingers then crawled along the tree line curving out of sight.

Lansky watched Nunez crawl away, unsure of what to do next. He needed to create a distraction, that was the plan, but what that would be he did not know. As Nunez snaked past the hole where the big gun had been buried until this, the last day, he could still feel the concussion released by each round.

The three-man Viet Cong gun crew had his patrol pinned down in the rice paddy behind him.

As he moved along, Nunez said a short prayer of gratitude to his Salt River Pima ancestors. They had visited his dreams often, and he now knew what they wanted. In these dreams, Nunez

5

was welcomed into a traditional willow branch and thatch hut joining a circle of his ancestors sitting around a fire. The fire was smoky, obscuring his vision, but he thought he saw his great-great-grandfather in warrior face paint rise and thrust a black lance into and out of the fire. The tale told about this iconic weapon was that his great-great-grandfather had used it to kill Apache at the Battle of Tempe Butte.

The lance was passed to his great uncle dressed in the blue uniform and yellow neckerchief of a US Army cavalry scout. His uncle admired the craftsmanship of the lance, its charcoal-colored oak shaft with blue quartz inlay and the shiny black obsidian spearhead attached to the shaft with fine copper wire. The obsidian blade was still sharp and ready for another battle.

Uncle passed the lance to Nunez's grandfather, a World War I veteran wounded at Belleau Wood. Grandfather was dressed in his Doughboy uniform with a row of medals above his left breast pocket. He raised the lance over his head and let out a lusty war whoop echoed by the others.

The lance was passed to Nunez's father dressed in the US Marine Corp battle gear of World War II. His father had told his son of being halfway up Mt. Suribachi on Iwo Jima when a group of GIs, including Ira Hayes, also a Salt River Pima, raised the Stars and Stripes.

Passed man-to-man, generation-to-generation, the lance was now held out reverently for Nunez to take. He always lost sight of the dream scene here, feeling suddenly cold and lonely, hurled into a deep darkness, free-falling through time. This falling sensation woke him with his heart pounding, short of breath, and a feeling of confusion.

He stopped crawling for a moment to examine the black stock, black pistol grip, and black hand-guard of his M-16. This was his obsidian lance. It had been given to him to silence the gun and square the circle. His ancestors had granted him the blood and iron to take the fifty-one out.

Now forty yards behind the gun, he worked his body into a comfortable firing position. Looking down the barrel, he lined up the rear sight notch with the forward sight bead and swung it onto the gun pit. The enemy gunners were hidden below the gun pit berm. The shot he wanted wasn't there yet. His squad was getting hammered and running out of time. Nunez now saw that his plan was a mistake.

It depended on Lansky to create a distraction that would pop the VC out of their hole. This would give Nunez his kill shot, but so far Lansky had not moved. Still concealed in the banana trees, Nunez stood to see how his patrol was surviving. He thought about charging the gun pit but hesitated, hoping Lansky would do his part. If Lansky didn't get going soon, Nunez would have to seize the initiative.

Sergeant Tiny jumped out of the far rice paddy, sprinted across the broad dike, and disappeared into the next paddy. It looked like he was going to try to flank the big gun not knowing Nunez and Lansky had already done it.

Tracers from the fifty-one arced toward Tiny but arrived too late. A long angry burst blasted the dike uselessly, the gun jammed with a loud clang.

Nunez heard excited voices jabbering in the gun pit, exhorting the gunner as he wrenched the bolt forward and back to clear the jam.

Vernon Huddle flopped out of the far paddy and joined Tiny by leaping across the dike. The bolt banged forward as Charles Laughton jumped out of the water, trying to follow Tiny and Huddle.

A short burst bracketed Laughton's legs. One of the rounds made contact taking his feet from under him. He spiraled head over heels onto the paddy dike, his weapon turning in the air and landing in the water. Huddle leapt from the protective cover of the paddy dike, snatched Laughton, and began dragging him to safety. The Viet Cong gun crew responded by firing a long volley of accurate fire toward the two Americans.

CHAPTER 1

September 7, 1971

A sly look sparked a nasty comment, gasoline on the flame of intolerance. Racial angst exploded. First one, then two, then a throng of black GIs leapt to their feet, blood in their eyes. White soldiers rose in a rage, fists balled in anger. Chairs flew, tables slammed on concrete. Wild punches cut the dense humidity. The fury of the effort made most swings miss. Men rolled on the floor; jumped through the air; kicked a downed adversary; shouted cries of pain, of fear, of loneliness—a primal roar. Table after table of GIs in the midnight chow hooch joined the brawl.

Deep into his first night in Vietnam, Private Ed Lansky felt surrounded by darkness. He'd plodded through his midnight KP detail in a weary languor, sleep-deprived, jetlagged, and sunburned.

Now he stood behind the food service counter next to the cook, Sergeant Chen, eyes ablaze, spooked out of his lassitude, watching the first action of his war.

Five MPs ran into the open-sided mess hooch, M-16s at port arms. One of them fired three rounds through the corrugated aluminum roof.

Most of the combatants stopped. One lone couple continued, a black guy had bulldogged a white guy to the floor, too angry to release his headlock, until the MPs separated them.

The white boy stood furious, glaring embarrassed that all eyes were on him. He breathed heavily, and his short hair stood on end.

A sergeant's bark broke the silence. "All right, you assholes. Fall out!"

Both sides were herded away, across the sand in two separate groups, and faded into the night.

Lansky said, "Are they going to lock all those guys up?"

Sergeant Chen smiled at Lansky. "No, FNG, they're going to yell at them then put them back on perimeter guard duty, those guys are our palace guard."

"Okay, that's a little frightening. Hey, why do you keep calling me FNG?" Feeling nettled, Lansky exhaled loudly.

"Because that's what you are, a Fucking New Guy who don't know nothing."

Lansky towered over Chen and outweighed him by thirty pounds, but looking down on the stout little mess sergeant made him realize confrontation was a mistake. The hard edge in Lansky's green eyes faded to acceptance. Respect was earned here, not given. He wiped perspiration from his broad forehead and subtle brow.

Sergeant Chen chuckled then stepped closer to Lansky. "Now, FNG, we also are of two different races, are we going to have our own little riot?"

Lansky leaned back. "No, no, we aren't."

"Good choice, FNG, good choice."

Lansky and Chen straightened up the chairs and tables, mopped the floor, and began putting away the leftovers.

As they rinsed the pots and pans, Lansky looked at Chen. "Maybe I didn't notice, but what were they fighting about?"

"Probably nothing. All it takes is a few wrong looks, and we got a race war on our hands. It's happened a couple times before. They come in from guard duty where they had a lot of time to think about how lonely they are. Puts them in a bad mood. They may be high. Blacks hold a grudge for being here to fight whitey's war. Some whites are prejudiced, but most are so self-absorbed they don't give a damn about the black man's anger. Those guys took a stand tonight, took a stand for the wrong reasons, in the wrong place, at the wrong time, but I admire them for drawing a line in the sand. What about you, Mr. Newbie, have you decided how you'll take your stand?"

"What do you mean?"

"Look." Chen lifted his left arm in front of Lansky's face. A long, intricate, red dragon tattoo wound down his arm. The dragon had large eyes, a long snout, flared nostrils, a scaled snake body, and bat wings. It rose in the air with a fish in its mouth above a lotus pond. "Are you a dragon or a fish?"

Lansky looked confused.

Chen turned his right arm into view and rolled up the sleeve on his T-shirt. On his right bicep, Chen displayed a golden dragon with a salamander body and large orange eyes that stared down his arm at a small musk deer. "Are you a dragon or a deer? Dragons eat deer."

"Sorry, Sarge, I'm a little overwhelmed at this point. Didn't sleep on the plane last night. I've been awake about thirty-six hours. I'm too frazzled to think."

Chen seemed amused. "That's okay. I may have something for that. Got a guy coming by here in about ten minutes to get me high. Maybe a little reefer would help you settle down and see my point."

"What about all the MPs that were just in here? Isn't it risky?"

"Listen, FNG, we run this place. I do this every night. It's no problem. Nobody will be around."

"I don't know."

"My man will be here soon. Let's go out for a breath of fresh air."

Lansky had lost his capacity for rational evaluation; anxiety had diminished his faculties. He didn't feel good about taking a risk, yet the fight in him was gone. Take a stand? He wasn't *capable* of resistance.

The screen door whacked shut as they slipped out the side of the secured kitchen area. A yellow fingernail moon glowed in an ebony sky. A sprinkling of stars flickered in the background. Crickets chirped, and moths swarmed the floodlights over the mess hall.

They waded through the sand to the 600-gallon trailer known as a water buffalo and shared a drink, using the same cup.

Someone approached them in the dark.

Chen called out, "That you, Whitey?"

"Affirmative."

Lansky turned to see a blond-haired GI in a tie-dyed T-shirt, jeans, and flip-flops standing in the dark. He stepped into the perimeter of light. Whitey's hair glowed. Even in the dim light, it was bright, shiny, and sun-bleached. An irregular part ran across the left side of his scalp. This unsteady line continued down across his face, where vague shadows gathered in the pockets created by the rise and fall of the line as it formed the obtuse chin, cheeks, and lip. It was as if that sliver of a moon had magically transported this man from some sunny San Diego street to this spot.

"White-man, meet an FNG," said Chen.

"Hey, FNG, welcome to Cam Rahn Bay."

"Yeah, well, can't say I'm glad to be here. How do you get away with being outta uniform?"

"Just like Stateside at Cam Rahn, man. Long as I do my job, I don't get no hassles. After hours, I can wear anything I want."

"Told you we run this place. Hey, Whitey, think we should let old FNG here do some dew with us?" Chen smiled.

"Never can tell about an FNG, might fuck up. How about we have him stand a coupla' meters down range in case he blows up while we're smokin'?" Whitey laughed.

Lansky didn't.

"Yeah, never can be too cautious when you're a short-timer. Hey, Whitey, how short are you, again?"

"Fifty-one and a wake-up!"

"Oh, not bad, but don't beat me, I'm forty-two and a wake-up."

They looked at Lansky.

"Well, if you mean how many days do I have left, I've got about three hundred sixty-four and a wake-up."

"Nooo, nooo, nooo, FNG, fuckin' up again. You've been here one day, so it's three hundred sixty-three and a wake-up." Chen smiled. "You never count the last day."

They all laughed.

"Not so bad now, is it?"

"Makes me feel a whole lot better." Lansky was catching up to their irony.

"Well, we're all gonna feel better in a minute. C'mon, Whitey, quit shamin'!"

Whitey pulled a blackened tobacco pipe and a small bag with brownish green herb from his pocket.

They looked around carefully, then Chen gave Whitey a light and the pipe went around, each man bringing the embers to a glow. Great bursts of smoke filled the air around them. The drug took effect immediately.

Lansky felt as if he was floating above the scene, dangling in the air, relaxed, looking down on the three figures, a birds-eye view. Those creatures down there didn't have a care in the world, their problems seemed small, concerns were remote, and troubles were floating away. Conversation was free and loose, laughter came easy, a moment of peace.

Chen relit the pipe for Whitey. Then it happened. Lansky's floating dream was shot down by three armed figures moving quickly around the corner of the mess hall. Back on earth, he noticed a pistol pointed at his nose.

Whitey froze next to him. Chen was gone, and a loud ruckus was building in the mess hall. The pistol sharpened Lansky's perception of the scene coldly and quickly as he observed the MP holding the weapon, aimed at him. A kid no older than nineteen with rimless glasses stood under the helmet.

"Don't move! Put your hands up! You're under arrest."

Lansky slowly obliged, looking dumbly at Whitey, who appeared very calm.

Lansky attempted to fight through his fear, to size up the situation. He had nothing illegal on him, but Whitey did. The running and shouting in the mess hall meant Chen had taken off with the pipe.

Two of the MPs were chasing him. They waited, silently listening to the scuffle of boots and curses as the MPs struggled with Chen.

Lansky studied the MP who stood uneasily in front of him: a curly-headed, skinny weed-of-a-boy, twitchy, unable to hold his weapon steady.

The look on this child's face was one of jittery resignation that belied the police uniform and pistol.

Whitey must have also noticed a crack in his façade. "Hey, mind if I get a drink of water at the buffalo over there?"

"What? No, don't move!" The kid shifted his weight nervously.

"Hey, you got us, man, I'm not going to try anything, my stomach's upset, and I want a drink of water, okay?"

The kid looked into the mess hall where the scuffling had stopped, yet loud voices continued to echo out the door. He looked at them, unsure of what to do.

"Okay, but don't try nothing."

"Thanks, man."

Whitey strolled across the sand, picked up the ceramic coffee cup on the trailer hitch, and turned himself a drink from the spigot. The trailer sat on the perimeter of floodlight illumination. Whitey had the pocket containing the bag of grass turned away from the MP, and his hand rested on his hip just above it.

The MP's concentration was now split between two points.

Sipping slowly, Whitey snaked his hand into his pocket, with two fingers pinching the bag.

The kid watched him closely but occasionally turned back to look at Lansky. Whitey's hand lifted the bag from his pocket and dropped it outside the perimeter. The MP missed it or chose not to pursue it.

Lansky and Whitey exchanged a brief deadpan glance of relief, then Whitey walked back toward them. Shouting voices moved closer.

The handcuffed Chen kicked the screen door open as he was dragged and pushed out of the mess hall. "Told you why I ran! Told you three times! We had a big race riot in the mess hall tonight. When I saw them guns, I thought it was blacks coming back to get us."

The prisoners were lined up in a row.

A short, intense-looking sergeant released his grip on Chen and holstered his .45. He lit his pipe, and the match flame illuminated bright black eyes, triumphant, pulsing with the excitation of the kill. "So what were you doing out here tonight?"

As he spoke, the sound traveled through the pipe, giving his words a reedy lisp.

"Takin' some air after midnight chow, Sarge," said Whitey.

A sarcastic grin came over the sergeant's face. He sucked saliva through the pipe stem, confident, juices flowing.

"You're under arrest for suspicion of smoking marijuana. Hardesty, take 'em back to headquarters, get some ID, and file 'em. I'm going to inspect the scene."

"Yes, Sergeant Snuflewicz!"

They were marched through the dark. Waves of fear and soporific disorientation swirled in Lansky's brain. A large green form flashed over his head, the air disturbed by the flap of a wing. When he looked up, he saw nothing but stars in the night sky. *Now I've gone too far*, he thought. *I'm seeing things.*

At HQ, they were searched, questioned again, and placed in holding cells—a series of wood frame and chicken wire cages. Each man had a separate cell, but only two had a thin mattress on the floor.

Chen's did not. He protested vehemently. "Hey, what-the-fuck? I'm ten months in country. I should get a mattress before an FNG!"

The large, sleepy, black guard looked at Lansky.

"You an FNG?"

"Yeah."

"Gimme that mattress." He opened the door.

Lansky couldn't believe it. He handed the mattress to the guard and sat on the concrete, staring ahead, dazed by the accumulated trials of the day.

Chen and Whitey whispered about the details of the story.

Occasionally, Chen would slide over and update Lansky. "Remember, say as little as possible, just a couple of dudes appreciating the moon, okay? It's no sweat. Whitey dumped his bag before he was searched, and I dumped the pipe in a big vat of fry oil. We're clean. And by the goddamned way, FNG, can you now see what I was talking about? You need to take a stand. I have my dragons to protect me, what do you have?"

"When we were being marched in here, did you see anything fly over us?"

Chen looked confused. "What are you talking about?"

"Something big flew over my head, it was green."

"No, I didn't see anything. You need some rest."

After thinking about it for a while, Lansky decided Chen was right. His brain was fried, and he must be hallucinating.

Time to focus on survival. He wasn't going to let the army or hallucinations get the better of him. This dark moment was a temporary condition, a pause in the flow of bright circumstance that found him when he needed it. Lansky believed himself the beneficiary of a natural law granting him a life filled with seren-dipity. Things didn't always go his way, but the steady accumu-lation of happy coincidence favoring him was well established. People noticed that his card fell at the right time, the wheel stopped on his number, his line drive to left landed just fair, and a stroll down Main Street got him a warm kiss. Currently, he was an infantry replacement in jail on his first night in country, but if he waited patiently, this too would change.

At some point, Lansky found sleep.

CHAPTER 2

September 8, 1971

The morning of Lansky's second day in Vietnam brought a large MP to his cell with a pair of handcuffs.

"Get up, hold your hands out, I'm taking you to breakfast."

Managing a breakfast tray with handcuffs was a new experience for Lansky; facing the quiet stares of the GIs in the mess hall was also different.

He looked at his two eggs sunny-side up with a curled strip of bacon below them, a happy face breakfast. Lansky smiled, this day would bring a change in his luck.

The MP eyed him, wary of the sudden change. "Now listen, dude. Don't go flaky on me. Hear?"

"Don't worry. I'm okay."

"I wanna have a peaceful breakfast. So just hang on."

"I'll be okay."

"Yeah, you stay cool."

Sergeant Snuflewicz was waiting for him outside the MPHQ when they returned. He had Chen and Whitey handcuffed and sitting in the back of the jeep.

"Get in the jeep. We're going in for your arraignment." The

night hadn't been kind to the weary-looking sergeant. He'd lost his swagger.

Whitey and Chen sat expressionless until the jeep started moving. When they were sure Snuflewicz was looking else-where, they exchanged the gallant glances of men with a cause. Chen looked at Lansky, the weak link, the FNG. Lansky looked back, straight and level, to reassure him.

The jeep sped along a beach road, passing brightly colored fishing boats moored in the bay. The water so translucent, the sandy bottom so white, the reflected sunlight so brilliant, it gave the illusion that the green, yellow, and blue boats were floating on air. Palm-covered islands dotted the far shore. The bay curved back on itself, ending in magnificent marble head-lands protecting the harbor. Dark mountains, obscured by morning haze, rose in the distance.

They passed oceangoing ships moored at deep-water docking stations. Giant cranes towered over the docks. Shipping containers stacked twelve high stood in long rows. Truck traffic slowed the jeep to a crawl as they followed a semi hauling a tank.

A gasoline tanker convoy passed in the opposite direc-tion. The first truck in the convoy was a deuce and a half with twin fifty-caliber machine guns mounted in the bed. A gun shield on the fifty had the word PERDITION painted across the top.

Chen tapped Lansky's shoulder, pointing at a road sign.

Drive Carefully
DON'T
Maim or Kill
Your Replacement!

They all smiled a momentary reprieve from the growing tension.

Turning off the main road, they entered the village. The jeep was stopped by a Vietnamese Army military policeman directing traffic from the top of a sandbagged bunker in the middle of an intersection. An M-60 machine gun poked out of the gun port.

Lansky looked into the market along the road. Hanging butchered animal carcasses caught his eye. They were about the size of dogs. A young butcher's helper swatted the air around the hanging meat, attempting to shoo the black flies away.

People pressed around the jeep. The ARVN MP signaled them to proceed. As the jeep inched ahead, Lansky swiveled around to scan the market, handcuffs dangling over the side of the crowded jeep.

A boy, no taller than the side of the jeep, ran up and grabbed Lansky's wristwatch. Lansky pulled away quickly and glared at Chen. "They try and steal your watch right off your wrist?"

"That's right, FNG. Be careful in the vil."

"Quiet back there!" yelled Snuflewicz.

Rows of barbed wire and guard towers came up on the right.

They passed through a heavily guarded entrance and drove up to a squat row of cinder-block buildings with CONEX shipping containers attached to the side. A large yellow sign with red letters proclaimed:

1st Company, 3rd Battalion
276th Military Police Headquarters
"Proud to Serve"

The sergeant signaled Lansky and the others out of the jeep. He then ran ahead, leaving the prisoners waiting at the door with the driver.

Snuflewicz walked across a red cement floor to an MP perched behind an elevated desk. The platform supporting the desk was so high that Sergeant Snuflewicz had to stand on his toes to hand the brief up to the man in charge. A large black and white wooden plaque depicting the Scales of Justice hung from the front of the desk, and an electric fan with blue blades pivoted mechanically, sending a strong breeze across the desk rattling the papers.

The desk sergeant dialed the fan back, skimmed the brief, then looked up with an acidic stare that melted some of Lansky's resolve.

"Hey, Snuffy, little bit of overkill here?" Last night's gin, the morning heat, and a disorganized brief conspired to give the desk sergeant a case of the ass.

"Just trying to get down all the facts and details."

"I'm going to need some time to go over these, Snuf. Put 'em in number three until I'm ready."

"Yes, Sergeant." Snuflewicz quickly escorted his charges along a row of iron doors with paper numbers over them. He ushered Lansky and the others into a hot metal box with small slits cut into the wall, allowing the morning sun to beat directly on them.

"This is a cell?" Lansky was astonished.

"This is CONEX, used as a cell."

The answer came from a pallid figure slumped in the corner. He was dressed in black pajama pants, Ho Chi Minh sandals, and a Three Musketeers-style puffy white shirt open to the waist. He smelled like a dead fish. Shoulder-length hair and absolutely white skin told Lansky this guy hadn't spent a minute in the sun in the last three months.

"Where you been?" Chen asked.

"Been gone. I duffed, took off, couldn't take the hassle, had me this little girl-san in the vil that I hid out with. Was great at first, but I couldn't go anywhere. If I went out during the day, the MPs would see me. If I went out at night, the VC would kill me. Matter of fact, they found out about me and were plannin' on gettin' me. So my girl and I tried to sneak out to her folks' vil, but the local militia intercepted us and turned me over to the MPs."

"How long you been gone?"

"'Bout six months, as best as I can guess. What month is it, anyway?"

"September."

"Guess I could be home by now, but I couldn't take the damn lifers hasslin' me."

"You're lookin' at a long time in Long Binh Jail, man," said Whitey.

"Yeah, don't wanna do no time in LBJ. I'm gonna duff again, if I can. This time for good. Me and my girl got a plan. We're gonna smuggle me out to her folks' place. It's gonna be Number One out there, man. I'm gonna be a rice farmer."

Chen stared at the man. "A rice farmer! Who you kiddin'? You wouldn't last a week in those paddies! You couldn't take the sun, the work, or the pay."

"My girl will get me through. Hey, we been through a lot already. She's great! She knows how to get over. We'll make it!"

"What about the VC?" asked Whitey. "You gotta know by now they got cadre in every vil. How you gonna live in the bush and avoid the VC? You ain't got a chance."

"My girl's old man is a big honcho in his vil. They have their own militia, no VC. We got connections. Believe me, it's gonna work out! It really is."

Lansky dead-panned him. "You mean you don't care if you get back home?" He couldn't imagine a life without his home.

The man gave no immediate response, but mentioning home

made his head start sinking. It stopped between his knees, the oily hair forming a perfect curtain. Then sitting upright, he smoothed his hair back with both hands. "Fuck the States! I was always in trouble there anyway. I'm from LA, lived on the streets all my life. It was a bitch, man. It's a lot better over here. Life is simple. I got my girl here, and she's really great. You should see her, she's beautiful. I never had nothin' like her back in the world. When we get out to her vil, we're gonna get married and live with her family. It's a whole different thing over here. They all live together and help one another. Her old man already sent word he wants her to quit her job at the post-exchange and come back home. She's gonna work out something with him so I can be a big honcho out there, too. Hey, really, it's my only chance for a good life. It's only Long Binh that's in the way."

"Only? Huh! You're nuts!" Chen shook his head in disgust. "You ain't gettin' outta LBJ for months. Girl-san will be long gone by then. She'll be back there livin' in that vil with some VC cadre, man. You're nuts."

The deserter stared off. He wasn't listening. The door rattled open.

"Okay, you're first, Thalacker." As the door clanged shut, Chen and Lansky crouched behind it to listen.

The desk sergeant read the charge against Walter "Whitey" Thalacker. It soon became clear Snuflewicz had confused the accused and their roles in the crime.

"So, you're the cook?" asked the desk sergeant.

"No, Sergeant, I'm a clerk."

"Clerk! Hey, Snuffy, c'mere. You got this guy mixed up with someone else. This Thalacker, Walter J., SP-Four, is the clerk. The other guy . . . lemme see here . . . the guy Chen, George C., E-Five, you got him down as the clerk."

Snuflewicz sounded embarrassed. "Musta got 'em confused."

"Yeah, you musta. Now let's get it straight. Who was the cook accused of holding the pipe, and who was the clerk accused of holding the bag?"

"Well, I guess Chen was the cook with the pipe and Thalacker was the clerk with the bag."

The desk sergeant flipped noisily through the volume of pages. "You got this all fucked up, Snuffy. Gonna have to do it again. Lemme see if I can straighten it out. Okay. Thalacker, what the hell were you doing last night, at oh-two-hundred in back of the mess hall?"

"Well, sir, I was out walking, couldn't sleep. I'm a short-timer and being this close to the end of my tour makes me nervous."

"Do you deny possession of the bag and smoking the marijuana?"

"Too short for that, Sarge."

"Yeah, okay . . . Gawddamn, Snuffy, you got this paperwork fucked up. Get the other one out here. Get Chen."

Chen and Whitey passed each other in the doorway. As the door closed, Whitey put his fist to his mouth and guffawed silently. Luck was on their side.

Lansky and Whitey hunched behind the door, listening to the desk sergeant questioning Chen. He spent more time asking Snuflewicz about the report than he did Chen about his pipe.

"Cheez, Snuf, I can't make anything out of these reports!"

"I'll square 'em away today and have them back in the morning."

"You better, ain't no doubt in my military mind this case is out the window unless you quit fuckin' up. Okay, may as well talk to the witness you brought . . . Hey, Snuf, you got your witness in the cell?" The desk sergeant sounded weary. "Why'd you lock up your witness, Snuf?"

"Oh, he's not a witness, Sarge. He's one of the accused, the FNG."

"You got him down here as Lansky, Edward R., PFC, a witness."

"No, that's wrong." Lansky heard humiliation in Snuflewicz's voice. "He's one of the accused. I made a mistake."

"You're the mistake, Snuf. Get him out here, will ya?" The desk sergeant smoothed his hair repeatedly.

Lansky attempted to compose himself, although his face was flushed. He stood under the desk sergeant's gaze, dumb, playing his role as the FNG. He wasn't laughing now.

"Straighten us out, young troop." The desk sergeant measured Lansky. "What's your story?"

"Well, uh, I only been in country twenty-four hours, I was on sand patrol all day yesterday, KP all night. We had a riot in the mess hall. I take a break, and the next thing I know I'm in the chicken cage." The craziness of his story made Lansky blanch.

The desk sergeant stared at Lansky with a cool regard. Lansky returned the look, not knowing what else to do. His heart rate increased.

"So, twenty-four hours in country, and you're in handcuffs?"

"Yes, Sergeant." Lansky was growing uneasy sweat darkened his fatigue shirt.

He was a terrible liar. The desk sergeant's stare made him uncomfortable. Lansky felt overmatched in an unfamiliar arena. He realized for the first time what trouble he was in when the desk sergeant said, "So, twenty-four hours in country, and you're in handcuffs?"

How could he survive a year when one day had become such a test? He looked up as the sergeant spoke.

"Well, when they were passing the pipe around, you didn't take any? Right?"

"Pipe, Sarge? What pipe? I didn't see a pipe." The words came out before Lansky realized he'd just avoided a trap. He exhaled quietly.

"Hmmm. That'll be all. Get this mess straight, Snuffy, and get the hell outta here. Next case."

CHAPTER 3

September 8, 1971

The heat of the day peaked in the chicken wire cages at Military Police Headquarters. Lying on the concrete floor, Ed Lansky snored so loud he woke himself up.

An officer arrived and told the three prisoners they were being released to await court-martial.

Lansky's deployment in country would wait on the results of his trial. Since deployment meant an infantry assignment, he took this as good news. The roller coaster of emotion that had taken him so low suddenly surged upward.

Stumbling into the sunlight, Lansky squinted at Chen and Whitey, not sure of what to do.

"Hey, Chen, the FNG handled himself pretty well this morning, didn't he?" Whitey smiled at Lansky.

"He did, they tried to crack him, but he danced around it." Chen broke out with a friendly grin.

"So technically speaking, he's not an FNG anymore because he didn't fuck up."

"You're right, White Man, so I guess we can't call him FNG anymore."

Whitey looked at Lansky. "What the hell is your name?"

"Lansky. I'm Ed Lansky from Wisconsin."

"Well, Mister Ed, since you're one of us, how about hooching in our barracks?"

"That would be great." Lansky smiled at Whitey.

"Yeah, you're gonna live in air-conditioned comfort."

They slogged off toward the enlisted men's barracks that housed the support company. Lansky noticed that these barracks were newly built and each room had an air conditioner in the window.

Once inside, smiling faces emerged.

"Got busted, hey, Chen?"

"I'm free now," he said, striding toward his room.

"Hey, everybody, Gorgeous George and White Man are out of the slammer!"

The first man into Chen's room asked, "How'd you get out so fast?"

"They got nothin' on us! Let's party, man, we're free!"

A gang of eight GIs crowded into Chen's room. Each of them found a place to sit—on the bed, desk, or small refrigerator.

"I'm goin' to get some tunes going. Who's gonna get me high?"

"Right here, Mr. Jailbait, suck on this for a while!" yelled a voice from the back of a group stepping in the door. He thrust a glowing bowl of marijuana at Sergeant Chen. After a long pull on the pipe, he blew a jet of smoke in the face of his accuser.

"Ain't no jailbait, and you can suck on this, jerk-off!" Chen grabbed his crotch and shook it.

"No, thanks. Take too long for me to find it."

"Up yours."

"So how you gonna beat this one?"

Chen squinted through the heavy haze created by three

large pipes going around the room. He attempted to talk while holding in his "hit" of marijuana.

"Nuttin'—to it—we're—clean. Foooohaaaaa, aah."

"What really did happen, George?"

"Well, me an' this FNG here—" He gestured at Lansky with his pipe. "—who, by the goddamn way, is no longer an FNG. His name is Lansky, from Wisconsin. Anyway, he was tokin' up with me and White Man behind the mess hall after midnight chow. The MPs almost got us. Luckily, I saw 'em comin' and duffed into the mess hall, dumped the pipe in some fry oil, and ran around until Whitey could get rid of his bag. So we're clean, man, squeaky, shiny clean! Ha, anyway, to top it off, Snuflewicz blew the indictment at our arraignment. He got us all confused, still doesn't have 'em right, so I bet we get off."

"What was the charge?"

"All they could come up with was suspicion of smoking marijuana."

"Sounds weak. You mean they couldn't crack the FNG?"

"Hey, he's one of us. They tried to trick 'em, but Lansky—and we'll call him that—Lansky didn't crack, didn't fuck up, so he ain't no FNG. Yes, sirree, we got ourselves a history maker here."

Chen moved over to put his arm around Lansky.

"Here he is, the first FNG in Vietnam to not fuck up! Why, if I was a lifer, I'd give him a medal or somethin'. Sooo, Mister Lansky from Wisconsin, meet the gang who run Cam Ranh."

Sergeant Chen introduced Lansky to some of the clerks, cooks, personnel, and payroll workers who operated the processing center at Cam Rahn Bay.

Lansky noticed how comfortable their barracks were: each had a bed with a thick mattress, sheets, tape player, refrigerator, and desk.

"You guys got it made here man. Is every room like this?"

"Yup. Told you, man, we live in style and run this place ourselves. Have another bowl." He jammed the pipe in Lansky's mouth and lit it.

More men crammed into the room and the crowd spilled out into the hallway. They all wanted to hear Chen's retelling of the story.

Lansky could see what tight camaraderie these men shared, men who spent their entire existence in the rear. For them, the real enemy was on their side of the barbed wire.

The lifers in their own army were far more formidable than the VC. The draftees just wanted to get high and get home. Insecure and defensive, they bunkered down, creating their own little generation gap in this microcosm of American society.

One of the men from personnel was giving Lansky a spaced-out description of how he was going to send Snuflewicz's personnel records to Greenland. Another man from payroll threatened to make some adjustments in Snuffy's payroll deductions.

Chen smiled. "See, man, told ya we run this place. Hey, c'mere, we found a room for you." He put his arm around Lansky and guided him down the hall to a vacant room. They walked in. The sarge brought the air conditioner to life. They stood in the cool breeze.

"You can put your gear in here, and I got a lock for ya in my room."

"Thanks." Lansky smiled at his good fortune.

"No problem. You're one of us. We take care of our own."

The party that night was intense. Lansky drifted from room to room.

Standing in the hall, he heard the sound of four tape players driving four sets of speakers, playing four types of music.

A baker from one of the mess halls elbowed by him, delivering a huge tray of sweet rolls to one of the rooms.

Lansky found himself sitting on a bunk next to a sleepy-looking soldier. The GI sucked a Kool cigarette down to its filter then fell forward, flat on his face.

"He's gone too far on that stuff again, man. He's totally nodded out," said one of the men as they picked him up and tossed him on a bunk.

Later, Lansky noticed the man struggling to a sitting position. He fumbled in his breast pocket until he found a small cylindrical vial containing a white powder, shaking a Kool from its pack, he rolled some of the tobacco out of the tip. Tapping half the vial of white powder into the top of the cigarette, twisting the paper shut, he rolled the stem between his fingers to mix the powder and tobacco.

He lit the cigarette with his Zippo, inhaled, and gagged several times. Smoke curled out of his nose, past his puffy downcast eyes, and through his disheveled hair.

"Try som'a dis," he said, passing the cigarette to Lansky.

"What is it?"

"Hooo-aah, this is smack, man."

Lansky took a drag, gagged, and bent over, dizzy, the room swirled. Conversation ebbed and flowed around him like voices underwater. Everything slowed. Euphoria. He couldn't talk. His mouth couldn't form words.

After a while, he was able to get out some simple sentences, but his voice cracked, as if he had something in his throat that couldn't be cleared.

The junkie looked at Lansky.

"So this is yer firs' day in country?"

"No, my second."

"An' yer smokin' this stuff already?"

"Well, I guess I am, you gave it to me."

Lansky watched the man suck down his Kool cigarette. How

strange, remote, and sad this character was. All these men were. No matter how hard they partied, the loneliness and estrangement twisting them would always be there when they sobered up.

Chen walked into the room.

"C'mon, man, got a tape I want you to listen to."

He put his arm around Lansky as they went down the hall.

"Maybe the guys in personnel can get you stationed here."

"What would I do here?"

"We always need guards."

"Yeah, maybe they could."

"Hey, someone is going to come by tomorrow and take you over to payroll. We can get ya paid. You're low on dough, right?"

"Yeah."

"Well, we can fix a partial advance on your first check. So hang around in the morning. Gotta wear your fatigues, though, don't show up in no civvies or the lifers'll be wise to what we're doin'."

"I didn't bring any civvies with me. I thought I'd have to wear my uniform."

"Well, first thing you do when you get paid is go shopping for civvies at the PX."

"Maybe I will."

At the end of his second day in country, Lansky felt overwhelmed. Even this stretch of good luck had an undercurrent of the unknown that made him suspicious. Where would the next thunderbolt come from?

CHAPTER 4

September 9, 1971

The next morning someone came by in a jeep and took Lansky to the payroll office.

He recognized the guy in the payroll cage from last night's party. Lansky got thirty-five dollars in military pay certificates and a wink that said, "See? We really do run this place."

On the way back, he asked the driver what there was to do during the day.

"Well, you could go to Burnout Beach."

"Where's that?"

"Down along the beach in front of the heroin rehab center. Don't expect a lot of volleyball, though. They send the burnouts out for some sun and air, but they mostly lay there like vegetables."

"Sounds like fun."

"Maybe not fun, but you probably shouldn't hang around the barracks. They'll put you on some detail to keep you busy."

"Okay, thanks."

Lansky left for the beach dressed in a borrowed swimsuit and flip-flops. As he walked down the rows of dark, two-story barracks toward the bay, the sun burned his shoulders and the backs of his legs. He put on his fatigue shirt.

The walk relaxed him, his first quiet solitude since arriving.

Lansky picked his way through diesel traffic and a labyrinth of ugly barracks, offices, and buildings.

Behind five rows of corroded concertina wire, aqua waves crashed into white suds. He ambled along the wire until he found an opening that led to the beach. The sea breeze gently massaged his hair and brought salt brine to his nose. Rhythmic crashing of the breakers calmed him.

Lansky stared out at the brightly painted fishing boats bobbing in the bay. Each of them had eyes painted on the prow to help guide them through the South China Sea.

He walked slowly out toward the water then down the beach. The warm sun hitting his face felt good.

Surf pushed dead, bloated jellyfish, spines expanded, up and down the wet sand.

A wilted collection of broken human figures sat on the sand in front of the heroin rehabilitation center. Lifeless, they stared out to sea, eyes glazed.

As Lansky passed the junkies on the beach, he felt the pull of some unspecific gravity, a force beyond his control, dragging him away from the familiar toward the strange. Something vital drained out of him with each odd occurrence. One day he, too, would be emptied, a lifeless figure on the beach.

Would his essence ever be replaced? He didn't know. But something had to happen in his favor if he was going to survive.

Lansky walked on.

A jeep drove down the beach, MP painted on the bumper in large white letters. Both driver and passenger wore MP helmets. When the jeep got closer, Lansky saw they were wearing gas masks and unusual rubber suits. Passing slowly, they looked at him, then continued down the beach beyond the wire.

Intrigued, Lansky watched them get out of the jeep carrying a large metal box. One man had a shovel and used it to dig a hole in the sand and drop the container into it. They buried the box and then drove back along the beach, staring at Lansky. He watched them bump slowly by. One of the MPs got out and opened the gate. They left.

None of the lifeless ones on the beach had noticed the MPs. *What the hell was that?*

Lansky needed relief—a swim in the South China Sea.

Wading into the surf, Lansky stopped to let the undertow pull cool water and sand under his feet. Lunging through the waves—the breakers lifting him free, swimming against the surf, tasting the saltwater, exhilarating—Lansky felt released. Clearing the swells, treading water, he bobbed along looking out to sea. He hung there, scanning the western horizon for several minutes, wondering if he was looking toward home, if anyone he knew was looking in this direction. He took comfort in the fact that he had a home and that someone on the opposite shore would soon think of him, maybe even miss him. Lonely now, Lansky turned away from the cruel beauty of the endless ocean.

He let the waves throw him back toward shore. As his feet touched, a sharp stinging sensation penetrated his thigh. Stumbling through the surf, he felt a burning pain. An egg-shaped, red welt about six-inches long confirmed he'd been stung by a jellyfish. The pain in his leg lasted several minutes. He lay on his back holding his leg in the air as the pain continued.

The welt symbolized the strangeness of recent events.

Letting his head fall back, Lansky closed his eyes. Too many odd occurrences were piling up. He'd never experienced so many bizarre events in such a short time.

These events were unworldly, his beliefs shaken, the premises he'd used to negotiate life were in doubt. He started praying, crying out, he'd had enough. Lansky now knew that his famous luck would not be enough.

Vibration split the air. A whirring friction pulsed across Lansky's face. His eyes opened to see broad green wings, a long neck, and a prehistoric head fly over.

The dragon banked over the ocean, climbed briefly, rolled sideways, folded its wings then dove beneath the waves. The force of the dive sent a splash of water high into the air.

CHAPTER 5

September 10, 1971

Lansky stared at the green dragon on the back of Chen's blue silk robe. *A coincidental resemblance to the dragon I saw on the beach? Or is it something more? A cosmic wink?*

The stout little mess sergeant placed a ceramic teapot and small cups on the low table. "Sorry, Ed, don't have a robe big enough for you." Kneeling on the tatami mat, he lit the joss sticks with a click of his Zippo.

"Get down next to me. She'll be here soon," said Chen.

Lansky did as ordered, then said, "So tell me again, who is this person?"

"Okay, I didn't know anything about dragons when I came to Cam Ranh. I'm from Sacramento, what do I know about dragons? Anyway, when I was an FNG, Sergeant Morgan, head cook for the night shift, took me under his wing. He was friends with the supervisor of hooch maids, Ly, an English teacher until she realized she could make more money working for the Americans. Speaks perfect English, highly educated. Morgan would always have tea with Ly at the end of her day shift before he went on night shift. I got to sit in. She told the most amazing stories."

"And she talked about dragons?" Lansky asked quietly.

"Shit yeah! Dragons? They're everywhere in Vietnam history. Ly told us all about them. So when you started talking about dragons flying over your head and diving in the ocean, I thought, this guy has gone over the edge, but then I started remembering Ly's stories. So I invited her by for tea. Maybe she can figure this out. By the way, I still think you're nuts."

"What were her dragon stories about?"

"The ancient king that founded Vietnam was the son of a dragon and his wife was a fairy. He commanded his people to cover their arms and sides with dragon tattoos for protection against monsters in the rice paddies."

"Sounds like superstition."

"So does a dragon flying over a guy on a beach."

"Got me."

They both laughed.

"After listening to Ly, I went on leave to Hong Kong. I saw a Chinese martial arts movie called *Dragon at the Gate*. Had to read the damned subtitles. But the star of the movie was Cheng Pei Pei, one of the most beautiful women I've ever seen. She could kick butt! She could fly, and I believed it because she was so sexy. The movie made a big deal out of her dragon tattoos and how they protected her from all trouble. I went out that night and started my tats. If it was good enough for Cheng Pei Pei, it was good enough for me."

They heard a quiet knock at the door.

Chen said, "Come in."

A small woman in black pajama pants, beige sandals, and a simple white blouse entered the room. Her posture and poise were perfect, her smile a thing of grace, her eyes crinkled in spontaneous joy. She warmed the room. Coming to the table, kneeling in slow and reverent grace, she glowed in appreciation of the tea ceremony honoring her visit.

"Hello, Ly, this is Ed Lansky from Wisconsin," said Chen.

"Welcome to Cam Ranh, Ed." Her large brown eyes gleamed. "Is Wisconsin in the east?"

"No, the Midwest, near Chicago."

"Ah, Chicago, I shall visit there someday."

Lansky watched Chen pour the green tea into three cups; small leaf flecks floated on the surface. Using a terry towel, he wiped the pot, then replaced it on the trivet. Eyes downcast, he lifted the first cup to Ly.

Accepting the cup, her smile lit the darkness.

Raising his tea, Chen said, "Here is to harmony with nature, and a quieting of our hearts. May enlightenment follow." They all took a sip from their cups. "Ly, Ed has a story to tell you."

Lansky hesitated.

Bemused by his boyish awkwardness, Ly said, "It's okay, Ed, you may speak freely."

"Well, a lot of unusual stuff is happening to me. Sergeant Chen and I got in a little trouble after midnight chow the other night. On the way to the lockup, something flew over my head. It was big and green. Then yesterday while swimming at Burnout Beach, I got stung by a jellyfish. Lying on the beach in pain, I'm overwhelmed, thinking about how I needed help. A big green dragon flew over and dove in the ocean. I must be going crazy, cause the dragon looked real."

Ly favored Lansky with a smile. "When you saw the dragon, did it relieve your pain?"

"Well, yeah, it did."

"So you asked for help, and it was given?"

"True, but that's beside the point."

"Maybe. Ed, are you a spiritual person?"

"No, not really."

"In Vietnam, we learn in childhood of the spirits around us. The dragon spirit is powerful. It goes back to prehistoric times when the Vietnamese people lived on rivers. They saw crocodiles in the rivers as the descendants of dragons. That's why so many modern day representations of dragons have crocodile heads. The ancients venerated crocodiles as living proof of the dragon spirit. To this day, seeing a crocodile is considered auspicious.

"Back in Wisconsin, you don't talk about dragons. But long ago in ancient times, people were of one mind. If you traced your ancestors back far enough, you could find one that believed in animal spirits. Right?"

"If I went way back, I probably could."

"The belief of your ancient ancestors in animal spirits is like a stream. It flows into a river. That is my ancestors' belief in the dragon spirit, one flows into the other, sometimes we don't know which is which."

"So you're saying this is something inside me that goes back to ancient times?"

"Yes, your emotions run strong, taking you deep within and far back in time for protection. Your ancient spirit is aroused and may reveal itself in many forms. Here in Cam Ranh, it assumes the form of a dragon."

"I've always been told I'm lucky. Maybe there's more to it than that."

"Luck comes to those who accept the guidance of their spirit." Ly put her cup down gently. "In Vietnam, people would say you had a vision, a rare and lucky experience. Could it be that the veil has been lifted from your handsome western eyes for the first time in your life? A spiritual gate has been opened for you.

Can you see the garden of serenity on the other side? Will you decide to walk through this gate that is open to so few?"

Lansky's eyes got big. "This is a lot of . . . stuff to . . . think about. Thanks, Ly. I'm more open to it than I was five minutes ago."

Chen looked at Ly. "Hey, remember the story you told me about the difference between Chinese and Vietnamese dragons?"

"Yes. Most of the dragon stories you see in the West are about Chinese dragons. They come down from the sky, breathing fire. They are evil, and man's task is to destroy them.

"Vietnamese dragons rise from the sea. They bring the water of life each monsoon season. They are good. Man's task is to live with them in harmony. To see one is considered good luck."

Chen pulled up the sleeve on his robe to show Lansky his red dragon tattoo once again. This time the dragon looked familiar rather than alien.

Lansky noticed a slight sly smile on the dragon's face.

"Your vision is a message from your spirit," Ly continued. "You need to pay attention to it. Use this dragon to help you on your way. It is a gift."

CHAPTER 6

September 17, 1971

While in Cam Ranh Bay, Lansky's days fell into a pattern: sleep late, then go to the beach, and party at night.

Each day he walked down the beach past the heroin rehab center to the spot where he'd lain in agony after the jellyfish sting. Ly's thoughts and insights were turning this spot into a place of peace and contemplation. He accepted her insight. The dragon, real or imagined, was a gift. What had seemed like a threatening shadow now revealed itself to be his warrior shield.

Lansky knew his future held many strange and dangerous events. He decided that whatever came along could be used as a tool to help him survive. Unexpected resources were being presented. Lansky had faith that now he was prepared to see them.

He realized he was a normal person having a normal reaction to an abnormal situation. Lansky would not get down on himself when the next shocking event occurred. He kept repeating the phrase, "I will survive."

* * *

At last, Lansky got some word about his case. It turned out that a lifer had observed them smoking behind the mess hall, phoned the MPs, and sworn out an affidavit.

A draftee in his barracks then swore out an affidavit to the effect that the lifer was so drunk he had no idea what he was doing. The case was becoming muddled.

One morning, as Lansky lay half-awake in his bunk, Chen burst through the door.

"Things are happ'nin', man, the charges are dropped. Gimme five! I told ya they would be."

Lansky reached over limply and blinked as Chen slapped his hand. Lying back, he looked up at the mess sergeant dressed in whites with a paper chef's hat.

"Well, that's the good news, now the bad." Chen looked serious.

"What do you mean, bad?"

"Yeah, the CO wants you outta here. Says you're a negative influence on the rest of us, so he's cutting orders to send you up country."

"I'm the problem? All this crap is my fault?"

"The CO is under the illusion no one smoked much dope until you got here. He's a lifer with no clue. What can you expect?"

"Where am I going?"

"Up to Chu Lai with the Twenty-Fifth Infantry. They call themselves the Americal Division. But they're headed home, so we don't know what's goin' to happen to you."

"Well, it's been great. Thanks for everything. I really appreciate you taking me under your wing."

"No sweat, GI. There is one thing you can do for me."

"What's that?"

"Let me give you a blow job."

This took Lansky by surprise. He stared at Chen.

"No, no. I don't want that."

"You sure?"

"Yes. Very sure."

"Well, okay," Chen said, embarrassed. "Hey, you won't tell any of the other guys, will you? They'd run me out."

"No, I won't tell anyone. It's okay. Am I going today?"

"Yeah, you'd better get ready. Go over to processing."

"Thanks. Say good-bye to everyone for me, will ya? I've learned a lot here." Lansky smiled at Chen.

"Yeah, okay, can do. One more thing, be careful who you tell about getting busted and then seeing a dragon. It's not the first impression you want to make in a new unit."

"Yeah, probably keep it to myself, my own private resource."

"Good luck, my friend."

CHAPTER 7

September 17, 1971

As soon as Lansky got his orders, he boarded a plane for Chu Lai. Only a few others, mostly officers, shared the jump seats in the C-130. Lansky fell asleep on the short flight, waking as the plane landed.

At the deserted air base, Lansky met a sergeant wearing the blue Americal Division arm patch, white stars of the Southern Cross embossed on the blue shoulder shield.

"So why'd they take so long to send ya up here, son?" The sarge's deeply tanned forehead furrowed at the sight of Lansky's orders.

"It's a long story."

"Cam Ranh hasn't sent anyone up here in two weeks because they know we're leaving. What the hell were you doing down there, son?"

"Well, they kept me over for guard duty."

"Guard duty? Humph." He pushed his salt-stained fatigue cap back and rubbed his forehead. "The CO isn't going to like this. What are we supposed to do with you?"

He stared hard at the orders. "Got no one in the reception center but a skeleton staff. We're leavin', ya know. Damn, I can't understand why you're here." He flipped through the orders, looking for a reason to send Lansky back.

"Well, Sarge, I don't generally talk about it much lately, but I'm going to confide in you." Lansky grinned.

The sergeant's eyes lifted off the orders.

"I'm here to present you with a puzzle only your salty self can solve. Does it really matter what went on in Cam Rahn? You could simplify your life by ignoring that question. What if you found a quiet little out-of-the-way place to stow me until nature takes its course?" Lansky gave the sarge an insincere smile.

"Oh, you want out-of-the-way? We got out-of-the-way."

Lansky found himself bunked alone in a hooch built to hold thirty men. The whole reception camp was deserted. Brightly painted photo, tailor, and curio shops were boarded up. Small bars along the beach were dark and empty. He had the camp to himself. The sea breeze and crashing surf were the only sounds. After a quiet night drinking in one of the empty EM clubs, Lansky turned in.

Next morning, in the Americal Personnel Office, Lansky was sent in to see the CO. An athletic-looking young captain, with friendly eyes and a big handshake, greeted him. "So, Lansky, is it?" The officer kicked back into his swivel chair and cracked the file. "So an eleven-bravo-ten, up here as an infantry replacement. I see you're a college graduate. Too bad you don't have two months under your belt, you'd go home with us. How the heck did you get up here so late anyway? We told Cam Ranh not to send any more grunts up here. You're screwin' up the works. What happened down there that made them want to send you way up here?"

Lansky thought he might tell the captain the truth but decided against it.

"Well, I was on guard duty, then they decided to send me up here because they didn't need me anymore."

"Guard duty? You must have messed up!" The officer's voice took on a coaxing, teasing quality for the next question. "C'mon. Just between two educated gentlemen, why did they send you?"

Lansky was beginning to sweat. "Well, sir, they didn't tell me a lot. I just got put on guard duty. Nothing happened . . . Here I am!"

The captain's deep blue eyes rested on Lansky's face, guessed he was lying, but remained amused. "Okay, troop, forget it. It's going to take me a while to find an infantry assignment for you. You know we're the last full-strength infantry division to withdraw from the field, First Cav is gone, Fifth Infantry is gone, and ARVN just kicked the NVA out of An Loc. I've even heard rumors about the Paris Peace talks starting up again. Looks like all the large-scale engagements that include American infantry are over with. The only action right now is up around Da Nang trying to keep rockets off the air base. Probably have to get in touch with the people up there. Until then, report to the personnel noncommissioned officer in charge next-door and you can help them get squared away until we leave."

Lansky reported to the NCOIC who told him, "Keep your boots polished and look busy when an officer is around."

"Yeah, but what should I do?"

"Do? There's nothing to do. In case you didn't know, we're leaving. We had the files all squared away last week. Don't touch 'em. Hey, how come you're here, anyway?"

Lansky was growing tired of the question. "Well, it's a long story, Sarge."

"Spare me."

"I'm the puzzle sent for you to solve."

"What?"

"Told you it was a long story."

"Get outta my AO! Get to the back of my office, an' don't never come up to the front while I'm here! Don't need no goddamn puzzles."

"Yes, Sergeant."

"I don't know how the hell you ever got here, but I'm gonna pretend you ain't here. You do the same!" the sergeant yelled. He sat down with a cup of coffee to read the *Stars and Stripes*.

Lansky walked back between the rows of spinning, pivoting fans whirring away on each desk.

The clerks looked down pretending to work. After several minutes, they began to introduce themselves. No one asked Lansky why he was there. Their only interest was the days left until they went home.

Lansky looked at the DEROS calendars on their desks. Big black Xs marked every day spent in country, tiny numbers in the corner of each date box counted the days left in country. One guy had the date circled that he was eligible for return from overseas. That date was September 25, 1971, eight days away. Most of them were down to single digits. Their time remaining in Vietnam was short.

They talked short talk, which was usually what they were going to eat, screw, and drive when they got back to the world. Then they went to short jokes: "I'm shorter than whale shit at the bottom of the ocean."

"Oh, yeah? I'm so short I could walk under a snake's belly and never bend over!"

Lansky longed to be short.

Soon he sat back in his office chair and turned on his fan as the heat peaked.

The men whiled away the afternoon with their feet on their desks, smoking cigarettes and reading magazines.

Occasionally an officer would come by. The sergeant at the front desk would yell, "Officer!" Then feet came down, magazines jammed into drawers, typewriters clacked, pencils flashed over D-D forms.

They all looked busy. When the officer left, the clacking ceased, forms went in drawers and the magazines came back out, feet returned to desktops. This went on for nearly a week. Lansky was bored.

One morning Lansky was polishing his boots when he heard, "Officer!" Quickly pulling out a D-D form, he started filling in the blanks with the name and background of some fictitious soldier.

Looking up guardedly, Lansky could see the noncommissioned officer in charge talking to three high-ranking officers, one of whom was a barrel-chested colonel. He had an entourage that included a photographer.

All of the clerks at the back of the office started exchanging worried glances, running down their mental checklists of mistakes made in the last few months. For a colonel to be here, they must have really screwed up.

Lansky kept glancing at the front and noticed the NCOIC pointing at him and laughing. When the NCOIC gave a crisp salute, the colonel moved out looking right at Lansky.

Sweat poured down Lansky's sides as the officers moved down the long aisle headed right for him.

Lansky looked at the clerk next to him for some guidance. He got a "drop dead" look in return. It was too late to run out the back door, they were next to his desk. Lansky pretended he was busy but eventually looked up.

The colonel smiled at him, didn't say anything, just smiled, for several seconds.

"Private Lansky?" boomed the barrel-chested colonel.

"Yes . . . Yes, sir," he said, rising hesitantly.

"Congratulations, son!"

"Congratulations? Ah . . . for what, sir?"

"Private, we have the honor of informing you that you're the last replacement for the American Division, the last in a line of courageous men who have served their country well in its struggle to staunch the flow of worldwide Communism. We are gathered here today to commemorate our proud tradition of excellence by honoring you."

"Me? Are you sure, sir?"

"Yes, you, Private. Here you are ready to serve just like your brethren in American. We're sure you're the aggressive, gung-ho type of soldier who would carry on our proud tradition. By honoring you, we'll remember all those who went before you."

"Well, I don't know what to say, sir."

"Of course you don't. It's okay. Now we have a presentation to make."

"Excuse me, Colonel," the photographer said. "If we could go outside, the pictures would be easier."

"Are you busy, Private?"

"No, no."

"Come with us, then."

Lansky walked outside with the group. The photographer pushed him next to the colonel. All the other officers were arranged around them.

"Okay, Colonel, go ahead." One of the colonel's aides put a shiny plaque in his hands.

"Private First Class Lansky." Rapid clicking and whirring of the camera captured every word. "I'm sure you're aware of what a privilege it is to serve with a 'can-do' outfit like American."

"Yes, sir." Lansky felt like crying out, like now was the time to start running.

"Private, you are replacement number ninety-five thousand, two hundred eighty-eight. We know you're the last but certainly not the least. We want you to accept this plaque in memory of our tradition."

Lansky looked at the plaque made of dark lacquered wood with a map of Vietnam on it, metallic South Vietnamese and American flags crossed at the top, and a large blue metal Americal patch was in the middle. At the bottom was a plate bearing an inscription with his name, rank, social security number, and the words "Last But Not Least."

"Well, I'm overwhelmed by this, sir," Lansky said. "Thank you." He was nervous. Would this turn into a joke that landed him in jail?

"Good show, Private." The colonel slapped Lansky on the back and locked his hand in a vise-grip handshake. All the other officers shook his hand.

The mood was up for these officers. The burden of command was about to be lifted because they were going home. The end needed to be heroic and ceremonious, even if it really wasn't.

One of the officers said, "How's it feel to be front-page news, son?"

"What?"

"Yeah, you're going to be on the front page of the *Stars and Stripes* magazine. They'll be reading about you from Tokyo to Saigon. Your picture will be seen all over Southeast Asia."

"Oh, I don't think that's necessary, sir."

"Don't be so humble, Private, this is a proud moment. By the way, the colonel has invited you to the officers' mess for lunch. He's going to personally grill a steak for you."

"No, I probably don't deserve it."

"Yes, you do. Report at twelve-hundred hours."

* * *

Later, as Lansky sat down with the officers, he was given a frosty mug of beer. They smiled at him, and he smiled back.

"How do you like your steak, son?" asked the colonel, standing at a gas grill.

"Uh, rare, sir."

"That's the ticket, never too rare is what I say."

"Yes, sir."

The officers made small talk at the table as the colonel took their orders. Lansky bobbed his head and smiled as if listening.

He tried to estimate how long it would take him to run out the door. Something visceral made him consider bolting. But it was too late now. They'd started crunching away on their salads.

The colonel served everyone and sat down, ate vigorously at first, and then slowed down to a more thoughtful pace.

Lansky could see a question forming as the officer looked at him.

"How's your steak, son?"

"Great, sir." Lansky nervously put large bites of steak into his mouth.

"So tell me, Private, I'm very interested. How is it you got up here so late? How did you become our last man? Why are you here? Get this down, will you, Bronson?" The colonel's aide put his steno pad on the table, and, pen poised over pad, looked at the honored guest.

Lansky was having trouble swallowing the giant piece of meat in his mouth. He held his finger up as a signal that he would answer when his mouth cleared.

All the officers put their utensils down and looked at him.

He was laboriously chewing the last mouthful.

Other conversations came to a stop. Men watched Lansky

swallow. The pause was long enough for all to feel a little tension.

"Well . . . Excuse me, uh-hmmm." The honored guest cleared his throat and looked at the door. "It's kind of a mystery to me, sir. I guess I could say a lot of things. All I know is I got volunteered for guard duty for a coupla weeks, and then I got sent up here."

"Damn lucky for all of us he did, right, men?" said the colonel, holding up his whiskey on the rocks with a twist. "Let's drink to Private Lansky, last but not least."

They all raised their glasses.

Lansky raised his. Taking a long draft, draining his beer, Lansky saw the colonel's white teeth smiling at him through the bottom of the mug.

"Thanks," he said, tabling his glass. "You've all been good to me."

CHAPTER 8

September 25, 1971

A few days after the Last Man Ceremony, Ed Lansky was put on a C-130 with orders to report to the 195th Light Infantry Brigade in Da Nang. A driver from Brigade HQ picked him up at the air base.

The large coastal city of Da Nang surrounded the air base with narrow streets abuzz with the sounds of commerce in open-air markets. Pedi-cab and pedestrian traffic clogged the street, so the jeep stopped often.

During one of the stops, Lansky looked into a tiny storefront. The faces of the merchants and customers, their animated expressions, suggested this was more than bartering. Troubled faces with skin pulled tight by great emotion, skin so tight the faces were only thinly veiled skulls.

A hole opened in the traffic, and the driver shot forward, then jerked to a stop.

Outside a small restaurant, the smell of pepper sauce, cooked rice, and exotic spices mixed with the diesel-urine odor of the street. Lansky looked into the humidity of the tiny blue and red shack. The patrons squatted with small bowls under their mouths, expressing rice to their lips using bamboo chopsticks.

Torrents of singsong conversation assaulted his ear. The faces were alike. Fervent.

No one studied Lansky's face. No one in the restaurant even noticed him. If they had looked past his occidental cheekbones, they would have seen his trepidation.

The driver started again, following a scooter through the crowd. The wall of people parted slowly, giving the jeep only enough room to creep along. The driver slammed his hand on the wheel in frustration as people dodged the bumper of the jeep.

"Happens all the time here," said the driver. "Never can get through this street."

The jeep pushed slowly through the throng.

Lansky stared at an open building supported on poles. Several monks in saffron-colored robes stood on a small dais swinging incense burners in a slow rhythm, filling the building with fragrant white smoke. Lansky smelled the sandalwood as the creeping jeep improved his view. Several rows of Vietnamese stood before the monks mumbling a chant at a very low octave. They were dressed in traditional religious costumes. Women wore brightly colored *ao-dais*, hair lacquered and coifed gracefully up and back. Men sat in a row, ochre-colored robes flowing, beating on log drums, others striking dulcimer-like instruments.

The crowd on the street focused on something in front of them, ignoring the driver's attempts to nose the jeep through from behind.

A rapid sequence of loud explosions pulsed down the street. Lansky's companion reached under his seat, pulled out a forty-five pistol, chambered a round and handed it to him. "Here, safety is on, keep it low, but be ready."

The crowd had pressed a young woman against the jeep. She frowned at the pistol in Lansky's hand. When he looked at her, she shook her head in disapproval. "Nooo! Haa-fest." She pointed out into the street.

Lansky tried to reason out what she said. Then it came to him. "Harvest?" He pointed with his free hand at the street.

The young woman's face blossomed with a relieved smile. "Yaaa—haa-fest."

Lansky looked at his companion. "The girl says it's some kind of harvest celebration."

"Just keep cool, let's see what happens." The driver's trigger finger drummed the magazine of the M-16, now in his lap.

The crowd became animated, a wave of energy rippled across the row of faces. Rhythmic clapping started. They cheered and pointed down the street, eyes wide with happiness.

Another sequence of explosions went off in the street.

"Fireworks?" The driver looked at Lansky.

"Yeah, we probably overreacted."

"You can't be too careful in the vil, but maybe you're right, this is some kind of festival. Let's take a look." They put their weapons between the seats and rose to a standing position.

The young woman smiled at Lansky. He offered his hand, inviting her to stand on the jeep floor, improving her view. She declined.

Out on the street, a ceremonial dragon swung from curb to curb in sinuous undulation. It had a green crocodile head, a white beard, glittering eyes, and a twenty-five-foot-long snake's body painted in multicolored detail.

A dance team marched under the dragon, holding poles supporting each of the twelve-hooped sections. They whipped the beast back and forth in a coordinated wave pattern.

Drummers in scarlet tunics marched behind the dragon, banging out a beat the dancers used to time their turns.

Fireworks popped and crackled in the street.

Lansky looked at the driver. "Seeing a dragon brings good luck."

"How do you know?"

"I learned about dragons down in Cam Ranh."

"Cool."

When the dragon and drummers passed, the crowd spilled out into the street and followed.

Lansky's driver sat down. "Let's go."

They drove across the empty street.

The driver pushed the jeep hard, roaring through town. Lansky pondered the faces of the people he had seen on the street as the dragon passed. They were serene. The faces didn't look like skulls, the desperation missing.

Oily exhaust corkscrewed through the air behind an ARVN soldier on a Berretta. The jeep pulled parallel with the soldier who stared straight ahead. His fatigue hat was pulled down over his dark face. His mouth turned down, and his skin was taut.

The jeep passed the lone cycle rider. Lansky's driver began to negotiate a series of switchbacks on the edge of town. They were climbing the broad hills guarding the western entrance to the city of Da Nang.

"Whooo haaaa! Made it through the vil!" The driver whipped his boonie cap off his head and held it high. He cracked a smile and looked at Lansky. "Ah'm another day shorter now! Got it made. How 'bout a beer, Mr. New Guy?"

"My name is Ed Lansky, from Wisconsin. Where's the beer?"

"Ah'm Sauers, George Sauers from Oklahoma. Look in the back, gotta couple back there. Cowboy cool by now, I s'pose."

Lansky reached behind the weapons sitting between the two front seats and grabbed several cans from the floor. Popping the first one sent foam down his arm. The driver took the can and raised it high over the windshield.

"Here's to bein' short, Lansky. Thirty-two and a wakeup."

He took a long drink, and the jeep swerved toward the drop-off. Lansky braced himself.

Sauers put the can between his legs, bringing the jeep back on course. Downshifting at high RPMs, he turned the jeep at full power, sending it smartly up the next switchback.

When Lansky opened his beer, foam sprayed the windshield. He held the can to his mouth until the foaming stopped.

It was depressing to be listening to this short talk again. Short talk only emphasized how long he had to serve. His perception of time was being stretched. A year was beginning to seem like a century. He had to get it off his mind.

Lansky craned his neck to look back across the city, the streets far below. His eyes passed across the blocks of cardboard and tin shacks to the open spaces dominated by long cement ribbons. Rows of concrete revetments served as rocket shelters and hangars for the Phantom jets. Lansky had counted fifty of them while waiting on the tarmac for the jeep to pick him up. Looking beyond the air base, several mountainous peninsulas separated the broad bays of Da Nang. The South China Sea sparkled on the horizon. His eyes returned to the unusual thrusts of land protecting the city and the coastline.

"Marble Mountain," Sauers said. He'd noticed Lansky's attention to the unique landmark. "That's Marble Mountain."

The jeep slowed then turned through a guarded gate. Sauers waved at the MPs on duty then coasted down the hill. The jeep whined loudly as it rolled toward the low row of tin roofs perched on the edge. Sauers stopped the jeep in a small turnaround.

"This is the One Hundredth Ninety-Fifth Brigade, Lansky. You're a grunt now. What company are you assigned to?"

"Uh, lemme look." Lansky pulled his paperwork from his trouser pocket. "Bravo Company, says here."

Sauers pointed at a row of barracks. "Down there, behind ya."

Now out of the jeep, Lansky grabbed his duffel and smiled at Sauers.

"Thanks. You know, all I've heard is short talk since I got here. How can a guy be sure he's gonna get short?"

Sauers looked at him seriously. "Wait, I guess . . . I really don't know. I wish I had a secret to tell you, but I really don't know." Holding the can up again in a farewell gesture, Sauers took a drink and roared away.

CHAPTER 9

September 25, 1971

Lansky entered the still heat of the Bravo Company area, duffel bag over his shoulder, beer in hand, ambling past ten or twelve plywood and screen barracks before he saw any signs of life.

Lonesome country music came from one and Lansky looked inside. A shirtless GI smiled at him from behind a desk. "Cain ah he'p ya?" Dialing back the noisy fan he turned down the volume on "Hello, Walls."

"Yeah, is this Bravo Company?"

"Sure is. You our new replacement?"

"Well, I guess I am."

"Well then, c'mon in."

Lansky climbed the steps and dropped the duffel in the cramped little office.

"Hey, Top! Our new re-croot is here!" the man yelled over his shoulder.

"Hokaay," an invisible voice growled in response. A squat, broad-shouldered man with a basketball belly filled the narrow hall, his fatigue jacket barely covered a giant gut making his legs look tiny.

Lansky was about to laugh.

The man marched down the hall eyes locked on Lansky's, keen eyes capable of control without words.

Lansky stepped back as the first sergeant marched up under his chin.

"Hi'm Pers Sergeant Bool Dawg Rodriguez off Bravo Company." The first sergeant shouted his greeting in a thick Puerto Rican accent.

"I'm Lansky, PFC. Here's my paperwork."

The first sergeant scanned the paperwork, and then looked up at Lansky, getting even closer.

"You wan lucky dick, Lansky, to be in Bravo Company."

"Yes, First Sergeant."

"Hey, I gonna introduce you to the company commander. He just flew in today to take care of a court-martial. He's flyin' back to the field tomorrow. You wait here."

As the first sergeant turned, he winked at the desk clerk then walked down the narrow hall to the back office.

The desk clerk grinned. "Top's up ta sumthin'. This'll be good. He always gets the CO goin'." He turned the fan and tape player off so they could hear.

"Got da new re-croot frohm Chu Lai here, sir! His paper-work up front. He jus' show hup."

"Oh," a disinterested and distant voice mumbled a response.

"Yeah, he hup front, sir. He ready to report to his commanding officer."

"Huh?" The man sounded preoccupied. "Okay . . . guess so. Bring him back."

"Private Duffelbag! Private Dilbert Duffelbag report for inspection by jor company commander!"

Lansky looked at the clerk.

"He means you. Go on back."

As Lansky entered the office, he could see the first sergeant looking at him from behind the CO's chair. He had a weird twinkle in his eye and jerked his head sharply right in a repeated private signal. Lansky decided to go along with the joke.

"Private Duffelbag reporting as ordered, sir." Lansky managed a snappy salute since this was a joke. The first sergeant smiled at him.

"At ease, Duffel . . . Bag." The CO's lips tripped over the name as if he just comprehended the preposterousness of it. He glanced at the first sergeant, who was staring deadpan at Lansky.

"Run up and get Private Duffel . . ." He looked at Rodriguez again. "Duffelbag's paperwork, First Sergeant."

"Yes, sir!" The first sergeant hustled off.

Lansky looked at his new commanding officer. Blond curls clung tightly to the broad boyish forehead, dark circles surrounded the light blue eyes with shadows of fatigue, pulpy lips seemed flaccid in contrast to the rest of his face, and high cheekbones dominated the young face. Some unseen force stretched his skin, making it creaseless, seamless.

"I'm Captain Robinson, Private, Bravo Company Commander." The man spoke formally, using the curtain between officer and enlisted man to conceal his disinterest. "First, Sergeant Rodriguez will assign you to a platoon. Tomorrow, you'll be taken over to supply and issued your field equipment. You'll not need to see the armorer until the morning of your first mission. That's five days from now. I'm going to let you stay in the rear until then. Use that time to get yourself squared away."

"Yes, sir."

"And keep your nose clean back here. Don't want to spend all my time on court-martials."

Rodriguez returned. "Here's the paperwork, sir. Py golly, I

fock hup! I must haf this man confused with someone else. He's Lansky, sir. See right here." Rodriguez pointed at Lansky's name. "I'm sorry, sir." First Sergeant smiled.

"Yeah, I bet you're sorry." The pulpy lips twisted slightly. "We'll have no more of this."

"No, sir!"

"Any questions, troop?" said the CO, reopening the legal file.

"No, sir."

"Get this man squared away, will you, Sarge?"

"Yes, sir." The first sergeant gestured Lansky out of the office.

"Mac!" the first sergeant barked at the desk clerk. "We gonna put Lansky in First Platoon. You go over to first platoon hooch and get Allen."

"Allen ain't gonna like this, Top."

"Too bad! Who da fock run dis company?"

"You do, Top. You do." The desk clerk jumped up and pounded the plywood out the door, skipped off the top step, and trotted off through the barracks area.

"Allen's in jor platoon, Lansky, he's in the rear getting his jungle rot treated. I'll have him show you 'round. Hey, priddy good one I play on the CO, huh?"

"Yeah, not bad. Surprised me. Not what I was expecting."

"We wasn't expecting you either, Lansky. We don't get too many guys sent up here by themselves. How come you here alone?" The first sergeant's face wasn't playful anymore.

"Well, when I was in Cam Rahn . . . ah . . . they put me on guard duty." Lansky could see a shrewd smile coming over the first sergeant's face. "And well . . . when I got up to Chu Lai . . . I was in American for a while . . . but they went home." Sweat ran under his fatigue jacket. "So . . . now I'm here." His hands flew out in a gesture of finality and then clapped back to his trouser legs.

The first sergeant's smile continued to grow, and his eyes narrowed. "You're a fock-hup, aren't you, Lansky? You been in trouble already, right?"

"Me? No, not me." The denial shot out too fast. He felt his face tighten.

"Dat's okay, Lansky. No big fockin' deal. You start over again here. You'll get plenty a chances to straighten out. In five days, you goin' to the bush. You ready to fock wid Charlie?"

"Well, yes, I am." He knew he wasn't.

"Charlie's gonna fock wid you, Lansky. You be ready."

"I will."

The clerk returned with another soldier. His companion stilt-walked delicately on tender feet, toes off the ground. One arm pumped dramatically, the other arm hung in a sling at his side. White skin glowed in contrast to the tan of the shirtless clerk, freckles blocked his skinny arms and bony shoulders, short waves of carrot-colored hair rolled under his rumpled boonie cap, and a pipe protruded from his broad mouth, pulling his lips back tightly, exposing his teeth.

The man seemed agitated. "Don't need no fuckin' new guy in my AO. Don't like it, I tell ya. I need some rest, goddammit! I got to hump the bush on these sore feet in five days. I'm on profile! How my feet s'pose to heal if I'm birddoggin' some FNG all over?"

"Sorry, Marty," said the clerk. He leaped the steps. "First Sergeant wants it this way."

"Hey, hey, help me up the steps. How'm I s'pose ta get up the steps?"

The clerk seemed exasperated now as he grabbed Marty's shoulder to pull him up the steps.

"Ah, ouww, slow down, will ya! Hurts my arm!"

When Marty made it up the steps, he saw the first sergeant

and became quiet. "You the new guy?" he said, looking at Lansky.

"Yes."

"Marty Allen. Welcome to First Platoon, I guess."

"You take care a'heem, right, Allen?"

"I'll do it for you, Top. Wouldn't do it for no one else."

"You get heem squared away and help heem be ready for da bush. Okay?"

"Wilco, Top. C'mon, let's go, new guy." Marty delicately negotiated the steps with small groans.

"Sounds like you're in pain."

"Don't worry about it. What's your name?"

"Ed Lansky. From Wisconsin."

"Not many guys from Wisconsin here. I'm from Pennsylvania. C'mon, let's hurry a little."

Lansky noticed that Marty moved with much less pain when out of sight of Company HQ. "Don't tell no one but I'm goin' to Maggie's tonight."

"What's Maggie's?"

"Korean restaurant down at the air base. You wanna go?"

"How're we going to get there?"

"I got a guy in Charlie Company gonna give me a ride."

"Okay, I'll go. Can you travel in your condition?"

"Sure, my feet are okay. I'm just doin' a little shammin' in the rear. Got sores and rotten skin on my feet, but I can walk."

"You mean you're faking?"

"Yup, wanted some time off, so I just complained about my feet 'til they sent me back here. Don't tell anyone."

"I won't."

"I gotta walk like this so they think it's still botherin' me. That way, all I've got to do is go to the infirmary once a day and *no* bush!"

"Sounds good."

"Yeah, I yell like hell down there when the medics take my bandages off. I put on a real show, especially when they pour that hydrogen monoxide on my sores."

"Monoxide?"

"Yeah, something like that. Today I rolled over backward off the gurney and claimed I hurt my shoulder, so they put it in this sling."

They were in the barracks now, and Lansky watched Marty look around carefully before allowing his feet to rest flat. He removed the sling and put on his shirt freely using the 'injured' arm.

"C'mon, let's go. We'll drop your duffel at supply before we go to Charlie Company. Just leave one uniform here.

"Okay, Private."

"Marty. Call me Marty." He flashed a smile and walked flat-footed to the door. Once outside he resumed the unbalanced stilt-walk, keeping his toes off the ground, free arm pumping furiously as his neck craned forward.

CHAPTER 10

September 25, 1971

Marty and Lansky walked through the small town of metal buildings that were the maintenance, service, and barracks areas at the air base. Marty led Lansky to a building that had a queue of soldiers standing outside it.

While standing in line, Lansky noticed the tortured condition of several of the nearby buildings. Two of them had their flat corrugated panels bowed out. The blue paint was scorched shades of black, gold, and rust. Both buildings had twelve-meter-wide holes in the roof. Twisted fingers of metal outlined the hole.

Lansky looked at Marty. "Must have had a fire in those buildings."

"Sure did. Anything that takes a direct hit from a rocket burns pretty strong."

"Oh, I didn't know that."

"Yeah, those two buildings were Maggie's I and Maggie's II. Charlie doesn't like the Koreans, he's always gunnin' for this restaurant, seems like he's frustrated since they built all those concrete revetments for the Phantoms. The last few times he fired us up, he went for the restaurant and put some holes in the runway."

"So we're standing on a bull's-eye." Lansky shifted his feet.

"Don't worry. Charlie won't fire us up until after dark. We'll be back at the base by then." Marty smiled at Lansky confidently. "Hey, you married?"

"No." Lansky smiled at the thought.

"Well, I am. See, here's a picture of my wife." He shook his wallet out of a plastic bag. "See, there she is."

"Pretty. You're a lucky guy."

"Sure am." The wallet slid back into the plastic bag. "Hey, you got one of these battery bags for your wallet?"

"No, I don't have any equipment."

"I'll have to get you one. Otherwise, your wallet will rot. I'm an RTO, so I get a lot of 'em. Hey, did you ever operate a radio?"

"No, I just went through regular infantry training."

"We need another RTO for the next mission. I'll teach ya how ta use the PRC-Twenty-Five."

"Okay." Lansky didn't respond to Marty's enthusiasm, the edgy discomfort he felt in this new and unknown world made him hesitant to speak.

"How about some poker later?"

"Maybe."

"I'm gonna get you in a card game when we get back to the company area. I love to gamble. I'll bet on anything." Marty kept up the barrage of questions all the way through the wait for a table and continued as they sat over their food. "I bet I know something about you."

"Like what?"

"You coulda been an officer, but you turned down your commission."

"How'd you know that?"

"When I first saw you in the HQ, all tall and serious. I thought you were an officer."

"I turned down my commission because it was an eight-year commitment."

"But you really turned it down because you've been demonstrating down at the university. You don't have military leadership in your heart."

"Got me again. How do you know all this stuff?"

"I'm an RTO. I have a good antenna. I can sense the important stuff about people."

"I hate the army. I'm only here because I got drafted to fight this senseless war." Lansky's anger grew he let his feelings go. "I'm glad we are on our way out, but obviously not fast enough because here I sit in Da Nang as a new infantry replacement. I feel used, misappropriated, enlisted against my will in an unjust cause." Lansky took a long drink from his Budweiser.

"In five days you will be in the war, like it or not." Marty bent to scoop noodles into his mouth with his chopsticks. *Sploot!* He sucked them in. Talking with his mouth full he said, "You wanna go home someday, don't you?"

"Yes." Lansky shifted in his seat and sweat formed on his upper lip.

"So do I and every man in Bravo Company. Right now you see me shammin'. I know how to sham in the rear. I also know how to be a first-rate infantry platoon radio operator. In five days, that's what you'll see from me." He picked up his bowl, draining the spicy contents. Belching, he grabbed his Bud and finished it. Pointing the can at Lansky, he said, "Tonight we begin your infantry platoon RTO training."

"Okay." Lansky's scalp began to itch.

"Okay? That's it? Don't get much from you, Lansky. You gotta find something inside you in the next five days. You fuck up out there or decide you don't wanna do something, you give old Luke the Gook an invitation to come creepin' round. He'll be watchin' you. You look half-assed, and he'll be in your face. You'll be dead, and so will a bunch of other guys. If you wanna live through the next year, your protest days are over."

Lansky did not finish his meal nor speak for a long time. The inescapable certainty that he was going to the bush hit him hard, a salvo to the gut, an internal explosion of panicky fear. He'd known this day was coming, but its immediacy released that which had been held back for so long in hopeful denial. Marty seemed to offer some hope of a way to go, a role in his unit, a place to take his stand. Lansky would do what Marty said, grateful the wacky fuck had decided to help. This possibility calmed him, his respiration slowed. His thoughts returned to Burn Out Beach down in Cam Ranh Bay where the dragon had flown over taking away his pain. He sighed, cracked his neck, and unclenched his fists. Events were in the saddle, beyond his control, he would wait patiently for the next resource to present itself. The phrase "I will survive," began looping through his consciousness. He wondered what form his warrior shield would assume.

After the meal, Marty managed rides for them back to the company area.

A poker game started in the back of one of the lonely barracks. The distraction made Lansky feel better.

One guy had a bottle of Scotch and a dirty glass. He poured the whiskey into the glass. Each man took a sip and passed it to the next.

Marty noticed Lansky's discomfort with this. "It's the way grunts do things, Lansky, we share, we're together. You'll understand once you've been to the bush."

Hot brass pipes followed the Scotch, pennies clinked on the bed, cards chattered.

Men groaned and laughed, they swore at each other, they loved each other's company.

The evening breeze cooled the room, the Scotch bottle emptied, warm beer started to get passed around, and the pipe followed. Conversation slowed and stopped, the cards stopped, some men slept.

Lansky was almost asleep staring at the floor, which now supported a pair of highly polished boot tips. Someone was standing over him, he jerked his head up and found himself staring into the face of First Sergeant Bulldog. Others were waking up and attempting to conceal the pipes and marijuana, Marty tried to find his arm sling.

"Ho, you fock-hups, too late for that. Could bust you if I want, I could bring smoke on jor ass!" Bulldog paused. "Bud I ain't gonna. Don't need the paperwork. Dat paperwork just like riding a bicycle." The corners of his lips turned up, the eyes remained hard.

A long silence passed with Bulldog standing over them. None of them moved.

Finally, Lansky asked, "Hey, First Sergeant, how come paperwork is like riding a bicycle?"

"Day both make my ass tired." The men smiled. "You fock-hups owe me one. I won't say nothing to da CO about this. But you owe me! Hey, who got a fockin' beer?"

One of the men found a beer under his bunk and gave it to the first sergeant. He took a long drink and walked toward the door then turned to look at his men. Lansky thought he was about to say something. Instead, he shook his head, turned, and walked into the night.

CHAPTER 11

September 30th, 1971

Red smoke curled over the log protecting the three GIs.

A bullet cracked the sky.

The sniper made Lieutenant Halverson jumpy. "Hey, Lansky, you got smoke? We need more cover."

Private Lansky raised himself on his left elbow to remove a smoke canister from his web gear. He felt a sudden change of pressure near his right ear. A pulse of energy glanced off the crown of his steel pot, ripping it from his head. Lansky flattened himself behind the log, heart pounding, eyes wide open, staring at his helmet lying in the dust. The sniper round had torn the camouflage cloth cover and creased the metal underneath. A strange sonic *zing* lingered in the air.

"Keep your goddamned head down, Mister New Guy!" LT was angry. "Believe me, it's good advice!" His eyes closed, a patient pause, opening his eyes, LT said, "You okay, Lansky?"

"Yeah, snapped my neck, but I can't feel any holes." His voice shook as he rubbed his scalp. "I'll keep my head down from now on."

"You're one lucky fuck, Lansky!" The anxious chatter from

the other end of the log could only be Marty Allen's. "That would have been the end of most new guys."

Lansky attempted to sound confident. "I am lucky, always have been." He rolled onto his back, removed a smoke canister from his web gear, felt his hands tremble, took a breath, pulled the pin, and lobbed it over the log.

Yellow smoke hissed from the canister as it rolled across the sand.

Another bullet snapped the air overhead.

"That papa-san is a pain where a pill won't reach," said LT.

"A mongrel nipping at the heels of innocents." Lansky grinned at the lieutenant.

"Fucking profound, Lansky. Fucking pro-*found.*" LT smiled sarcastically, surprised by the new guy's quick recovery.

"You musta read that somewhere, Lansky," Marty yelled. "You ain't that smart."

"Okay, okay. I read it."

"Gimme the phone, Lansky, switch to air support."

Lansky changed the frequency on his field radio and gave his officer the radio handset.

"Time to give Pops something to think about while we make our getaway."

Lieutenant Halverson depressed the talk button. "Tomahawk Four-Niner, this is Lonely Boy Actual, over."

Lansky noticed sweat dripping off LT's chin.

"Tomahawk, this is Lonely Boy, have sniper fire from the tree line at the top of the ridge. He's three hundred meters November Echo of my smoke, over."

A dust geyser erupted behind them.

"Roger-copy, Tomahawk, thanks, over and out." Looking at Lansky, LT said, "He's going to make his run now to cover our pickup bird."

A growling spot fell in the sea-blue sky. Gaining size and lethal shape, the gunship arced toward the ridge.

"So long, Pops," said LT.

Hidden hammers struck invisible anvils. The gunship opened with a long burst of cannon fire. Mushrooms of gray smoke and flying debris trampled the ridge, a fractured tree trunk bounced down the hill. White flame broke from the gunship, the mini-gun buzzed, evil, unnatural, the sound of five chain saws revved to full throttle. Wild dust clouds danced among the trees, suddenly stripping away leaves, branches, and bark. Flames exploded in the dry vegetation.

"Hey." The lieutenant nudged Lansky.

Behind them, helicopter vibrations grew suddenly intense. Flying below eye level, gaining cover in a sunken riverbed, the pickup bird closed on their smoke. Flashing above the riverbed, the Huey fanned sharply, sideways for a second, scrubbing off speed and then leveling into a delicate landing.

Ducking under the rotor blades, Lansky ran to the bird. He noticed a smile on the pilot's face. A bug-eyed caricature of the screaming eagle decorated his aviator's helmet.

They took off in a tight circle, increased gravity pinned Lansky to the chopper floor. He caught a brief glimpse of the burning ridge. His dangling legs rose gently as they dived toward the water. The pilot leveled off twenty feet above the shallow river. As the Huey accelerated, emerald foliage on the bank blurred, and the bird swayed side to side as the pilot negotiated each bend in the river.

A sampan blew into view. Three frightened river sailors hit the deck as the whirling machine shot overhead.

Looking back, Lansky saw a conical straw hat turning in the air. The wind caught his long legs, pushing them back. Pulling them in, leaning against the bulkhead, he extended his large hands across the aluminum decking. His sodden uniform hung loosely on his semi-athletic frame.

Cool air rushing by dried him. He felt the exhilaration of being lifted out of a tight spot. Smiling easy now, his green eyes gleamed under his subtle brow.

Climbing, they flew straight across dry rolling hills dotted with villages and roads. A small, brightly painted green bus bounced along the dirt path below. Passengers sitting on the roof and hanging in the doorway looked up briefly as the Huey flew over.

The abandoned air base near Phu Bai came into view. Passing over the hangars, they landed on a long concrete runway. Familiar, fatigued, dirty faces watched them step off. Lansky and Marty moved among the supine figures sprawled along the ribbon of concrete.

"Hey! Where ya been?" a sunburned, grimy soldier yelled at Lansky.

"Had to wait for an extra bird since we didn't get a ride on the first lift-out."

"That sounds like trouble."

Lansky lifted his steel pot up for all to see. "Had a sniper take a few shots at us. I think the Cobra got him."

A small group gathered to inspect the helmet, passing it man-to-man, fingering the creased metal and cracked inner liner.

Huddle shook his head. "That's about as close as she gets, Lansky."

"He's one lucky fucking newbie," commented Marty who sat near the group chomping on C-rat crackers.

Third Platoon was chattering about catching Charlie in their ambush.

Lansky dropped his pack, and then knelt to get out a can of spaghetti. His shaky hands fumbled with the tiny can opener unable to attach it to the rim.

Huddle watched silently then approached, taking the items from Lansky's hands. He deftly punctured the lid and levered it open. "Here you go, man. Take it easy, you survived your first mission."

"Thanks, Huddle." Lansky felt somewhat comforted by Huddle's sympathetic support.

Four ancient C-119 transports lumbered across the sky, turning to approach the landing strip. Seemingly hanging in the air, they floated toward the runway, whirling propellers reflecting sunlight, their black noses slightly raised. Each engine trailed a black veil of exhaust. The first transport touched down with a squawk. Wings sagged and bounced as she rumbled by, engines racing in reverse. The rest rolled past, shabby and tired.

They lowered their cargo bays at the far end of the runway. A company of ARVN disembarked from each. Four ARVN companies would be replacing one US company in this area. The Americans were pulling back, leaving this map grid to the Army of the Republic of Vietnam.

Bravo Company, 3rd Battalion, 20th Infantry of the 195th Brigade was leaving. The last American infantry unit in Vietnam was turning this area of operation over to ARVN. Some of the GIs stood and yelled, "Good luck, ARVN, Charlie is mad as hell."

Lansky sat on the ground, spooning meatballs from a can.

When he finished eating, he lay back on his pack, closed his eyes, wiggling his legs and shoulders into a more comfortable position, and thought back to the start of this, his first mission . . .

Smiling, he recalled LT's annoyance as he sat in the door of that crowded chopper. Every time Lansky fired a burst, LT caught hot brass in the face. Whenever he stopped firing, the door gunner poked him to continue. Looking back into the bird, Lansky saw there was no place for LT to go.

The door gunner pumped tracers into the near tree line as the chopper descended. He stopped to poke Lansky again. Hot brass pinged off the lieutenant's helmet, face, and chest, he leaned away covering the side of his face with his helmet, but it wasn't enough.

The ground rose in front of them. All six choppers fired from both sides. Angry orange tracers bounced across the horizon.

Hot brass rebounded off LT, three feet from the ground he'd had enough. Jumping into the prop wash, the officer sprinted for the nearest tree line. First Platoon followed, full packs rattling.

Silence of the hilly prairie replaced the roaring whine of six helicopters. Lansky looked over his shoulder at the birds, now specks across the distance.

The platoon lay on line in the underbrush, listening.

Lansky noticed an unusual irritation inside his uniform. He felt movement along his arms and legs, a slight stinging sensation. Red ants raced in and out of his shirt sleeve, a row of red bumps dotted his arm. He was lying on a fire ant colony.

"Motherfucking ants in my pants!" he whispered. "Damn!"

The lieutenant looked at him. Lansky started squirming in reaction to this emergency. LT Halverson whispered, "What's the problem?"

"Ants."

"Well, keep quiet."

Lansky took off his pack and started searching for his bug juice bottle. The sound of a lone helicopter approaching distracted him. While his hands fumbled for bug juice, a freshly-painted, olive-drab helicopter stopped and dropped three men. They bounced out of the bird on a dead run right at him.

He recognized the Bravo Company commanding officer in the lead. The CO seemed short next to his radioman and forward observer. His helmet bobbed over his eyes then back off his head. The CO cursed. They paused while he recovered his headgear. With the CO's helmet in place, they ran on, panting heavily by the time they stopped in front of the lieutenant.

"Halverson, what kind of a fuck-up are you?" The CO tried to catch his breath.

LT's jaw muscles began working.

"Stand up when I'm talking to you!"

"Yes, sir!" Halverson stood slowly.

"Where's the damn RTO?"

"Lansky, here, sir." As he stood, the insects pressed the attack, making it difficult to remain still.

The CO got right into Lansky's face. Pulpy lips and watery blue eyes stared up at him. "So, the new guy is fucking up!" He looked at LT. "How come you got a new guy on the radio, Halverson?"

"He volunteered, sir."

"Shit!" He spat. "What ta fuck you doing up in that bird, trooper? I told you to switch to air support frequency. Called you three times, can't you hear, boy?" The CO's face turned red. He shouted as loud as he dared.

The ants were grinding away. Lansky started to wiggle. "The door gunner wanted me to lay down support fire, so no, I could not hear you, sir."

"You can hear me now, right?"

"Yes, sir." Lansky shook his shoulders.

"We got half the damned air force up there waiting to help you and you ain't listening! If it was a hot LZ you'd be lying and dying now, wouldn't you? And stand still when I'm talking to you."

"Yes, sir." Lansky bent over.

"Have that handset at your ear on every insertion or your butt is mine, got it?"

"Yes, sir!" Lansky lifted his right leg and shook it.

The CO had attempted to ignore Lansky's gyrations, but they were too overt. He stepped back and looked at the nervous lieutenant.

"What's the matter with this man, Lieutenant? I never saw a man dance when I was chewing him out."

"Ants."

"Ants?" The CO's lips flattened into a hard angry line. "You gettin' weird on me, boy? Don't make me any madder than I am."

"No, sir! Ants! Got 'em everywhere."

Lansky couldn't suppress it any longer. He started shaking his uniform and jumping foot to foot, trying to shed the ants. "Gotta get some bug juice, sir." He hobbled off.

Tight as a banjo string, the CO clenched his teeth. The CO's RTO and FO fidgeted uneasily. Heavy silence filled the air.

Not knowing what to do, the young lieutenant smiled and pointed at the ant colony. "Lansky was lying right in the middle of it."

Exasperated, the CO said, "Call my bird back before I do some permanent damage around here."

The medic stood at Lansky's side. "Dude, you gotta strip off every stitch of clothing, then shake out the ants, and douse your fatigues wid bug juice." He handed Lansky a white tube. "Rub some a dis cortisone on your bites, everywhere, gonna sting, but that should clear yer pestilence and stop da itch. You got any allergies to bug bites?"

"No." Lansky put the cortisone tube in his pocket.

"See me later. I'll give you an antihistamine if you have a reaction."

Lansky was out of control. He grabbed his bug juice and weapon then labored off into the bush. Before disappearing, he yelled, "Don't nobody shoot me."

Quiet laughter passed along the platoon line. A muffled groan came from the bush.

LT laughed as he said, "I'm taking First Squad out on patrol to find a night logger. Don't nobody shoot Lansky."

The incident put the young soldiers in a light mood that carried into the evening.

The platoon found itself on top of a barren hill that overlooked a long stretch of rolling wooded prairie.

As the sun set, LT made his evening rounds inspecting the perimeter of his night defensive position. He noticed no one had dug in. Ordinarily, he ordered everyone to dig a hole, and then inspected each for depth. Under the influence of the day, he ignored standard procedure, saying, "I'm not forcing anyone to dig a hole, but it won't be me sitting on the perimeter all night."

This comment made everyone think seriously for a moment. But still, no one dug. The moon rose, bathing the night logger in silvery light. Restless, LT stood on the perimeter with the first watch.

Lansky lay on top of the hill listening to LT tell yet another version of the ant story. Muffled laughter followed. Lansky covered his head with his poncho.

The ground quivered. Lansky uncovered. A boiling chaos lit up the valley floor. It exploded with a sibilant *whoosh*, edged with a hornet's buzz. White flashes and red tracers erupted in the small woods across from them. Intense firing directed at a small area. Green tracers arced skyward. The *bump, thump,* and *boom* of explosions and then secondary explosions followed.

Metal shovels began clanging on dirt at the edge of his perimeter.

Lansky noticed LT standing and laughing as several GIs dug furiously. Firing and explosions echoed across the valley.

LT made no attempt to take cover or kneel down. Even when the first stray rounds and ricochets began whistling and wobbling overhead, LT stood his ground, teasing the frightened GIs who were suddenly motivated to dig.

Fragments of metal continued to whisper and hiss over their position.

Lansky crawled to the opposite side of the hill. Scanning the company frequencies on his radio, he found out what was happening. Third Platoon had a lot of movement in front of their ambush and had opened fire.

The sound from across the valley began to diminish and digging ceased. The lieutenant came padding up the hill and lay down near Lansky.

"Hey, was that Third Platoon's ambush over there?" LT was full of enthusiasm.

"Yup."

"Looks like they kicked booty."

"Sure sounded like it."

"Great day, huh?"

"Yeah. Good night, LT." Lansky fell asleep that night with the handset at his ear . . .

Looking back on his first day in the bush made Lansky smile. The mission was over, and he could relax. The ant incident and creased helmet were entertainments, something to laugh at, a diversion from the daily tensions of platoon life. It had opened a door, which Lansky walked through an accepted member of First Platoon.

He brought his mind back to the present. His legs had become numb from lying in one position while he daydreamed. Lansky shifted his body and squinted at the four chubby transports parked at the end of the runway. The ARVN reclined nearby waiting for their mission to begin.

Lansky wondered how many missions he had left.

A large wad of brown liquid struck the ground.

"Mail call, Lansky."

He looked up at Sergeant Massey noticing how the chaw in his cheek distorted his Howdy Doody face. Sarge dropped a letter in Lansky's lap.

The young soldier caressed the plump pink envelope. His first letter from home made him feel lonely. Round girlish handwriting in the return address corner read:

Sheila Jensen
2477 Prairie Circle, #27
Whitewater, Wisconsin

He opened the letter.

Dear Ed,

I've thought about you so much since you left. Hope this letter reaches you in good spirits.

I feel bad about some of the things I've said. I never intended to hurt you. You're not naïve. You're sensitive and innocent, too. These are good qualities, the things that attract me to you. Don't be so self-conscious.

You're lucky, too. It's your special quality. Everybody has always said that. When you're in trouble, things happen and you find a way out. This won't change. You'll come home and we'll—

An incoming rocket blast shook the ground behind Lansky. A compression wave rolled over him with such force his shirt collar slapped the side of his neck.

The letter ripped away.

Lansky flattened himself, covering his head with his steel pot. He felt the heat and flash of each detonation. Blast fragments rattled off an upright object suddenly in front of him. Lansky lifted the edge of his steel pot. Two large dragon feet stood inches from his face, talons dug in the dirt for stability. Debris from each explosion caromed off thick armored scales above the feet. The next ground burst shot grit in his eyes blinding him for the moment. The volley continued its march out along the runway toward the C119s.

After eight rounds, the barrage was over.

Lansky stood and shook chunks of clay off his shirt. The air base was shrouded in smoke and burnt cordite odors hung in the air. As the ashen haze lifted, he could see nothing was hit. The confused, young soldier did a slow scan around him searching for the dragon, but the beast was gone . . . or maybe never was there.

Lansky searched for his letter, finding the first page by the airstrip. Tiny flashes of pink paper turned in the smoky breeze rolling along the cement runway. The missing pieces of the letter blew toward the ARVN.

Pieces of his life would soon be in ARVN's hands.

The next months would be a test. He wondered how many lucky marbles were left in his can, how many hits his warrior shield could endure.

CHAPTER 12

October 20, 1971

Bedeviled by the vagaries of luck, Marty lamented his loss.

"Yup, the day I get back, I'm going to the track, and this time I'm betting that trifecta! I was on a hot streak picking ponies all day. So my wife says go for the big money, bet the trifecta. I had three nags picked perfectly, just didn't go to the window. Six hundred bucks I lost. My wife almost killed me. She sent me to the window, but I saw one of my picks in the paddock and started doubting him."

Lansky smiled at the slight figure squatting on his steel pot, fatigues still blackened by last night's drizzle. Marty waved his canteen cup of coffee as he talked.

"Boy, did I blow it! Boy, oh, boy, I shoulda just gone to the window and bet. Won't happen again, I'll tell you that!"

Lansky laughed. "What happened?"

"Dunno, dunno." His voice lowered as his head sank. "I just couldn't pull the trigger." He shook his head, studying the ground. "Every time I think about it . . . Sheeesh!"

Lieutenant Halverson broke through the foliage, interrupting Marty's daydream.

"Morning patrol is going out. Whose turn is it for RTO?"

"Mine, mine," said Marty. "Lansky went yesterday." The redhead, sometimes known as "VC" because he was so thin, gulped down a last swig of coffee then shouldered his weapon and radio. Walking toward the trail, he paused over Lansky. Looking up dreamily, he said, "Sure woulda been somethin' if I da' bet that trifecta. I da' been in the money. Six hundred bucks!" He put his thumb and first finger together, rubbing the imaginary money. "I was on such a roll, kissed by fate. Do you ever have that feeling, Lansky?"

"Sometimes it comes to me when I'm playing poker."

"Me, too, did you ever wonder why good luck runs out?"

"Not really. I just hope mine lasts."

"Allen!" A hoarse whisper came from the head of the trail.

"Yeah, coming. Lansky, gimme a commo check when I get out there, okay?"

"Roger that."

Marty stumbled through the brush to the head of the trail.

Lansky took off his sodden fatigue shirt and laid it on the rock in the morning sun. He took a deep breath as he surveyed the green hills and trees. GIs called this place Charlie's Ridge.

The radio receiver by his pack crackled out Marty's muffled voice: "Tango Two-Two, this is Ranger Six, commo check, over."

"Ranger Six, this is Tango, read you loud and clear, over."

He knelt and rummaged through his moist rucksack. A small olive-colored can with black letters labeled "Pound Cake" surfaced. He placed it on top of the pack with the label facing him. C-rations were not home cooking. This batch had the issue date of 1962. Everyone hated most C-rations, but a few were acceptable, even good. Pound cake was considered the ideal breakfast, treasured, even fought over. Lansky had won his in a card game.

Next, he pulled plastic explosive from his pack and pinched off a chunk of the waxy bar. It made him wonder who had discovered that C-4 could be used for cooking. When burned instead of detonated with a blasting cap, it gave off a brief but intense blue flame. Coffee could be heated or food steamed in seconds. He placed the white substance in a perforated cookie container used as a stove.

Reaching into the pack, Lansky brought out instant coffee, cocoa, and cream packets. Unfolding the collapsible handle of the canteen cup, he placed it on the stove. Holding all eight packets in his left hand, he ripped the tops off with his right and dumped the contents into the cup.

The pound cake can waited on top of his pack. He took a deep breath and reached for it, then cut the top off with his can opener.

Next, he picked up his canteen and poured water into his cup, forcing two sizeable ants out over the side. Lansky peered into the mixture of powders and water rising with one ant swimming frantically in the middle, his grimy finger spring-boarded it out into the wilderness. He paused for a moment, looking at his craggy unshaven reflection in the oily liquid. Grabbing an unwashed plastic spoon, Lansky stirred the contents.

His last book of matches was a little soggy. The third match set the C-4 ablaze, steaming the coffee in thirty seconds. Carefully placing the cup on a flat rock, he prepared another chunk of C-4 for the pound cake.

A feeling of well-being came over him. The anticipation of eating cake during a quiet morning made him feel good. As he reached for the pound cake, a low *wumping* sound rolled over the night logger. Lansky dropped the can and stood up, looking in the direction of the explosion.

The sound of surprised men stumbling over equipment came

through the trees. A muffled rattle of weapons being picked up ripped the glow off his mood.

Sergeant Massey's voice whispered from the command area, "Lansky, get on the radio, First Squad got hit and Second Squad ran out after them, those fools. See if you can hear what's going on."

Before he could pick up the receiver, another *wump* boomed over their position. This one more closely, followed by cries of the injured. It was now obvious both squads had been hit. Lansky picked up his radio handset. "Ranger Six, Tango Two-Two, sit rep. Over." He called Marty but got no answer.

Marty should be yakking like crazy if it was trouble. Lansky tried several more times with no reply. He didn't like it. Marty should be on the horn. "Tango Two-Two, Ranger Six, sit rep! Over." No response. He threw down the receiver in disgust.

Lieutenant Halverson came bursting through the bush, bug-eyed and red-faced. "Get on the radio and go up to Alpha Golf! Get a medevac bird out here. They're hauling in Second Squad. Some of them got dinged up."

"What the hell happened?"

"Allen stepped on something. Second Squad ran out to help. One of their guys tripped something off. Third Squad is hauling them in. Now get that medevac up! And bring that radio over to the LZ on the other side."

Lansky lunged through the brush, dragging his radio and weapon, calling in the request for medevac. The dispatcher told him to change to another frequency and wait for the pilot to signal him.

The LZ crawled with action. Several men, stripped to the waist, were hacking a wider perimeter with their machetes. A security cordon with weapons pointed over their heads stood behind them.

Second Squad stood on one side looking sheepish rather than injured. Three men had caught shrapnel from a small landmine. Their trousers were shredded and red. Several holes punctured each one's fatigue shirt, the wounds superficial, with minimal bleeding. They refused any treatment, acting like embarrassed victims of a practical joke.

The handset glued to Lansky's ear came to life with the vibrating voice of a chopper pilot.

"Tango Two-Two, this is White Bird Delta approaching your position. Pop smoke in five minutes."

"White Bird this is Tango Two-Two, Roger, wilco, over. Pop smoke in five minutes," Lansky yelled at Sergeant Massey.

The sarge waved the two smoke canisters he had ready.

One of the men in the security cordon crouched, his shouldered weapon aimed at moving brush. He lowered it as the point man for First Squad pushed into the LZ. Three men in bloody shirts followed. They were carrying Marty. His pants were completely gone. A long red gash split the skin on the inside of his leg. It was raw and swollen. The calf had a flash burn and several small punctures that bled.

As they walked, his head bobbed on his chest. Tears came to Lansky's eyes. They laid Marty on the ground with the other wounded. Rushing to his side, Lansky noticed the pallid skin and vacant eyes.

Grabbing his hand, Lansky said, "C'mon, Marty. Hang on. You crazy fuck, no sleeping on me! Stay with me, man."

The medic tightened a tourniquet on Marty's upper thigh and applied large compresses to the wounds. His head rotated slowly, sleepy eyes turned in Lansky's direction.

"Gonna bet that trifecta when I get home."

"Yeah, you are! You sure are! Gonna be Mister Easy Money living large at the track picking ponies on a sunny summer day."

Sergeant Massey popped the two smoke canisters, casting purple and white smoke over the perimeter.

They could hear the *woppity-wop* of a distant helicopter flying flat out and low. Within a minute, the gleaming white machine swung over the horizon, cutting a swath through the smoke. It climbed briefly and carved a tight circle around the valley.

"Tango Two-Two, this is White Bird Delta, wind check, over."

Lansky paused for a moment before advising the pilot on wind direction. Looking at the smoke and position of the sun, he made a quick guess.

"Delta this is Two-Two, north to south, over."

An angry voice cut in, "Check that, Delta, it's south to north." Lieutenant Halverson was monitoring several frequencies on radios in the command area.

The medevac dropped to the deck at the far end of the valley and came straight at them. As he lowered his tail to slow his approach, the chopper moved sideways. The pilot was coming in too hot, tail rotor nearly in the dirt.

A hurricane of dirt and debris blew over the wounded. They winced in pain and tried to turn away. Marty rolled on his side and covered his face. The medic tried to shield the wounded leg.

With stinging eyes, Lansky watched the pilot struggle to save the landing.

It looked like the chopper was going to fall right on the wounded. A sudden forceful wind shift knocked the bird to the ground in a hard landing. The dragon blazed down on the chopper, wings beating madly. Lansky's eyes streamed with irritation from the turbulent dust, yet he was sure he saw the dragon save the landing.

By the time he rubbed his eyes clear, the wounded were on the heavily laden chopper. As it lifted off, Marty raised his head and looked at Lansky. He held up his arm rubbing his first finger and thumb together, giving him the, "in the money" sign.

Tears came to Lansky's eyes again as he nodded his head. The bird passed slowly over the tree line and was gone. The dragon had disappeared.

"Tango Two-Two, this is Delta. I nearly lost it in that crosswind with your directions." Lansky almost said, 'thank my lucky dragon you fucker,' but chose, "Sorry, Delta, out."

The group walked back toward the night logger without talking. Halverson glared at Lansky, who returned the stare momentarily. It was obvious LT didn't hear the last radio transmission, nor did he see the bird almost crash, nor did he know the dragon had saved his ass, and Lansky knew he couldn't say anything about any of it.

Back in his area, the young soldier decided he felt good about not confronting LT on his miscalled wind direction. He had no words to share with any member of the human race about what was happening, or what he thought was happening. He felt empty, alone, drained and in no mood to argue or explain, didn't want to talk, didn't want to see anyone. He just wanted to be alone with his pound cake. Back in his AO Lansky found the black ants were enjoying carving tunnels through the yellow sponge. He envied them. They were on a run of good luck.

CHAPTER 13

November 1, 1971

Lying on that giant rock all night made Lansky's whole side numb. A dull glow of opaque light grew in the fog. Signs of morning came as a relief to the wet, stiff soldier. He could now see the boulders, stream, and evergreens in the dim morning light. His squad had lain there all night attempting to ambush a VC rocket team sneaking down the mountain.

Lansky was hungry. Having not eaten for a day, his stomach growled. Resupply choppers had been grounded by the fog.

He decided to move his numb leg, which made a rough scraping sound on the rock that was way too loud in the early morning quiet.

A large cold hand clamped around his neck, quietly but firmly reminding him of the need to maintain noise discipline.

The hand of Tiny had been laid upon him, a hand that Lansky respected. Sergeant Tiny was six and a half feet tall and weighed 250 pounds, a ranger on his second tour.

Growing daylight made it obvious that the ambush was over. Charlie wouldn't be moving at this time of day.

Tiny acknowledged as much by sitting up and looking around. "Okay, Lansky. You can move now. Sorry about putting the clamps on you, but sometimes it's the last few minutes of an ambush when something happens."

"It's all right, Tiny. I was just so stiff."

"Yeah, me, too. Willis! Go on up and get that claymore. Lansky, radio in, tell them we're coming up the hill."

"Will do, Tiny." Willis stretched again, knelt for a drink, got up, peed in the bushes, then jumped upstream, zigzag from rock to rock.

Lansky watched him disappear into the fog, glad he never had to disarm the unpredictable claymores. His radio work kept him busy.

They were all standing by the stream, stretching, or urinating in the brush.

As Tiny knelt for a drink, Lansky marveled at his mountainous build, the waist-long and V-shaped, swelling into enormous shoulders, and a neck so thick it made his head look little.

A loud blast from upstream froze everyone. Tiny motioned them down with a hand signal. The sound of pulverized rock raining down came through the fog. All eyes fixed on the foliage upstream.

White smoke oozed through the trees. It blended with the gray fog forming a dense curtain that rolled over them. Each man squatted alone, motionless, muzzle pointed upstream.

Seconds passed before they heard footsteps on the rocks. Each barrel traced the sound. Fingers slowly moved safeties to auto, resting lightly on the triggers.

Tiny yelled, "Identify yourself!"

"Willis!" came a cry. "It's me, Willis, man! The claymore went off before I got there. Musta' been the moisture. Boy, that was close. Lucky it was pointed in the opposite direction."

Lansky's radio crackled with the lieutenant's sleepy voice. "Alpha Fox, this is Lonely Boy Actual, sit rep, over."

"Lonely Boy, this is Fox. Situation negative. False alarm. Will be returning to November Lima. Over."

"Roger, Fox, watch out for a certain E-Five type, first letter of last name begins with motel. He's crapping in the brush off the trail you'll be on. Over."

"Lonely Boy, this is Fox, wilco, over and out. Hey, Tiny, watch out on the way back up, Massey's taking a crap in the brush."

"Picked a hell of a time for that. Don't like it. I'll take point."

Sergeant Massey was hunkered down in the brush, unaware of the eight VC lying in the rocks and bush twenty meters behind him.

The point man of their rocket team had tripped the claymore and lay in the brush next to them, bleeding out. A large boulder had shielded the rest from the blast. Their long, crude aluminum rocket lay beside them.

If Sergeant Massey hadn't stumbled down the trail to squat next to them, they would have gone back up the mountain.

Now they had to wait.

The leader signaled the man closest to Massey. Knowing what was needed, this black pajama-clad figure moved quietly around the rocks separating him from his prey. He raised the Marine Corps K-bar knife and extended his other hand, preparing to grab Massey's mouth as the knife plunged in.

Massey's severe diarrhea attack was consuming all of his concentration. It had kept him up all night.

The VC picked a target on Massey's back.

Lansky's patrol noisily climbed the trail.

The VC froze then began a slow, stealthy retreat, back behind the rocks.

Sergeant Tiny heard squirting, farting noises off the trail and raised his hand. The patrol knelt, weapons at shoulders, muzzles pointed at the earthy sound. Tiny looked into the bush.

"Identify yourself!"

"Huh? Wha—? Hey, it's me, Massey. Don't shoot."

The patrol lowered its weapons, recognizing Massey's voice. Tiny parted the evergreen shrub with his weapon, smiling. "Hey, Massey, caught you with your pants down, eh?"

"Gawddamn, Tiny. Got a case of the Hershey squirts that just won't quit! Been shittin' all night next to my hooch. LT got so disgusted with me, he made me come down here." Completing his toilet, Massey stood and hitched up his pants. His movements were slow and painful as he climbed back to the night logger defensive position.

As they entered the perimeter, Massey walked up to the hooch he had shared with LT. "Almost got my shit blown away. Wish you wouldn'a sent me down 'ere."

LT was lying under his mosquito-net hooch.

"Wish somebody would blow that smell away, Massey. The way you stunk last night, you were so close to death, they'd have done you a favor. Got real tired of listening to your short rounds go off all night."

Massey, pallid and drained, knelt and started crawling under the mosquito net.

LT Halverson raised his head to stare at him. "You coming in here, Massey?"

"I've had it, LT, I gotta lie down." Massey crawled onto his poncho liner and collapsed.

"Next time I'm in the rear, I'm going to get me a gas mask issued for sleeping with you."

Lansky smiled then headed for his rucksack. He noticed how unique each man's rucksack was as he passed them on the perimeter. Each had a different shape. A ruck assumed the personality of the man who carried it.

Tiny's pack was simple—filled with extra ammo, not extra ponchos. When it rained, Tiny got wet, and he didn't care.

Lansky recalled the ranger who had been in the platoon on his second mission. He'd reported from Ranger School at Fort Benning, Georgia. Being assigned to an average line company like Bravo had disappointed him. He considered himself superior and wanted an elite assignment. Fort Benning had been hot, but it wasn't 110 degrees in the shade as it was on his first patrol in Vietnam.

Lansky called in a dust-off rescue helicopter while standing over the hyperventilating ranger. The squad had poured all of its water over the man, taken off his boots, and loosened his clothes. Several of the men were fanning him with their shirts. His overloaded system continued to fry itself, a serious heatstroke began to develop. He was slipping into unconsciousness as the dust-off came *thwack-wacking* over the treetops. They lifted him out and climbed to maximum altitude. The cool air revived him before he suffered permanent brain damage.

The ranger was quiet when he returned. He no longer looked down on Bravo as an average company.

Tiny was a contrast. This giant with a booming baritone voice was a natural soldier, a real ranger.

Later, Lansky heard Tiny speaking patiently to the men in his squad. They were complaining about being hungry.

Tiny gave them the few meager rations remaining in his rucksack, explained again how the message of their urgent need for supply had been radioed in. He reassured them that a resupply bird would be out as soon as the fog lifted. Looking around optimistically he said, "I think it's going to clear up!"

Willis, only eighteen, wasn't going with the program. His emotions got the best of him. He made the mistake of saying, "If they don't resupply us today, I ain't movin'! I'm gonna stay right here, and so are the rest of the guys!"

This talk stoked a flame in Tiny's eyes, yet he tried to ignore his anger.

Willis didn't give up talking to the rest of the men about forming a protest group. He wanted them to refuse to move until they were resupplied. As he continued, Lansky could tell Willis was growing more irrational. Tiny couldn't ignore it any longer and told the young soldier to knock it off.

Willis yelled, "Forget it, you big creep, we ain't movin'!"

Tiny exploded. He charged the young rebel, plucking him off the ground by his shirt collar, shaking him violently, stumbling over equipment, but not falling. Willis's feet never touched the ground. "I'm tired of your fuckin' crybaby whining, you little worm! Put a sock in it or you'll be sorry. We're all hungry! Your complainin' don't help. So shut up! Got it?" He held the frightened man's face one inch from his own. Giving him one last snarl, Tiny dropped him in the dirt.

The squad area was quiet after that.

Fog and drizzle lifted enough that afternoon for the resupply chopper to find them. They were given double rations, and each man ate well before the afternoon move.

CHAPTER 14

In the afternoon, Tiny took the point leading his platoon up the mountain into a world of rock and cloud. The trail led over stones and boulders-steeply up, then straight down, across a narrow ledge, then descending through loose talus, climbing past fiercely vibrant purple rhododendron piercing the interstitial rock. A misty drizzle fogged the day.

Six VC lay in the brush off the trail counting the number of Americans going by. They looked for signs of alertness, condition, type of weapons, and how much ammunition each man carried. They had shadowed Lansky's platoon for several days. The Americans were obstructing a major rocket-smuggling route that the VC would fight to keep open.

Tiny felt a visceral discomfort as he walked that trail, uneasy, a scent of danger. *Charlie is here.*

The big man's uniform began to itch as it had on his last tour. Charlie's presence irritated his skin. He checked his men to make sure they were alert. Looking off the trail, Tiny hunted the bush and rock for movement—a glint of metal—any clue to Charlie's location.

He felt Charlie.

That night, he carefully placed each man in his quadrant of the night logger perimeter. He staked out a field of fire for each position, checked each man's weapon and condition of ammo. As dark crept in, he assigned a fifty percent alert: one man awake, one man asleep, all night.

He gave a serious talk at each position. "Charlie is here, man. I can feel him. Watch out. He's going to be sitting right out there in front of you tonight, waiting for you to go to sleep. Give him a chance to waste you, he'll take it."

Stepping back, Tiny surveyed his section of the perimeter, satisfied that his squad was ready.

Tran Thi Gung, Viet Cong commander, lurked in the underbrush outside the American perimeter watching every move Tiny made. Madame Tran, petite, distinguished by a jet-black braided ponytail was an inspiration to the men under her command. Famous for her slow, low-crawling penetration of the enemy perimeter, she'd return with a map of gun positions and strong points, ready to lead the attack. When these Americans had turned back one of her rocket teams, she decided to take command of the response. The flow of Katusha rockets toward the US air base at Da Nang was crucial. A hole in the runway prevented the morning flight of Phantom jets from taking off to bomb North Vietnam. She had prowled the trees around the American perimeter looking for her entry point.

A huge American was organizing a tight sequence of defensive positions. He seemed to look right at her as he pointed out the field of fire for each gun. The Americans were alert. There would be no penetration of the perimeter before the attack.

As the sun set, Tiny walked through the mist to the command area and found LT and Lansky.

Halverson was on the radio. Because this was active enemy territory, the Americans knew they could not hide. Since the potential for attack was high, LT was working with the artillery officer at the firebase. They would zero in artillery support with airburst illumination over the night logger. LT Halverson could then adjust it. He could have five 105mm howitzers pounding at the border of his perimeter within two minutes. Once the fire mission was established, it was given a code corresponding to its position. If LT radioed in his code, he would get artillery support where he needed it.

In the dark, Tiny could barely see Lansky and LT but heard their stiff, wet ponchos crackling in the breeze.

"Hey, LT, I got a feeling we're not alone up here. I think Charlie is right on top of us everywhere we go."

"Well, the CO says that this is one of the major rocket-smuggling routes."

LT's handset crackled with news that the first shot was out. It sang as it fell toward them.

Paaaa-wooooa.

Two hundred meters south of the night logger, bright white phosphorous strobed the darkness.

"Steel Chucker, this is Lonely Boy Actual, give me another willy-pete airburst one hundred north, over."

The next round came in louder and closer. Scratching the air, metallic sizzle growing in volume, silent just before detonation.

Paaah-woooooa.

The round flashed one hundred meters from the perimeter. Bringing in a real fire mission at that range would send shrapnel inside the perimeter, but he wanted it snug and took a chance on having it too close.

"Steel Chucker, this is Lonely Boy. You got it where I want it. File it. Over and out." LT handed the handset to Lansky. "Well, Tiny, if Charlie is up here I wonder what he thought of those fireworks."

"Don't know what he's thinking, but I do know what he's doing, crawling around out there watching our guards, looking to overwhelm us where we're weak. He wants to find the easiest way inside our perimeter."

"Yeah, probably true."

"I got an itch, LT. I know he's out there. Why don't we call in a fire mission? See if we can stir up young Charles's observation post he got going out there."

"Well . . . I don't know, Tiny. I'm not authorized to call in arty for no reason."

"Listen, LT, I was never wrong on my last tour. When I had the itch, Charles was close. We could fire a barrage on each side of the perimeter and see if we could get him moving. If we get movement, we got a reason for a fire mission."

"Might be okay to fire a probing mission. The CO would understand that. Make the first move instead of waiting for Charles to do it—Okay, creep around the perimeter, and tell everyone what's going on. Tell them to get down and cover up. I'll give you fifteen minutes."

"Roger, LT."

The six members of the VC cadre looked at Madame Tran with surprise when they heard the rapid popping of barrels coming from the firebase. The first barrage slammed into the side of the perimeter farthest from them.

Ca-Ca-Ca-Ca-Ca-Chowoooooaaa.

It stamped a line one hundred meters outside the perimeter.

The VC became uneasy.

The second series of pops sent a fusillade over their heads singing a deathly tune. The rounds struck an area one hundred meters from the corner of the perimeter adjacent to them.

Ca-Ca-Ca-Ca-Cachowwwooooooaaaa.

The white flash of the last two rounds could be seen from

where Madame Tran lay. Experience told her they were next. She signaled for a slow, stealthy retreat. They rose from their prone positions to begin quietly sneaking away.

A third rumble of artillery barrels popped behind them.

The VC fled, breaking brush, unconcerned about the noise.

Tiny ran to the machine-gun position. As he picked up the M-60, the artillery rounds touched off to his right.

Ca-Ca-Ca-Ca-Cachowwwwooooooooaaaaaa. A sequence of rapid detonations steamrolled a line a hundred meters outside the perimeter.

A little slice of hell unfolded in front of Tiny. Shrapnel buzzed and fluttered by him, mini-knives sliced the night. He showered the area with automatic fire. The rest of his squad opened up with their weapons. Long bursts of orange tracer sailed into the white shroud of explosions.

Yelling to Willis, he said, "Tell LT we had movement on this side of the perimeter. Tell him to walk the arty down the mountain."

Willis took off to give LT the message. The artillery flash died, and only the hop and skip of hot rounds remained, flying into and out of the dense smoke. Tracers struck large boulders, bounced off at sharp, crazy angles, arcing into the night, whining, pinging, and humming as they struck different textures of rock and wood. The heavy chatter of M-60 fire reverberated and echoed in between bursts.

By moving, the VC had avoided the pulverizing effect of the direct blast. One of them did catch shrapnel in the shoulders, back, and neck. Another caught a piece in the spinal cord. He fell, tumbling past them. They picked him up by the shoulders immune to his cries.

Madame Tran looked up the mountain at the shroud of smoke. Hot tracers burst from the cloud in all directions. Some passed directly overhead, cracking the air. Other rounds could be heard zinging and thudding off rock and brush, a metallic buzz, the twang of impact. One of the ricochets caught her in the foot, knocking her down, she wore an angry expression as she hobbled down the hill, resting on her comrade's shoulder.

The artillery pursued them. Each time they stopped to rest, another stick of explosions walked by them. Their determination and experience saved them. They pressed on. The man with shrapnel in his spine begged them to leave him behind.

In the morning, the lieutenant sent Tiny and some of his men down the hill. He found two blood trails and followed them for half a kilometer, which soon disappeared. Tiny stopped and looked down the mountain.

"I knew Charles was out here. I knew it. Now we got to watch it. He's going to be ticked."

They humped back up the hill, and Tiny reported to LT. "We found a coupla blood trails, LT. We dinged up Charles pretty good."

"No bodies?"

"No, sir. Charles never leaves anyone behind."

"Think we stopped them from carrying rockets down to the vils?"

"For a while. They'll find a new way."

"Will we see them again this mission?"

"Count on it."

"I want you to pass the word to be extra alert when we move. You, too, Massey, tell all the squad leaders."

"Okay, LT."

That afternoon the fog thickened.

Madame Tran picked three men and sent them back up the mountain then set up an ambush with the remaining men where she hoped to lure the Americans. Her men found the blood trail of one of their comrades then followed it through the fog to the last patch of rock and brush outside the American perimeter. They lay waiting all afternoon for the sound of Americans breaking camp.

The platoon was leaving through the opposite perimeter. Sensing the moment, the VC crawled through the fog up to the perimeter. The tail of the American column was walking away. Standing, the VC emptied their weapons on full auto. Each of them threw a grenade, then ran and slid down the mountain, engulfed by fog, hoping for pursuit.

Tiny's squad was last in line, and he reversed course as the firing started. The men at the rear returned fire. Tiny ran forward until he had a clear field of fire.

The enemy was gone, crashing brush down the mountain. Tiny fired into the fog. Running past two wounded men, he threw a grenade over the side.

When he returned, the two wounded men were being cared for. Willis had taken a round in the butt cheek and needed an immediate dust-off.

Lansky knelt by him calling in the request. The other man had shrapnel in the arm and hip. It hurt like hell, but he wasn't fatally injured.

Tiny walked back to the side of the hill. He considered a headlong plunge over the side—his hate almost strong enough—but he knew, the VC would be waiting below.

He returned to where the wounded were being treated. Approaching the lieutenant, he said, "I'd like to volunteer for tonight's ambush, LT, I know a good place for one."

CHAPTER 15

November 7, 1971

They sagged against the side of the gully, fatigued to the bone. In the beginning, Lansky counted the saddles and ravines his patrol traversed, but the sun had withered his interest in numbers.

Lansky rolled onto his elbow and scanned the country he'd just crossed. Monsoons had washed deep cuts into the rocky hills. Leached grainy soil, cacti, wispy grasses, dense thickets of stunted trees, and clumps of woody shrubs with small, hard leaves lay in the folded topography that rose steadily to become the Annamese Cordillera.

Climbing this sandy soil was like walking on a treadmill. Descending was like skiing, feet churning up small stones, clattering down the side. They made too much noise. The more tired they got, the more noise they made.

LT decided to stop and rest. "We gotta check out a few more of these ravines, then we can hang 'er up." He drank from his canteen while looking at his map. "I figure two more, then we can swing back." He handed his canteen to Lansky. "The CO says they're using these gullies and washes for their resupply patrols headed up to Charlie Ridge." Studying his map, he traced a dirty finger along his intended line of march.

Lansky took a long pull from the canteen and handed it back. "They got patrols out in broad daylight?"

"Yup, they're desperate. You guys ready? Let's go look at another dam gully." LT sounded tired.

As they stood, Lansky noticed only small patches of olive remained visible on their sweat-blackened uniforms.

Lifting his leg to take the first step up found him remaining in nearly the same place, as the earth parted around his sliding boot. He duck-walked on the insides of his feet to decrease the back-slide. His ankles and legs hurt from hours of straining at unusual angles. The sand collecting in his boots chaffed his skin. He looked up to see McGowan, the point man, pause at the top of the ravine scanning the next one. His casual, tired survey ended abruptly. Crouching, he signaled LT forward.

"We got five or six Charlie types walking along the trail below!" the point man whispered, chest heaving.

McGowan, Lansky, and LT crawled across the top of the narrow ridge and looked over the side.

Six, small, brown men dressed in black pajama pants and peasant shirts walked along the trail at the bottom. Each of them carried a pack and an AK-47. LT motioned the rest of the nine-man squad up the hill.

"On line. Fire when I do," he whispered hoarsely.

Charlie had passed their direct line of fire. They would be shooting up the ravine instead of directly down into it.

A crackling burst from LT's M-16 set them off. All nine men emptied their thirty-round clips in a sustained volley. The *wump* of Jackson's M-203 grenade launcher continued while the others rattled new clips into firing chambers.

The VC jumped at the first report from the top of the ravine, dropped their packs into the spraying sand, sprinting forward. One of them collapsed and was dragged by his comrades into a dense thicket on the side of the trail.

"We only got one of them?" LT yelled incredulously. "Keep putting rounds into the shrubbery. Fire on semi, and this time aim at something! Give me that radio, Lansky." He snatched the radio handset. "This is Rover One Actual calling Lover Boy Actual. Have contact. Over."

"Rover, this is Lover Boy, Roger copy, wait one for Actual. Over." It surprised the LT just how quickly the Command RTO got his CO on the horn.

"Rover, this is Lover Boy Actual. Sit rep. Over."

"Okay, Lover Boy, got six armed Victor Charlie types pinned down in a ravine about one klick west of position Golf Zebra. Over."

"Roger, Rover. Have a Cobra up. Need some support? Over."

"Affirmative, Lover Boy. Over."

"Okay, Rover. Go up to Alpha Sierra and ask for Black Lancer. Give me a minute to raise him first and relay your positions. Over and out."

"Roger wilco, over and out." He looked at Lansky.

"Cack up, Alpha Sierra."

Lansky pulled the yellow and black plastic code card out of his shirt. He looked at the tiny wheel in the middle labeled with the letters of the alphabet. Lining up the guide letter of the week with the number of the week on the outer ring of the cack-card, Lansky matched "A" and "S" on the inner wheel with the outer ring numbers.

"Forty-five."

The lieutenant switched frequencies.

"This is Rover One calling Black Lancer. Over."

There was no response.

"Not close enough yet. Keep trying, Lansky. I gotta see what's goin' on." He handed his RTO the handset.

The squad laid a steady fire on the clump of stunted trees keeping Charlie in place. Occasional muzzle flashes erupted from the woods. Jackson fired his grenade launcher and swore at himself.

"Sonuvabitch. Lieutenant, them cocksuckers keep movin' round in that thicket, and I can't put it on 'em."

"You've seen movement?"

"Not in the last minute, but they're still in there, still shootin' back at us. No way are they gonna get outta that ravine without us wastin' 'em."

He fired again. LT tracked the round to the middle of the copse: a dull flash and muffled explosion, then gray smoke oozed out of the brush.

"Hey, LT, why don't we jus' run along this ridge an' go down there to get Old Charles?"

"'Cause we got a Cobra inbound soon."

"Yo, LT! Got the Cobra up," Lansky yelled from the other side of the formation.

The officer waded behind his men in the uneven footing and grabbed the handset.

"Black Lancer, this Rover One Actual. Over."

The chopper pilot's vibrating voice bounced out of the receiver.

"Rover Actual, this is Black Lancer. Have received your position and situation from Lover Boy Actual. Where are they from your location? Over."

"Lancer. They're a hundred fifty meters east in a thicket at the base of the ravine. Over."

"Roger. Copy. Rover gonna do a flyby to eyeball it and see if I can spook Charles into confirming his position for me. Then I'll make my run. Pop smoke on your position. Over."

LT put the receiver down and pulled a smoke canister from his belt. Pulling the pin, he laid the canister on top of the ridge next to his men. A yellow fog formed over the men lying on line, firing into the thicket.

Their weapons were overheating, frying the LSA lubricant coating each part. Smoke curled out of the barrels, handgrip vents, and ejection ports. McGowan had nearly emptied his shotgun vest of the grenade rounds. He continued to fire and curse, never seeing if he was hitting anything.

An airplane-like helicopter with a sleek fuselage growled over their position. The jet engine whined, and the rotor blades rumbled as it dove down into the ravine, buzzing the thicket.

A muzzle flash pulsed from deep in the copse as the Cobra passed over. Sparks ignited on the birds under armor.

The gunship climbed steeply out of the ravine turning away in a high, wide circle, gaining altitude effortlessly. Grinning shark's teeth and beady eyes decorated the nose painted several shades of camo-green. It bristled with armaments.

"He's coming in, LT," yelled Lansky.

"Cease fire men, the Cobra's coming in. See if he spooks young Charles out of the briar patch."

"Bet he's gonna smoke Charlie's butt, huh, LT?" yelled Jackson.

"We'll see."

They put their weapons up to watch the show. The gunship was several thousand feet over the ravine and went into a steep dive away from it. Turning 180-degrees, the pilot pointed the Cobra's grinning teeth right at the ravine. The *woppity-wop* of the blades grew louder as he closed on the target.

Two puffs of white smoke erupted from the wing-like stabilizers. Rockets cut the azure sky, emitting red tracer trails, each five hundred feet, to help the gunner guide them to target. They hissed past the GIs and slammed into the ravine fifty yards in front of the thicket. Geysers of dirt and rock streaked into the sky. A *chug-chug-chugging* came from twin canisters mounted below the fuselage. Exploding forty-millimeter cannon rounds marched up the ravine and through the thicket. The impact sounded like a row of boxcars slamming together.

A desperate figure stumbled out of the woods, staggering up the ravine.

Multiple black barrels protruding from the shark teeth flashed white-orange flame. A buzz saw at high RPMs, the mini-gun lifted broad curtains of dirt and rock over the man and much of the rest of the valley. Clouds of hot brass rained from the mini-gun ejection port. Shiny shells caught sunlight as they fell to earth, hitting the valley floor, *pinging* like tiny bells.

Diving deep, the pilot held the screaming mini-gun on target, its reverberation chattering off the valley walls.

Secondary explosions erupted with a thud, igniting a powerful burst of heat and light. Waves of intense orange flame rolled through the thicket. Plumes of oily black smoke twisted skyward.

The smiling teeth flew over the target, jet engine hissing, climbing out of the valley, then circled for another pass.

A rolling dust cloud formed over the ravine, rising above eye level. Flames from the trees spread. Dry vegetation on the valley floor caught fire, glowing and crackling through the haze. Lansky had the handset to his ear.

"Rover. This is Lancer. Softened them up for you. Want another pass? Over."

"Hey, LT, do we need another pass?"

The lieutenant had been surprised by the ferocity of the attack. He turned slowly to Lansky. "Negative. If that didn't do it, nothing will."

"Black Lancer, this is Rover, negatory on the pass. Over."

"Rog, Rover. This is Black Lancer, will circle until you give the all clear and confirm my KIA count. Over."

"Roger copy, Lancer. This is Rover. Over."

They all stood now looking into the ravine, weapons at their sides. The odor of high explosives hung in the air. Dust began to settle. Small fires continued to snap in the scrubby brush. There was no movement. The man who had fallen out of the thicket in an attempt to escape was not visible.

"Don't tell me that damn dink got away. Gimme the glasses."

One of the men handed LT a pair of binoculars, and he glassed the ravine.

"Can't see him. Better go down and look."

Their initial steps down were slow and careful. But as the footholds gave way they began sliding and jumping. A small avalanche of rocks preceded them to the bottom. Caution returned as they formed on line across the trail and stepped off up the ravine. They stopped at the collection of packs dropped on the trail.

"Looky here, LT. These packs are just sandbags and rope."

"Yup. You guys watch the trees. I'm going to look inside."

He knelt cautiously, visually inspecting the packs from several angles before touching them. Pulling open the carefully knotted cinch string at the top revealed rice and candy. Chewing on the candy, the patrol moved past the rocket craters toward the smoking thicket.

The offensive odor of burnt hair and flesh stopped them short.

Much of the foliage was gone from the small trees on the

fringe. All the leaves and branches were stripped from the interior trees. The trunks were split like toothpicks; jagged holes punctured the remains. The earth was charred down to dirt.

As they moved closer, their boots stirred a fine ash that mixed with sweat that darkened their faces.

Charlie tried to hide behind the trunks of some of the larger trees. It hadn't worked.

"Think they're dead, LT?"

"A thousand times over. Where's the one who ran? Shiiit. Look over there!"

They all looked up the side of the ravine at the missing man, lying on his back, head down, legs up about five feet above the trail. Empty eyes in the upside-down death mask stared at the sky.

"Must of gotten blown up there." Jackson was surprised.

"Gawddamn." McGowan marveled at the violence.

Jackson shook his head. "All this for a few dinks."

"Yup." LT had grown quiet.

Lansky turned away, overcome by the carnage.

Too busy with the radio during the attack, his feelings were catching up with him. His hands shook. Fear, excitement, and disgust welled up inside him. Slowly, his arms stretched tautly skyward, his head tilted back, a fierce expression of anger came over his face, then deep anguish.

"Why am I here?" Lansky whispered to himself. "Why am I here?" He knelt, facing away, looking down the ravine.

"Lansky, call Black Lancer. Give him the all clear, then the CO. Tell them six KIAs," said LT.

Lansky followed orders. The CO was enthused with the report. Lansky's disgust grew as he listened to his commander's excited voice. It expanded when the CO ordered the bodies be prepared for lift-out.

His eyes closed, his heart raced. It took a while to gain the composure required to tell LT.

"The CO wants us to get the bodies in place . . . for a lift-out."

Lansky could see discomfort in LT's face at the thought of dragging the bodies down the trail.

"You got smoke, Lansky?"

"Yeah."

"Stay on the horn and bring in the bird. Pop smoke for him when he's inbound. We'll lift the bodies out right here."

"Okay." He put the handset up to his ear and made the call.

Later, Lansky stood in the prop wash, as the KIAs were placed on the chopper. The bodies were pocked with penetration trauma and blistered flesh. Some had missing limbs.

When the Huey was gone, Lansky withdrew, ignoring the others on the back trail. The labor of climbing the sandy sides of the washed-out ravines brought a quick sweat, stinging his eyes. Wiping his forearm across his brow cleared his vision for the moment. After an hour of steady slogging, they paused at the top of a ridge, and he drank from his canteen. The water tasted like boiled plastic.

The green dragon landed on top of the next ridge. Lansky blinked, trying to clear the crusty salt from his eyelashes. His vision remained foggy, eyes irritated from continuous rubbing.

The dragon unlimbered its wings, blue-green in the pitiless sun, stretched its long neck, raised its prehistoric head, and leapt out over the wash, diving down, gaining speed. Banking down the defile, it began flapping its wings—the snap of heavy canvas in a strong wind—climbing off toward the sea, a spot in the distance . . . gone.

Lansky's breathing slowed. Water from the canteen tasted sweet and cool.

The dragon's flight drew something hard and dark from his

soul, taking it away to drop in the South China Sea. His warrior shield had been struck but remained in its place.

The patrol moved out, sliding down the sandy ravine then walking along a dry arroyo. They would soon be back at the night logger. Then he would be able to rest.

Lansky repeated a phrase to himself over and over, "I will survive."

CHAPTER 16

November 14, 1971

Nguyen watched the American column labor along the trail toward a banana tree grove bordering the swamp. Oppressed by the pre-monsoon heat, he took a warm soda from the case and sipped it, while squatting at the water's edge.

He'd been shadowing this American patrol all morning, hoping to make a sale. The GIs stopped in the shady grove and now rested in its understory.

Nguyen smiled when a thirsty Lansky appeared in the saw grass across from him.

Lansky waved Nguyen over, holding a roll of military pay certificates—MPC—in his grimy hand.

"Hey, GI Number One," said Nguyen.

Swinging the case of Coke cans to his shoulder, the eleven-year-old plunged into the knee-deep swamp. Each step released a rancid, sour-smelling gas. His feet sank into the muck and made popping sounds as he pulled them out. A trail of bubbles rose to the surface of the coffee-colored water each time he put his bare foot down.

Looking at Lansky on the bank made him smile in anticipation of cash in his pocket. He even smiled at the GI back in the trees, aiming a weapon at him.

Pausing on the slippery bank, Nguyen picked several leeches off his ankles then struggled up to solid ground.

Lansky looked over his shoulder, then down at the boy.

"How much?" The towering American with the curious foreign face smiled at Nguyen.

"Tan." He held the fingers of both hands up and said it again, "Tan."

"Too much! Ohhh, okay." Lansky stuffed two orange notes in the kid's hand. Grabbing the case, he sliced through the saw grass and was gone.

Nguyen felt pride and elation as he waded back across the swamp. He'd made enough in a few hours to keep him in candy, rice, and cigarettes for a week. Life would be easy for the next few days. Much better than the time right after he lost his family. During those months, he had nearly starved to death. He survived by stealing and begging, until he learned how to deal with the Americans. Bartering on the black market, Nguyen bought peace medallions, film, soda, and other comforts of interest to the Americans. The price they would pay for things astounded him.

His hardworking rice farmer family rarely had any money. Most of the people in his village only had cash after the sale of their crops. Yet it spilled out of the Americans' pockets like a monsoon-swollen river. He was making more money than his parents had ever dreamed they could make.

His hard, bare feet found the trail back to the village. Lighting a cigarette, he took a deep breath and swung his arms like a marching soldier.

"Won, two, tree, four."

As he approached the main road, the sound of truck traffic came to his ears. Scrambling up the bank, he walked along the shoulder in a dust cloud kicked up by the trucks.

The road passed the American firebase at Nam Phat Lam. Soldiers referred to it as "Fat City," an ugly scar on top of the only high ground on this plain of rice paddies. Shabby black sandbagged structures broke the horizon at the top of the hill. An American flag unfurled itself occasionally in the slight wind. A chain of bunkers surrounded the hill, shielding artillery positions. Row after row of concertina wire stretched down the hill toward the road, then curved off to surround the perimeter. Some of it was strung two or three rows high, supported on metal posts.

Nguyen slowed, discreetly studying a section of wire he had secretly marked to see if anything had changed. He could see spots where careful clipping and crimping made it possible to open and close the wire like a door.

It was difficult to notice the cuts because of the care with which it was hooked together. The wire appeared whole. Only Nguyen's trained eye knew where to look for the nearly imperceptible breaks.

The metal chopper pad at the base was empty now. Three days ago, it had been crowded with GIs in full field dress. Another rotation of platoons was being made from the field to guard duty at the firebase.

Buddha had favored Nguyen. The changing of the guard brought forty new customers to his territory. He smiled at his good fortune. A fresh set of squads on patrol thirsty for a Coke and green guards on the perimeter meant he could try his trick again.

His hunger hurried him toward the village. The sharp briny odor of *nuoc mam* greeted his nose.

Entering the village, Nguyen stopped at a flyblown hut with an open front. An elderly mama-san spat betel nut juice and smiled as he held out one of the orange bills. The boy squatted next to the huge wok with a fire burning under it. Steam rose lazily from the stew as she filled a bowl with the rice and fish head mixture. She gave him his change, the bowl, and chopsticks, then squatted to watch him eat. Flashing brown betel nut-stained teeth at him, she asked how he had come by so much money.

As he lifted food to his mouth, he explained how he had sold Coke to the Americans. She warned him about the danger of being out there.

He responded that it was no problem for a brave man. Thanking her and returning the bowl, he ambled into the street and lit a cigarette. His Zippo lighter closed with a metallic *chimp*.

Passing some of the other shops, a handsome gold watch in a tiny display case caught his eye. He entered the shop and extended a polite greeting to the proprietor. He'd long dreamed of owning a watch like this. It would give him extra status among the children of the village. He could see himself showing it off and being a "big honcho." The watch was a Seiko from Japan.

Nguyen tried it on, held it out at arm's length to admire it. Putting it next to his ear, he noticed the shrill sound of the battery. He began to barter with the merchant, their voices sang and clucked for several minutes. It was too much. The boy smiled and bowed as he left, thinking about how he might steal it. He really wanted it, so he would have to steal it or do his trick on the Americans.

Back at the firebase, Sergeant Gordon H. Tippler inspected the guard positions his squad would man that night. After thirteen years in the army, he remained an E-5, the lowest grade of sergeant. His wife never wrote him anymore, but the bank did. They were repossessing his Chrysler Imperial. He wondered what his wife was doing with the money he'd been sending her to make the payments.

Worst of all, his squad had no respect for him, nor did his commanding officer, Lieutenant Halverson. The squad mocked him openly for the way he scrambled the English language. He wasn't permitted to forget about the large words he attempted to use but could not pronounce.

When he had a spare moment, Tippler read army manuals kept in his pack. He attempted to quote memorized regulations from the manual, but somehow he always broke down.

His squad set him off for entertainment. Even when the consequences were extra duty and dirty details, they just couldn't resist getting him going.

The latest problem occurred on the platoon's last day in the bush. Two of his men fell asleep on guard duty.

LT found them wrapped in their ponchos, snoring at their perimeter guard positions. One entire flank of the night logger was unguarded.

Halverson stomped off to Tippler's sleeping position and roughly kicked him out of his poncho. "Hey, shit-for-brains, did you know both men at your guard position are asleep on the perimeter?" LT was pissed.

"Sleep? Huh? Well, I better get down there."

"Yeah, you better get down there and make sure your squad covers its position at night. Have them see me today to sign their Article Fifteens. Next time it happens, you get one, too."

Tippler didn't need another Article Fifteen on his service record. His face got red as he approached the squad guard position. Davis and Bohanan were snoring innocently. He kicked them rudely.

"Hey, Sarge, why ya breakin' foul on us like that?" cried Bohanan.

"Because yer sleepin' on guard duty."

As he chose his words, the pages of the army manual turned in his mind. "You'll be reportin' to the lieutenant today to sign your AR-Fifteen papers. This is clearly neriglection and deliction of duty."

They were half-asleep.

Tippler noticed his error. "I mean it is clearly deliction and relection of duty."

Slow, sleepy smiles crept across their puffy faces. They looked at each other.

"What was that again, Sarge?"

"Hey, you know what I mean. Now don't fall asleep again!"

"Didja hear that one? Haw-haw! Neriglection and rediction? Oh, brother! That's a good one."

"Give him a break. He's not fluent in the English language." Davis coughed up morning phlegm while laughing.

The sarge stormed off.

"Hey, Sarge! Did you mean dereliction and neglect?"

As they sat around the LZ waiting for lift-out to the firebase, Davis and Bohanan mock-lectured each other about neriglection and deliction of duty, while Lansky reclined, reading, on his rucksack. For a while, he found Davis and Bohanan entertaining, but it got old soon. He almost felt sorry for Tippler.

Eventually, LT said, "Knock it off. You're in enough trouble as it is!"

Tippler suffered silently. Halverson noticed how upset Sarge was, and, in a rare moment of compassion, attempted to counsel him about, "not letting them get to you."

* * *

Sergeant Tippler now walked between the rows of concertina wire to place his claymore mines for the evening. He found an elevated piece of ground with four holes drilled into the hard-baked clay. The same spot he had placed his claymores the last three nights.

"Okay, Bohanan, put one of your claymores on this mount."

"Gee, Sarge, putting it in the same place every night seems so predictable. Shouldn't we change the position? A dude from Echo Company says he had one of his claymores stolen here." Bohanan seemed genuinely concerned.

"Steal a claymore? No way anyone is gonna make it through a hundred yards of wire and steal a claymore sitting in front of a machine gun."

"Well, that's what the dude said."

"Just put it where I said, Bohanan!"

"But, Sarge, it's so obvious sitting up there."

"Put it where I said, and don't bug me."

The private unfolded the metal legs on the bottom of the green elliptical mine and plunged them into the holes. He grumbled while inserting the blasting cap and stringing the detonator cord back to the sandbagged firing position. Using a screwdriver, he wired the cord to the clacker, a pliers-like firing device.

Now Bohanan stood behind the M-60 looking out across the wire and decided that Tippler was right, no way in hell anyone was going to steal that claymore.

CHAPTER 17

November 14, 1971

Sundown in the village found Nguyen gathering pieces of cardboard on a side street.

The shops were closed now, motorbikes and pedicabs quiet. Most of the villagers were in their hooches, hoping for a quiet night.

Nguyen dragged the cardboard into an alcove between two shops. He fashioned a bed from the pieces, as was his custom.

Smoking a few cigarettes while lying on his bed helped him relax enough to attempt some sleep. As his eyes closed, he saw a gold watch and visualized the sequence of events he would undertake that night.

A few hours later, Nguyen woke up, checked his wire clippers, and walked behind the village, off the road, toward the firebase.

The *wump* of artillery grew louder as he got closer.

Crossing the road, crawling through the ditch, he stopped next to the wire, lying there for an hour, watching and listening.

When the artillery flashed, he checked the position of the bunkers and plotted his course.

Patiently approaching his secret spot, unhooking the first row, Nguyen moved it only enough to squeeze through. Each row was left open to facilitate a hasty retreat.

Artillery rounds hissed over his head.

Pausing a few minutes at each row, looking ahead, listening, then resuming his slow, low crawl, the little phantom closed on the American firing position, movements cautious and measured.

Nguyen was now less than ten feet from the claymore. Perspiration broke out on his upper lip as he inched ahead. His face was almost touching the mine. He could hear his heart pounding. He froze for a moment worried the Americans could hear it, too.

The fear passed, and the wire clippers came out of his back pocket. An artful reach around the mine allowed him to cut the detonator cord. Rolling to his side, he pulled the mine out of its anchoring holes.

With it in his shirt, he made his way back out through the wire, carefully closing each row behind him.

Morning routine at the firebase included retrieving the claymores. When Sergeant Tippler saw one was missing, he sizzled with indignation.

Bohanan and Davis had been on duty in the pre-dawn hours at the firing position. No one was in the mood for the lecture that Tippler was about to begin.

Lansky could hear the arguing as he and Lieutenant Halverson approached for morning inspection.

"You guys at it again? What set you off this time?" Halverson wasn't happy.

"Hey, LT, someone duffed with a claymore, and Tippler's trying to blame us," Davis yelled.

"Well, you were the last ones on duty." Tippler took an assured tone.

Bohanan sulked, staring at the ground. "Wasn't our fault."

"No one was out there during our watch!" Davis replied in a rising voice.

"No one was out there during my watch either!" Tippler was shouting now.

"Oh, yeah? Well—"

"Shut up, all of you." LT jumped on the sandbagged wall. His eyes followed the cable to the spot where the mine had been. "How come you put the mine in the same spot as last platoon, Tippler?"

"Well, it seemed so perfect."

"Told ya not ta put it there, Sarge," Bohanan said angrily.

"Shut up! You don't tell me nothin'. Why, if LT wasn't here now, I'd—"

"You'd what? What would you do? Huh, what?"

Tippler was nose to nose with Bohanan, daring him to swing. LT started laughing. Bohanan and Tippler backed off to look up at the lieutenant. His chuckle grew into a belly laugh as he pivoted on the sandbagged wall to look down at Tippler.

"Ya know, Tippler, it just occurred to me that this is very funny."

"Funny, sir? I don't get it."

"Well, you're blowing up all the time, right?"

"Huh? Yeah."

"And these guys are always setting you off, right?"

"Well, I guess so."

"Know what I'm going to call this squad from now on?"

"Hmmm." Tippler didn't answer, braced for the insult.

"Claymore and the Clackers! Get it? They're settin' you off, and you're blowin' up. Get it?"

Some of the other men smiled. Lansky looked away in disgust as the claymore controversy had become tiresome.

LT walked away, laughing and shaking his head.

Later in the day, Nguyen walked up to the main gate of the firebase. He showed the claymore to the guard at the gate. The guard called his CO, who came out to talk to the boy. The CO paid Nguyen fifty MPC for the mine.

Nguyen skipped into the village and bought his watch. He had enough left for rice, candy, and cigarettes for a month. He was now "Big Honcho" among the boys in his village.

They stood in the dusty street admiring the shiny watch. Nguyen held his arm up to each boy's ear to hear the hum of the battery. The boys rubbed their ears and chattered excitedly in reaction to the exotic sound. Each of them envied Nguyen. A guessing game started, inquiring how he had acquired such a beautiful thing.

He cut the chatter with a wave of his hand then lit a cigarette. Expertly executing a movie star French Inhale with the spent smoke, he gave them a gallant smile.

Turning, he swaggered down the street, never revealing the secret of the wire.

CHAPTER 18

November 25, 1971

Surges of monsoonal air raced down the Asian coast ripping into the tropics, heating the atmosphere and growing in force. Warmer latitudes pumped water into the clouds. Swollen moisture-laden curtains of angry air billowed into the stratosphere. Gaining weight and height, they advanced like a herd of rutting water buffaloes. The great beasts lowered their heads for a charge. Nostrils flashed lightning, mouths belched thunder. Huge hooves of wind stomped a puddle called the South China Sea. Winds of sixty knots whipped and lashed the waters. Fishermen raced to moor their boats. Birds didn't fly. Animals hid.

The storm drove inland across the mountains and down into the jungle lowlands. Rain pelted the top of the canopy. Wind forced its way down through the layers of exotic, water-loving plants, bushes, trees, and vines.

Lansky watched the point man hack a tunnel through the rounded green flesh of the jungle. Gigantic fronds, creepers, and brush fell to the ground. The slashing machete released an acrid, pungent jungle perfume.

Rain washed the jungle floor and released the rotted odor of decaying plant tissue.

Green and yellow snakes slithered through the foliage. Earthworms, slugs, and leeches reveled in the rich mud. The leeches filled the boots of the soldiers as they crossed pools of water.

Each man squirted bug juice into his boots and up his pant legs to relieve the sting. They pulled their boots off to remove the leeches when they had a chance. Pant legs were bloused into tightly laced boots. Fresh leeches would soon replace those just defeated. Sores would soon fester on the legs and feet of the constantly wet soldiers.

They moved on silently, taking turns with the machete, hacking the heavy foliage.

LT studied his compass and plastic-wrapped map. They were lost. They'd been lost since the storm started several days ago.

The officer looked up at the canopy, trying to catch a glimpse of the sky. He hoped for a break in the weather, a change in their situation. Solid gray showed through the few gaps in the green.

Looking at his watch showed that daylight would soon fade away.

He told the squad leaders to have their men cut a perimeter for a night logger. Machetes and banana knives came out. Men began whacking crude corridors into the languorously waving jungle.

Marty, on his first mission after his hospital stay, decided to hooch with Lansky.

Marty got out his collection of shoestrings. Lansky cut bamboo poles and stakes. They snapped the rubberized plastic ponchos together, then tied shoestrings to the metal eyelets and staked the whole thing down. The rain made a drumming sound on the taut ponchos. Gusts of wind flattened foliage and flapped their tent like a bird, which withstood, surviving on its own.

The two smiled at each other.

"Hey, I got another poncho in my pack," Marty said. "Let's rig it to the front of the tent so we have a dry place to heat some food."

"Okay, I'll cut some more poles."

Soon they were squatting under the poncho, heating their C-rats.

As the dark crept in, they crawled into the muddy tent. Marty produced another poncho to cover the ground. They stretched their poncho liners across it and rolled up inside them. Both men were able to sink into sleep.

Wind and rain continued to whip the jungle and shake the tent. A violent gust stirred Lansky. When lightning flashed, he noticed a small rivulet streaming through the tent. It washed a small gully under his poncho.

As he shifted his body away from the little flood an alien odor—something briny, the smell of the sea—replaced the earthy sour-mud atmosphere of recent days. The next lightning flash outlined the dragon sitting in the foliage, a few paces away. An animal reflex deeper than his bones jolted Lansky wide-awake. Suddenly chilled, he shivered painfully, feeling disarmed and helpless, frozen by fear.

Then the five leeches on his legs dropped off, all at once, an unlikely event since leeches were tenacious. The timing made Lansky wonder if this was some kind of dragon alchemy, the beast's way of letting him know that he was safe because his warrior shield was sharing the stormy night with him. This thought helped him catch his breath, yet it took a long time for his body to stop trembling. The spark of visceral fear, once lit, glowed on toward the dawn. Lansky re-wrapped himself in his sodden poncho and attempted a fitful night's sleep. When the lightning flashed he did not look for the dragon, he'd seen enough for one night.

He awoke to the steady drumming of the rain. A burst of wind laid the shrubbery over and lifted the tent. It billowed and tugged on the stakes pulling one of them loose.

Marty looked at Lansky's muddy face. "Can you get that, dear?"

"Why, yes I can." Lansky smiled, relieved that he had survived the night. Marty was in a good mood, despite everything, and Lansky felt comforted by his presence. It helped him turn to the page on last night's startling events.

He crawled out of the tent and shoved the stake back into the mushy ground. Standing, he surveyed the perimeter. The jungle continued to rise and fall in the stream of wind and rain. No sign of the dragon. Water and air hissed against the dense tangle.

Five days earlier, Lansky was uncomfortable in the rain. Now he accepted it, having become accustomed to being soaked. It was bearable, as long as it stayed warm. He rinsed the mud off his face and arms with his wet hands. "Hey, is today Thanksgiving?"

"No. I think it's a coupla days off," replied Marty.

"What's the date today?"

"Ahaaah. Think it's the twenty-third."

"Naw, couldn't be." Lansky frowned. "It's the twenty-sixth. Thanksgiving must be tomorrow. Bob Hope's supposed to be in Da Nang. Going to put on his show for the rear echelon motherfuckers."

"Da Nang is probably taking a real pounding in this weather. Bob Hope's flight might be delayed." Marty smiled in mock sympathy.

"Too bad. Those REMFs will be disappointed."

"Lucky for them, we're out here keeping rockets off Bob Hope's ass." Marty sat under the poncho with his right boot and sock off and his pant leg rolled up. He was examining the long pink gash that went up his leg.

"Hey, how's the leg?" Lansky moved closer to look at Marty's wound.

"A little tight. Hard to put weight on it all day, but it's mostly healed."

"Thought for sure that would be your ticket home."

"Me, too. The doctors thought otherwise."

Lansky sat on his pack removing his slimy boot and sodden socks. The leeches had not bothered him after the dragon sighting. But now that he was moving around in daylight, he found one engorged leech clamped to his shin. "Gonna burn you, sucker! Marty, gimme your lighter!"

Marty flipped his Zippo to Lansky. It smacked the palm of his right hand. Flicking it open, spinning the ignition wheel with his thumb, holding it under the leech, Lansky smiled as it crackled in the flame and dropped off.

"N'other one bites the dust. I'll notch my Zippo," Marty said.

Lansky examined the sores on his leg. Tiny swollen holes in the pallid skin dotted ankle and shin. Some were scabbed over, others oozed pus.

Sergeant Massey came through the bushy corridor. "Mount up. We're movin'."

Lansky pulled his boots on and began assembling his equipment. Soon he heaved his pack on their back and fell in with the rest of the platoon, moving slowly through the jungle.

The storm seemed to be lifting, the wind drier and less volatile.

As the morning move wore on, they reached their first view of the horizon in days. Rocks and earth from one of the sandstone cliffs jutting out of the jungle had let loose. A muddy landslide had flattened trees and bush between them and the cliff.

The lieutenant studied the cliff, estimating time and difficulty of the climb. "Let's stop here. I'm gonna climb that cliff with Third Squad and see if I can figure out where the hell we are. Third Squad, follow me. Sergeant Massey, post your guard. The rest of you can fall out."

Lansky watched LT and Third Squad wade through the slippery mud up the hill toward the cliff. He decided to make some coffee and have crackers, then reclined on his pack in the mud, and pulled a book out of his ammo box.

The story absorbed Lansky's attention, so he didn't notice the weather moderating.

By the time LT returned, the wind had died down. He could hold the book in one hand without the pages flapping much.

The lieutenant was muddy and smiling. "I know where we are."

"Huh," Lansky grunted.

"Let's stop here for today. We're supposed to get resupplied either today or tomorrow."

"Okay."

Marty and Lansky set up camp and sat playing cards in front of their tent. Huddle and Eberhardt drifted in and whiled away the afternoon playing penny-ante poker.

Squinting at his cards with one eye, Huddle said, "Boa, boa, boa, them leeches was all over me last night. Reminded me of a girl I knew who lived outside of Bogalusa."

Eberhardt grinned his long-toothed grin. "Yeah, bet she had a face like a leech, too."

"Shadup, Neverhard!"

Massey squished along the path. "Need volunteers to cut an LZ. First Sergeant's coming out with Thanksgiving dinner tomorrow, we gotta cut an LZ big enough for his bird to touch down." Eberhardt and Huddle volunteered, following Massey through the jungle. Marty crawled in the tent to take a nap. Lansky opened his book. A cool, dry wind blew through the jungle. He put his book down, got up, emptied his pack, and hung everything out to dry.

In the morning, the men stood around the LZ as a chopper came *whacking* across the treetops. First Sergeant Bulldog hung out of the hatch as the bird carefully beat its way down to the ground.

Several of the men ran to the chopper, removing the pressed aluminum trays of food, canisters of coffee, duffel bags of beer on ice, and other more typical resupply items. When the bird was emptied, First Sergeant saluted the group and smiled as the chopper rose, then hurried out of sight.

Shards of shrubs and leaves stirred up by the chopper drifted down on the scene as the men formed a chow line.

Huge turkeys, stuffing, gravy, potatoes, cranberry sauce, pumpkin pies, beans, rice, shrimp, and other dinner items sat on the jungle floor.

Lansky loaded his plate. It was his first real meal in weeks. He balanced his food in one hand and pulled a cold beer out of the duffel bag, then sat on the jungle floor with Marty and others. The richly flavored food satisfied. He couldn't remember enjoying a meal that much.

Lansky decided to propose a toast. Standing with his beer can raised, he said, "Here's to First Sergeant and to all of those close to us but so far away."

It was silent for a second as they all raised their beer cans, then laughter and loud talk broke out among the men, the first laughter Lansky had heard in days.

Sunshine poked through the clouds and lizards began to sing.

Marty looked at Lansky thoughtfully. "Nice toast."

"Thanks."

"Makes me think of home in Pennsylvania. My old lady is over at my folks' house for dinner. My mom always gets up early to cook Thanksgiving dinner. She cooks a mess of food. We eat about midday, then watch football and burp. Boy, wish I was there now."

"Yeah, we all wish we were home." Lansky sounded sad.

"What are your folks doing at Thanksgiving?" asked Marty.

"Well, they had Thanksgiving already, and my dad is deer hunting up in Sawyer County. My mom is home with my sisters."

"Deer hunting, huh? What's it like?"

"Oh, it's a great time. Party atmosphere. That whole part of the state shuts down to go hunting. Everyone around there believes that going up north will solve all your problems. My dad would always say, 'When you go up north, problems seem to solve themselves.' People look forward to it all year." Lansky smiled, thinking back.

"Did you ever go?"

"Sure, I went a couple of times. Ha, boy, some funny things happened."

"Like what? We could use a funny story," said Marty.

Eberhardt and Huddle were listening. Even the new guy, Nunez—a Native American called Chief, who had yet to speak to anyone—moved closer.

"Well, one time, my dad and I were the first two up at the shack. That's what we call our hunting camp, 'the shack.' So we started a fire, had dinner, and sat around waiting for the others to show up. A couple of my dad's friends came rolling in. Let's see . . . it was Boney from Baldwin and his friend Baldy. They had this old stuffed deer head, an eight-point buck, one of those mounts with a curved neck. The head looks sideways.

"They took it out into the woods and nailed it to a tree.

With the yard light on you could see the face, antlers, and neck looking around a tree. Looked like a deer was really standing there. Along comes the next guy, all primed for the hunt. His name was Leo, comes in all smiles because that's everyone's attitude.

"He draws himself a beer and walks over to kibitz at the card table. We'd arranged the chairs so he'd have to stand behind us to see the game. At the same time, he's looking right out the window. He's standing there for quite a while bullshitting and getting ready to get in the game. All of a sudden, his beer cup hits the floor, and he yells, 'Buck!'

"We played it cool and said, 'Huh?'

"He's jumping up and down now, pointing out the window yelling, 'Buck! Buck! Buck! Who's got their rifle? Look, a buck!'

"My dad says, 'Yeah, a buck, go get him, Leo. Our rifles are buried under our sleeping gear.'

"Leo tears out the door, opens his truck, and starts loading his rifle. We followed him outside and watched him, trying not to laugh. So, he says in this hoarse whisper, 'Is he still there?'

"Baldy says, 'Yeah, Leo, but hurry, will ya?'

"'I am! I am!' he says.

"We almost break out laughing right there. By this time, Leo's loaded, raises his weapon, and *blam, blam, blam*, empties the rifle. 'Sucker's still there,' he says.

"We're yelling, 'Reload, reload, you missed him.' So he reloads, empties his weapon again. The deer head hasn't moved. Leo stops and stares at the deer. By this time, we're rolling on the ground, laughing. He looks at us, completely confused. Then he walks out to look at the deer head, which is all tore up from the rounds he put through it.

"We heard, 'Sons-of-bitches.' Leo comes running back to his car and starts reloading his rifle, mumbling, 'Gonna hunt me some pranksters.' He's mad. Everyone took off, deep into the woods. He let a few loose rounds go and called us every name in the book. We hid for an hour before Baldy could talk him into calming down and letting us come back in. Froze our asses off. But you know what?"

"What?"

"The next guy that came into camp, Leo plays the same trick on him!"

All the men laughed for a long time. Lansky noticed the new guy, Chief, staring at him with a happy gleam in his eye. Then the laughter died, and they became serious and quiet. Lansky's story had focused their thoughts on home, on their own Thanksgiving stories.

The light mood passed as the rain started again, the wind picked up, slanting rain rattled the empty aluminum trays.

Running off, they all looked for a place to keep dry.

CHAPTER 19

December 3, 1971

Lansky stood atop the seventy-five-meter guard tower along the beach at the Chu Lai Army Hospital on a rare monsoon day of light winds and little rain. Pale shafts of silver sunlight mottled the azure-gray ocean. The dull routine of guard duty made his commanding view of the South China Sea to the east and the bustling city to the north hard to appreciate.

Lansky's boredom was relieved when a dragon rose from the ocean lifting a broad curtain of water. Its wings beat against a gathering breeze. As the dragon passed through a cloud, it disappeared. Propelled by a gentle zephyr, the newly formed rain cloud drifted on shore.

Now hundreds of dragons ascended to the cloudscape, each clutching a curtain of falling water. They passed through the cloudbank and evaporated leaving a light mist that fell across the horizon.

The young soldier shook his head and blinked his eyes attempting to comprehend what he saw, or thought he saw.

Marty walked across the tower decking, "What ta'fuck Lansky, you look like a deer in the headlights."

"Have you seen anything unusual out over the ocean in the last ten minutes?"

"Unusual? Fuck yea, it stopped raining a while ago for the first time in about a hunerd' fuckin' years! But now it's back, makes me fuckin happy."

"Okay, sorry, been up in this tower too long. I'm glad our shift is almost over."

Marty pointed to a village girl walking along the beach. "Hey, ready to lose some money?"

"Why not?" Lansky faked some enthusiasm feeling grateful Marty was distracted by an opportunity to wager. "Betchya she makes it!" Lansky leaned into the railing.

"Yer on. Five P says she gets her pants wet."

The young Vietnamese girl stood on the beach studying the waves.

Her densely populated hometown of Chu Lai surrounded the hospital. All morning the two soldiers had watched the citizens walk along the beach socializing or doing some fishing.

Living in a city with no sewer system, it also was a place to take a morning dump. Timing the interval between the big waves, waiting for a roller to crash and then recede, they chased it out as far as they dared. Dropping their pajamas, getting their business done, hoisting pants, and hopping through the surf, splashing ahead of the next big wave. Those slow afoot got swamped.

The girl they had bet on made a quick entrance into the surf. Squatting for several seconds, she did what was needed. A big breaker closed on her.

"C'mon, baby!" yelled Lansky, pounding on the rail.

"C'mon, roller!" Marty countered, leaning over the rail, waving his arm.

On her feet, running, nimble steps carried her ahead of the

rolling water. She hopped on shore with the wave crashing behind her.

"Five P. Pay up!" yelled Lansky, his excitement insincere.

"Hey, wait till she turns around. I think there's some water on her pants."

"No way!"

"Wait now, might be something on her little backside."

"Double or nothin' her backside is dry."

"Done!"

Lansky whistled and waved at the girl, making a circling gesture with his left hand. "Hey, turn around. Hey, down there, turn around."

The girl looked up at Lansky, not comprehending. Eventually, she walked back toward the vil. As she did, they could see that the back of her pants was dry.

"Her pants are dry!" Lansky smiled falsely. "Pay up!"

"Buncha crap!" Marty turned away to open his wallet. He always turned away to open his wallet. No one had ever seen its contents.

"Here ya go, ten!"

"Thanks, buddy."

A head poked through the ladder-well on the tower floor.

"Hey." It was Huddle.

"Hey," said Lansky.

Eberhardt came through the well next. He swung off the ladder, stretched, and looked out to sea.

"Nothing happening here, Huddle. We're gonna go back to the barracks." Marty swung himself over the ladder and started the long, slow climb down to the sand with Lansky following.

The light drizzle continued. Lambretta, pedicab, and diesel traffic growled along the road outside the wire.

They dodged puddles on the way back to the rundown guard barracks, then stepped off the guard tower path, and waded through the sand toward the maze of sagging buildings.

A man lay on the sand near the entrance to their barracks. Davis was down-on-the-ground drunk, semiconscious, doing what appeared to be half an Australian crawl.

Marty looked down at him in disgust. "Davis, you're blotto again. Hey, it's not that bad."

"Let's haul him to his bunk," said Lansky. Marty grabbed him by the collar. Lansky grabbed him by the belt.

"Wait, he dropped his pistol."

Lansky went back to pick up Davis's sand-covered .38 revolver. They hauled him into the smoky barracks.

As they dragged him, Marty looked at Lansky. "Why's he need that pistol?"

"He doesn't need it. Seems to have some fetish about it, always cleaning it and playing around with it."

Finally, they reached his bunk and threw him roughly onto it. Looking for the safety, and finding none, Lansky put the pistol under the bunk.

A freshly demoted Sergeant Tippler, now Private Tippler, lay on the bunk next to Davis, watching the scene. Pulling on a fifth of whiskey, he commented, "Davis has been out there all morning. Got drunk at sunup. Won't stay in his bunk. Keeps crawlin' out on the sand."

Davis rolled off his bunk, hitting the floor hard and dragged himself along with one elbow, head down, eyes closed.

"Hey, Allen, ya in?" The call came from the marathon poker game at the end of the barracks.

"Yeah, I'm in. Don't need any more of your money, but I like to watch you cry."

"Hey, make room for the pigeon!"

Marty sat on one of the bunks, lit his pipe, and joined in the chatter of the game.

Lansky lay in his bunk looking at Tippler. He had little sympathy for the man. Officious and incompetent, Tippler was one of the few guys Lansky hated. "How do you like the EM barracks, Tippler?"

"Sucks."

"Too bad about losing your stripes."

"That sucks, too. My mistake, din't tell Davis where 'ar ambush was that night. Should'a told him it was three hundred yards at his twelve o'clock. Nine guys out there're bound to make some noise. Davis heard 'em. By the time I got down to his position . . . damage was done."

"Ya, sure was. When's your court-martial?"

"Doan' wanna talk about it." He took a pull off the bottle. "Gonna see what's at the gate." Getting up, Tippler stumbled out. The bottle hit the floor, rolling noisily, banging into the wall. It came to rest with the amber liquid dancing out of the neck and bubbling onto the floor, releasing the strong smell of spirits.

One of the card players heard Tippler say that he was going to the gate. "Whoa, Tippler's going to the gate at ten in the morning. You'd think he'd have the decency to wait until eighteen hundred when everyone else goes."

"Yeah, you'd think he'd have some decency. Ha, ha, ha!"

Lansky closed his eyes.

The gate was where the prostitutes hung out. The commanding officer of the hospital had made prostitution legal on base so GIs would leave the nurses alone. Young girls would gather around the gate at dusk for selection, but some girls could be found there almost any time of the day.

Restless, Lansky vaulted out of his bunk, stepped through the warped doorframe into the salty gray air, and listened to the surf pounding the beach.

"Davis! What are you doing out here?"

The sad sack lay unconscious, coated with sand. "C'mon, let's get you back inside."

Lansky grabbed him by the collar and belt and began dragging him back to his bunk.

One of the card players noticed the entrance. "Here's Davis!"

Lansky heaved him into his bunk. The man couldn't get comfortable, mumbled and rolled around listlessly. When he hit the floor and crawled out the door, Lansky said, "Must need to be outside." He opened his ammo box, pulled out a book, and started reading.

Tippler arrived with a short little girl no older than sixteen, throwing her roughly onto his bunk.

She tried taking her clothes off carefully, but Tippler tugged at them, popping some of the buttons off her peasant blouse.

Drunk and impatient, he attempted to pull his pants off over his boots, but they got stuck.

The guys playing cards stopped to watch.

Frustrated, Tippler unlaced his boots and removed his pants. The girl covered herself with Tippler's poncho liner.

"Hey, Tippler," said Lansky. "Couldn't you do this in the pleasure palace?" He was referring to the private bunk at the end of the barracks that was blocked off with cardboard and pieces of plywood.

"Na." He crawled under the blanket and got on top of the girl. "Gonna get it right here."

The card game resumed, but the players' attention was directed at Tippler. "Hey, Tips, you foul fucker, couldn't ya do that somewhere else?"

Tippler's head swiveled toward them. His face was drunk and sad.

The little Vietnamese girl's eyes were shut. Eyes shut in pain. The bed rocked with the rhythm Tippler created driving himself into her.

Davis appeared at the door, covered with sand, eyes puffy and swollen. Lurching forward, he shuffled down the aisle, stopping to look at Tippler.

Lansky put his book on his chest.

"Tippler! Hey, Tippler!" Davis seemed ornery, irritated, and hung over. "Fucker! Where's ma booze?"

Tippler turned his head. "Hey, I'm busy."

"Wersit?" Davis took a threatening step toward Tippler, face flushed.

"Hits over der, by the wall." Tippler motioned with his head.

Davis started wobbling in between the rows of bunks, looking for his bottle. He saw it under his bunk and got down on his hands and knees to reach for it.

Lansky could see the .38 under the bed.

The drunken soldier picked up the pistol and the bottle.

"Hey, Davis, why don't you let me keep that pistol for you? I'll give it to you later," Lansky said, sitting up.

Taking a long pull off the remains of the bottle, Davis ignored him. Holding the bottle at arm's length, he gave it a long drunken study. "Tippler, you drank all of my booze."

Tippler tried to ignore him.

Davis fixed his gaze on Tippler, moving around the bunk, tripping over its edge.

Lansky felt stupid for not emptying the pistol when it was in his hand.

Stopping next to the bed, Davis raised the pistol to Tippler's ear.

"Hey! That's not funny." Lansky stood up. "Put your piece up, man, you don't need more trouble."

Lansky measured the distance between himself and the pistol. He considered diving for it.

The card game stopped. Tippler lay still. The cold blue barrel touched his ear. The young girl looked up at Davis in silent terror. Tension began to build. Rising together, the card players started moving slowly toward Davis.

"C'mon, man, 'nuff jokin', put it away," said Marty.

Another card player tried to distract him. "Hey, buddy, c'mere, I got a bottle of Chivas Regal I been savin'. C'mon over and have a few shots with me."

Davis turned his head slowly. "Back off."

The card players froze.

A smile came over the troubled face, a drunken, incongruous smile. "Don't nobody move."

The hammer on the pistol went back slowly then fell forward. *Click.*

Tippler collapsed on the girl.

Davis let the gun fall to his side and looked at the card players, smiling. "See, it wasn't loaded, I was jus' foolin' with you guys." He laughed. "I was jus' foolin', just messin' with you guys. Wasn't loaded." He raised the gun to his own temple.

Click.

"See, not loaded. Ha, ha, ha, ha." His head tilted back in painful laughter. Tears ran down his cheeks.

"Let me keep it for you, Davis, you don't need it, man," Lansky said.

"Naw, it's mine. It's okay. Not loaded. See?" He raised it to his temple. *Click.*

Turning, he walked toward the door. "See! Ha! Not loaded." *Click.* His voice took on the quality of a child. "See! Ha! Not loaded."

"I'm gonna get that thing and bury it," said Lansky.

"Don't want any more scenes like that," Marty said.

They began following him out the door.

The report of the .38 broke them into a dash through the door. Davis was nose down in the sand, gun in hand, head bloodied, sand blotted black.

Lansky knelt beside him. "Get me a bandage. Shiiit! Get me a bunch of bandages. Call the lieutenant. Let's put him on a blanket. We'll take him to the hospital."

Another monsoon storm rolled in that night. The wind got under the corrugated aluminum roof, rattling it. As the storm strengthened, the clatter became an eerie moan. Rain pounded the roof and water piddled through the cracks.

Lansky and Marty completed three hours in one of the guard towers. They returned windblown and wet to an empty, silent barracks.

Marty collected steel pots, putting them under the leaks, to keep the floor dry.

Soon they were sitting across from each other, staring at the lonely candle on the floor, the flame guttering and flickering in the breeze.

The card game had broken up. Most of the men were on guard duty.

Staring at the candle, Lansky said, "CO asked me to get Davis's personal stuff together and bring it down to HQ in the morning."

"I'll help you."

"Sonavabitch, isn't it?"

"Sure is." Marty shook his head. "Where's the pistol?"

"They took it for the investigation. I should have emptied it when I had it in my hand." Lansky's eyes closed.

"Not your fault."

"Feel bad about it."

"Me, too."

Lansky noticed a briny presence in the room. The dragon lurked behind him, barely perceptible in the candle shadow. He did not look for the beast, he didn't want to be shocked by its appearance or disappointed by its absence, its aura was too comforting to take a chance on seeing that it wasn't really there.

CHAPTER 20

December 15, 1971

Mud sucked Lansky's left boot off his foot. He stood stork-like in the mist, quietly cursing his footgear sunk in the mire.

Should have taken the time to tie the laces.

Lansky surrendered to the mud, sat down with a squish, and reached for his left boot. What did it matter? He was muddy yesterday; he would be muddy tomorrow. The boot came loose, oozing slime. Lansky managed to tie it on his foot, not much muck had gotten inside.

He looked out across some of the highest peaks in the Annamese Cordillera. Monsoon clouds, heavy with moisture, shrouded the black ridges, limestone escarpments, and granite peaks.

Below, a solid bed of white fog glided gracefully through the defiles, curling and turning through the dark passages. Broken in patches, it revealed the gnarled gray branches and green canopy of the tropical rain forest.

Lansky's position gave him an unusual view of the zona verde. Instead of looking up at the canopy from the forest floor, he looked down on it from above.

His immediate surroundings weren't as interesting. The remains of Firebase York, an ugly scab on the land, sat atop a sheared-off peak, waiting for its end.

The American Army was pulling back, preparing to withdraw from the field, so York was no longer needed. Lansky's platoon was on deconstruction detail, taking the firebase apart.

A week of deconstruction during the day and peering into the fog at night had been tolerable. He could handle it. The thing that got him down was the rain. So confining and relentless, it made everything slippery, heavy, and mucky.

At night, he wrapped himself in his wet poncho liner and shivered until dawn—a water torture: slow, steady, and pitiless.

The dull sameness of the days was tiresome. He felt depressed. Worse yet, he was beginning to feel sorry for himself.

He sat in the open now for the first time in a week without being rained on.

A flock of yellow birds broke above the white fog. Something had spooked them out of the canopy. Swirling in a panic, first left—glowing by a trick of the light, blue stripes accentuating yellow wings—then right, losing light, colors muted.

The dragon followed, its colors similar to the forest canopy. Only the motion of its wings showing it to be distinct, animate. It became a black silhouette as it crossed the fog bed. The dragon did not chase the birds, it just flew; climbing through the valley, banking around the mountain Lansky sat on.

He felt a light drizzle come over, surrounding him in cool mist, cutting his visibility to twenty yards.

A sound like the snapping of a canvas sail in fair breeze came from the mist. Then it repeated slowly, like bird wings flapping—large bird wings cutting a broad volume of air, slowing for a landing. It roiled the mist, a small turbulence.

Lansky saw motion through the vapor. He stood and

walked forward, feeling no fear. A little voice inside him said this was safe.

The dragon landed on a pile of sandbags along the perimeter of the firebase twenty feet away. Taller than Lansky, its large red eyes perched above a rectangular head, a long snout, and prominent nostrils. Crocodile teeth spiked from the upper and lower jaw. Green scales on the neck shimmered with an iridescent wet quality. Large bat wings folded around the midsection. A long bumpy tail switched slowly back and forth across the ground. Five large claws on two splayed feet punctured the sandbags.

"You look like you're really here," said Lansky. "I know this is my imagination at work, but you look so real." He was starting to accept his vision, a comforting gift from the universe. It came when he needed it, and he always felt better afterward.

The dragon stood motionless.

"I think I see you, but you're not there. What I think I see does not exist. You are not there, you are here." Lansky pointed to his head. "But no matter where you are, I am grateful for your presence."

The dragon blinked, eyes wider, glinting in the available light, thin lips drawing back. A sly smile?

"Thanks for being here with me. It makes me feel better."

Lansky heard the sucking sound of footsteps in the mud. "Who you talking to, Lansky?" He turned to see a soldier slip-sliding through the mist. Huddle walked up to him, head down, with the effort required of a man struggling through heavy mud. Straightening himself up next to Lansky, he looked out into the fog. "Who ya talking to?"

"Well, it was kind of a spiritual conversation."

"Huh, well, I been prayin' myself, lately. Prayin' for a day without mud. Just don't say my prayers out loud."

Lansky recognized this comment as Huddle's reminder of the importance of noise discipline. By the infantry code, he was making himself a target in two ways: talking out loud and standing in profile on a ridge against the skyline.

"This weather is making me a little goofy," said Lansky.

The dragon was gone. Lansky stared into the quiet void.

Huddle looked at him with concern. "You okay, Lansky? Did you see something? Kinda' funny bein' out here alone talking to the fog."

"I think my eyes are playing tricks on me."

"The fog has played a few tricks on my brain, too. You keep lookin', thinkin' you see somethin', then it goes away. Nothin' was there. Gets you worked up."

"That must be it," Lansky said quickly.

Huddle looked at the ground, shook his head, and smiled. "Come on back to my hooch. I'll make us some hot chocolate."

"Okay."

As they slogged along, Lansky heard the snap of canvas overhead. He looked at his friend. Huddle was intent on the difficulty of walking in deep mud and so heard nothing.

The dragon had helped Lansky again. It wouldn't do to try to explain. Even if it only existed in his imagination, he needed his dragon, didn't want anyone trying to convince him it wasn't there.

CHAPTER 21

January 17, 1972

The kid plowed into the river unafraid of its depth or what was in the saw grass on the other side. LT and Lansky exchanged nervous glances. This ARVN "Kit Carson" scout that had been sent as a guide needed a lot of watching for a guide. Having grown up in the sandy delta country of the Song Vu Gia River, the teenager should have known better. Phong acted like the impulsive sixteen-year-old he was.

"Goddamned, Kit Carson's going to put us in a bad spot charging around like this," said LT.

The scout's next few steps sent him plunging in over his head, his flat face and weapon dry for a moment, then the current carried him under. A leg came up. LT grabbed it, pulling him to the shallows. After a few choking coughs, the teenager stood, pouring water out of his weapon.

LT glared down at the tiny figure.

"Phong, you fuckup! Goddamn, you're something. Get back at the end of the column before I hurt you." He pushed the kid by the neck to make sure he got the message.

"Permission to take the point, sir?"

LT looked at Ramon Arocha who never had been at point but seemed anxious to try.

"Okay, Arocha, take over. Let's find a way across this river."

"Yes, sir."

"Hey, Lansky, you crossed here yesterday, right?"

"That's right, LT, walked right across hip deep."

"The river must be rising. Hey, Massey, go back there and keep an eye on old Phong, will you? And help him clean that weapon when we get back to the night logger."

"Okay, LT." Sergeant Massey patiently told Phong in Pigeon-Vietnamese-French-English how careful he must be. Phong nodded his head as if he understood.

Arocha tested the depths of the river, wading out carefully, scanning the water and far shore. The rest of the squad followed. Arocha startled at something he saw downstream. "Gator!"

"What?" LT wrinkled his nose in disbelief.

Arocha turned toward the bank, head and upper body wrenching in great effort, the water holding his legs in slow motion. "Gid out!" he yelled. "Gid outa da water!" Splashing up into the shallows, he approached the lieutenant.

LT looked surprised. "You're telling me you saw a gator?"

"Ya, a gator floatin' in the middle of the river around the bend."

"Christ Almighty, I guess we better get out of the water."

They sloshed out and stood along the bank, dripping water, waiting for LT to decide what to do.

"I gotta see this," said LT. "C'mon, Lansky, let's walk around the bend and look."

Pushing through the saw grass for five minutes gave them a view downriver. A gnarled log floated on the water.

Lansky's second look noticed that several of the knots on top of the log were looking at him. He wondered if this was his dragon. "Hey, LT, did you know gators are the descendants of dragons? To see one is considered auspicious."

"Sounds like a folktale."

"It is."

"So this is an auspicious moment?"

"Count on it."

"Well, you are in luck." LT grinned.

"How's that?"

"High water and gators are making me think this patrol is over."

"You mean you're going to hang up a patrol early?" Lansky smiled.

"I think so. The river is getting deeper, and the current is too fast. We'll stay on this side for today."

"Whoa, man, I better write this one down! The day that LT let us quit a patrol early!"

"That's not so funny. I can be nice once in a while."

"Oh, I know, I know!"

"Stuff it, Lansky! Let's head back to camp. Call in and let them know we're coming."

"Roger that, LT."

Back in the night logger, Lansky opened a can of crackers and jam, reclined on his pack and watched the huge post-monsoon clouds roll by. Patches of direct sunlight flashed at him between the gaps. He felt the drenched earth baking itself dry. Shimmering humidity rose around him.

The monsoon was passing. It was good to feel the warmth again. Lansky got very comfortable and fell asleep. A sudden cloudburst drove hard rain into his face and sent him scrambling for the protection of the nearest tree.

Phong ran under the same tree. They smiled at each other.

Hailstones bounced and ricocheted off the ground. They shared a laugh at the men running for cover. Small puddles formed around the tree. Their gazes met.

Phong's flat face became animated as he pulled his wallet bag from his pocket. "Hey, Chee Hi, look a numba' wan!" Phong opened his wallet to the picture compartment.

Lansky was surprised that Phong had no relatives or girl-friends in his wallet. Each little plastic sleeve contained fashion pictures clipped from some American catalog. Flipping through the wallet, Phong grinned at Lansky, fingering the pictures of adolescent Americans wearing bellbottom pants, ruffled shirts with high collars, beads, and medallions. "Ahhh, beau coupe numba' wan, ha, Chee Hi?" It seemed as if Phong was asking for Lansky's fashion opinion.

He smiled. "Ya, hey, Phong, that's some pretty sharp threads you got there."

"Ahhh." Phong's face moved slowly up and down in agreement. He pointed at the picture, then to himself several times. His narrow eyes opened wide. The dream of dressing like an American excited him.

Lansky put his arm across Phong's boney shoulder. "Someday, Phong, you'll be dressed in style." He pointed at the picture. "Number one, huh, Phong?"

Phong nodded his head as he closed his wallet.

"Hey, Phong, I'm Ed. You call me Ed." Lansky was pointing to his chest.

Phong's eyes smiled. His lips parted. "Ad."

"Okay, close enough." Lansky checked his watch. "Gotta go now, Phong." He pointed to his watch. "Gotta di di—guard duty." His voice rose as if loud volume would make him more easily understood. Phong waved as he walked away.

Lansky took his rifle and a can of pork and lima beans to

the head of the trail for his three hours of guard duty. He sat on a downed tree off-trail. From this position, he could see, but could not be seen.

Listening for a few minutes, becoming very still, Lansky explored the hundred meters in front of him. Removing his soggy boots and moist socks, he examined his toes and feet, pulling small strips of dead white skin from under his toes and across the top of each foot. The puffy patches itched. Lansky wrung out his socks and draped them across the log.

Drawing the bolt back on his weapon allowed him to observe the tip of the copper-jacketed round as it slid into the firing chamber, which always made him feel safe. He listened again for a long minute. Satisfied with the quiet, he opened his pork and beans. Cold, greasy pork and hard beans needed hot sauce, but he'd forgotten it in his pack. He ate it anyway.

Twilight brought the night sounds: barking dogs in the nearby villages, occasional bursts of AK-47 fire, a distant thump of artillery, bugs, crickets, and frogs creating a sonata in the dark.

Even the rare and unique lizard that Lansky hadn't heard for a while joined in. GIs called them the "fuck you" lizards because their tiny shrill voices sounded as if they are saying, "Fuck you!— Fuck you!—Fuck you!" Sometimes it wasn't recognizable, especially the first few attempts, which were muddy and inarticulate. After fifteen minutes, the lizard's voice would become louder and more recognizable. "Hup hoo!—Huck hoo—Huck hoo— Huck you—Fuck you!" The little creature didn't get it perfect every time, but when he did, Lansky couldn't help but smile.

Several hours passed easily, and Lansky enjoyed the evening. He checked the time, fifteen minutes left of guard duty. He wiggled on his damp socks and slid them into his cool, clammy boots. Walking back to the trail, Lansky knelt, waiting for the next man on watch.

Chief, a man of no words, walked down the trail. Three months in Bravo and he had spoken to no one. Lansky nodded at the Native American. Chief nodded back.

"Quiet on my watch," said Lansky.

Chief silently acknowledged the comments.

Lansky walked back to his sleeping position. Lately, he'd been hooching with LT who'd snapped two ponchos together and strung them out on stakes to make a tent. He'd even hung a mosquito net inside. Lansky crept inside the little shelter and saw his poncho liner laid out with a towel wadded up for a pillow. He wanted to thank the lieutenant for arranging his AO.

Lansky could barely see the prone form of the officer with the radio receiver resting on his neck. The thank-you could wait.

He curled up in the fetal position and soon joined LT in a soft snoring contest.

CHAPTER 22

January 18, 1972

Lansky woke up wet, poncho liner soaked, nothing unusual, so he tried to go back to sleep. Two minutes later, dirty river water filled his mouth, making him choke, waking him up again. LT woke up coughing at the same time. They were lying in six inches of rising water. Men in the other hooches were yelling in surprised reaction.

One of the sentries knelt at the entrance to the tent. "Hey, LT, wake up, man. We got water everywhere."

Lansky and LT crawled out of the tent with their weapons and the radio. Water rose over their boot tops at an accelerated rate. Men started gathering around the tent in the dark.

"What's going on, LT?"

"Must be some kinda flood. Get everyone over here!"

All around them, men splashed in the dark. Strained whispers and curses of the confused drifted across the area.

LT said, "Anyone with a flare, shoot it off. Everyone over here on the double! Arocha, you here?"

"Yo, LT."

"Get going to some higher ground. We have to get out of here. Lansky, you and me got to walk the perimeter to make sure everyone gets out."

"What about equipment, sir?"

"Forget it. Just grab your weapons. We got to move."

The *pop* of a flare echoed across the water, a low star over the night logger. Lansky could see only water now, waist level in some places. They were wading through a river. The flare saved them the walk around the perimeter. Men were forming in a close file, following Arocha.

"Hope we aren't leaving anyone behind," said Lansky.

"Yeah. C'mon, let's move forward and have each squad leader do a head count." LT started wading toward the front of the line. Most of the squad leaders had collected their men. They accounted for everyone.

"Lansky, call the CO and give him a sit rep. Tell him to fire illumination on the night logger position. I'll correct when the first round comes in."

"Roger, LT."

Lansky complied. As he finished his radio transmission, he heard a splash behind him. Phong emerged from the water, hair in his eyes. Flares dangling from tiny parachutes revealed men stumbling in potholes, tripping over unseen rises in the ground. One of the new men, Giancarlo, started singing and laughing. A rifle butt to the chest silenced the frightened soldier.

Illumination flares and splashing sounds marked their position. If Charlie had an automatic weapon on high ground, they could all be dead. Stuck in the water, unable to maneuver, tense and tired, the men followed Arocha until he stopped.

Chief stood in front of Arocha. He had been ahead of the column and pointed his rifle in a different direction. Wading a step, he looked back and waved the column along. Chief wanted everyone to follow him.

Arocha yelled, "Hey, LT, I don't know where I'm going. Chief has an idea. Let's follow him."

The water rose steadily. The current accelerated.

"C'mon, Lansky, let's get up front and see what's going on," said LT.

Phong sloshed along at Lansky's heels. The shorter men, especially Phong, would be swimming soon. The river emptied into the ocean three miles away.

LT took out his compass. Staring at it for several seconds, he said, "Last time I looked at the terrain map, high ground was over there. Chief is right." He pointed across the bleak brown water in the direction Chief was going. "Everyone follow Chief!"

With his weapon at high port, the Native American waded away.

The hiss of large wings cutting humid air came to Lansky's ears. The dragon flew past one of the parachute flares on the same line as Chief, confirming his heading.

Lansky plunged into a hole, water up to his neck, lost his balance but managed to plant his feet and lean into the current.

"Ad, Ad!" Phong started drifting away.

"Grab my weapon!"

Phong lunged at the barrel and hooked his hand around the front sight. Lansky felt the water trying to lift his feet. Somehow, he managed to hold his footing and pull Phong a few yards. His feet found a rise in the ground. Lansky pulled Phong to it and held him by the collar until he could get his feet planted. His M-16 surfaced like a submarine in his hand.

"Hope there's no gators around now," said Lansky, looking at the dripping, useless weapon.

The howl of incoming artillery grew behind them. *Paawooooo!* A flash of illumination rolled over them. The round had airburst over their night logger. The water sparkled with a brightness that lasted a few seconds.

"Okay, Lansky," yelled LT, "that's our illumination. Tell them to correct five hundred west and continue airbursts."

"Got it, LT." Lansky called in the correction. The immediate response surprised him. His soaked PRC-25 was still working.

The wail of artillery rounds grew louder. *PAAAH WOOOO!* It cracked like thunder overhead. One rolled in every thirty seconds. The men cheered when they saw land ahead. Small bits of debris from the nonexplosive rounds *whizzed* by them and *ploinked* the water.

Lansky's ears were ringing from the blast and compression. One round burst directly overhead, his hearing was gone. The front of the exhausted rank reached the bank. After slipping, Lansky crawled up the bank on hands and knees until he was several feet above the water.

He turned onto his side to look back at the column. Men fighting the current struggled toward him. Luminous glitter twinkled overhead, decaying to darkness. Each thirty seconds brought the fulgent blink of white phosphorus. Smoky vapors rolled over the water.

Lansky lay entranced, unaware of LT yelling at him.

"Call in a cease-fire! Hey, Lansky. Enough. Call in the cease-fire." LT finally grabbed him by the collar. "C'mon, Lansky! Cease-fire! Call it in!" LT yelled in his ear. Lansky could barely hear him. He made the call automatically, unable to hear his own words. The message must have gotten through because the firing stopped after about a minute.

Lansky lay watching the primordial scene fade to black. Just before it dissolved, he saw the dragon flying low and fast over the struggling column. It came right at him, wings flapping at full extension. As it passed overhead, Lansky's hearing returned.

Most of the men were on the bank, flopped over in exhaustion. The tail end of the column struggled blindly out of the water. Wet, slippery bodies slithered all around Lansky. They bumped and slid off one another until they were all on land.

LT got up and asked for volunteers to find the top of the hill. As he finished his sentence, he turned to see Chief gesturing with his rifle. He pointed off into the dark.

"You know where the top of the hill is?" asked LT.

Chief nodded, pointing again.

"Okay, whoever is able, let's follow Chief."

Several men slowly followed Chief out into the dark, searching for a safe night logger.

Lansky didn't move.

When LT returned, he said, "Okay, men, we need ten more minutes of discipline. I know you got it in you. Charlie knows we're here. Our shit is weak. We got to get up to the top of this hill and form a perimeter. After we post our sentries, most of you can rest. C'mon. Let's go."

They slowly rose, slogging to the top, and each squad took a quadrant of the hill. Guard duty was assigned. LT and Sergeant Massey checked the perimeter. When they returned, Lansky was sprawled on top of the hill, asleep, radio receiver next to his ear.

In the morning, they looked across the plain. The water had receded. Saw grass was matted in places, some trees were bent, and puddles of water remained in the depressions. Otherwise, it looked as it had the night before. The flash flood had passed just as suddenly as it had risen. The brown Song Vu Gia had returned to its banks snaking off in the distance toward the sea.

Most of the men wanted to go back to search for missing equipment. LT formed a patrol for a return to the night logger. Lansky was the RTO.

"Okay, Chief, head out," said LT. "Let's get back and grab that equipment before young Charles does. Sergeant Massey, you stay here and handle the resupply choppers. If the colonel shows up, tell him I'm busy."

Covering the squishy ground in the daylight was easy. When they reached the night logger, LT posted a small security cordon. The rest of the men began assembling the sodden equipment.

The rising sun beat on the soaked ground creating an intense humidity. Each man broke into a severe sweat. Ponchos, packs, boots, clothes, rusting ammo, and mud-choked weapons were piled in the middle of the perimeter. Once the area had been searched, they shouldered the equipment and started back.

A low-flying helicopter nestled on top of the hill beating purple smoke into the air. Lansky and the rest humped up the hill past the sentry. The colonel stood over a pile of resupply materials. Water, Cs, LRPs, mail, ammo, socks, and a change of clothes waited for everyone.

Each squad resupplied itself with rations, ammo, weapons lube, cleaning rods, letters, and packages. Others took long drinks at the water blivet and filled canteens. Filthy fatigues and socks smelling of river water were dropped in a pile. Soldiers picked through the clean pile until they found something that fit.

Phong approached Lansky as he was dressing. "Beau coup numba' wan, Ad," said Phong. He mimicked himself plunging underwater and being dragged up by Lansky. Phong acted out the scene with adolescent vigor and sound effects, finishing off with boyish laughter and a grin so broad his eyes crinkled to slits.

Lansky put his arm around Phong and said, "Glad I was there for you, man."

Mail call brought a package of cheese and crackers from Lansky's mom. The gift was in a cardboard case shaped like Wisconsin. He opened one of the tins and dipped a cracker into the cheese.

Handing it to Phong, he said, "Try this, Phong. Wisconsin cheese!" The dark eyes examined the processed goo on the cracker. He nibbled it with quivering lips, eyes tightly shut. His first taste of cheese brought a smile to his face. Phong took another cracker and dipped it, chomping greedily.

Lansky opened a letter from his girlfriend, Sheila, and started reading it. Brian Hazuka and some of the guys from Second Squad happened by and asked if they could have some cheese and crackers.

Lansky said, "Okay," without looking up, absorbed in the letter. Sheila described life back in the world on the university campus where she was a member of the newly-formed girls' softball team. Women's collegiate athletics was just getting started, and Sheila was proud to be on the first university team. They worked out in the gym several days a week getting ready for the season.

As children, Sheila was the only girl to join the boy's sandlot football games. Her team had two plays: pitch to Sheila left and pitch to Sheila right. She wasn't just faster than any boy out there, Sheila had moves. At times, it seemed as if she was taunting the boys with her athleticism. Sheila rarely got tackled, but any boy who did bring her down bragged about it for days. All the guys had crushes on her. When she surprised Lansky with a kiss and said, "You'd make a beautiful girl with those eyelashes," he knew that he possessed rare luck.

In the small town of St. Bernadine's Crossing, her football exploits were big news. Lansky's dad showed up to take eight-millimeter film of Sheila the running back. Then he invited all the parents over to watch the movie.

When drinks were poured, and the lights were dimmed, they rolled the film over and over laughing and shouting at her surprising abilities. The best scene captured Sheila running right at the camera blue sneakers digging up dust, blazing past the boys, ponytail streaming, sweatshirt flowing over her willowy feminine frame, face flushed with pure joy.

During her senior year in high school, the coach of the boys' football team had her come to a few of the fall practices as a pass receiver.

If his defensive backs could learn to cover Sheila, they were ready for any receiver in their small city, north woods football conference. Even though she would never play a down, Sheila was recognized as the best athlete in town.

Several minutes went by before Lansky stopped thinking about Sheila and noticed Hazuka and second squad smiling at him. Each man's mouth was stuffed with cheese and crackers. Two of them were dueling with crackers, trying to knock each other's hands away from the last tin of cheese. The other tins were strewn around the area upside down and empty. One cellophane sleeve with two sesame crackers remained in the package.

"You assholes," Lansky said, "I wanted some of that stuff."

They just knelt there smiling at him, cheeks full of cheese. Hazuka finally swallowed his wad. "Uh, hey, Lansky, got some water? I'm sorta dry."

"Get outta here!"

"Sorry, Lansky, hee, hee, didn't mean to eat all of it. Hee, hee."

"Yeah, sure."

They got up to leave, and Lansky noticed the two remaining crackers.

"Hey, you forgot something. You missed two crackers."

"Oh no, go ahead. We don't like sesame. Hee, Hee."

"You assholes."

"Shh, don't break foul. Look, priests."

Hazuka pointed at the Catholic chaplain and two other ministers conducting simple services for a few men.

A pleasant breeze rose, and Lansky lay back on his pack, watching the field Mass. Sipping from his canteen, he reflected on his Catholic upbringing and how it had caused him to resent religion. One incident in particular still vexed Lansky when he thought about it . . .

On the first warm spring morning of his freshman year at St. Bernadine's Crossing Catholic High School, he impulsively skipped the school bus, jumped on his bicycle, and peddled the five hilly miles to school just to get some air in his lungs. He told Rita, the girl who lockered next to him, about how he had enjoyed riding his bike to school in the warm sunshine. Tired of the school bus, she asked Lansky if he would give her a ride home on his handlebars. As they rode down the hill in front of the school, the spring breeze pressed against Rita's cotton blouse outlining her breasts . . . it also lifted her pleated skirt above her thighs. She smiled bravely at the catcalls and whistles coming from the students on the sidewalk headed home. An innocent spring lark would now turn into something horrible.

The next day, Rita's ride was the only topic of conversation. Girls made catty comments to her in the cafeteria and boys whispered insults in her ear. Lansky tried to defend her. He kept saying, "Hey, what about me? It was my idea. You should be criticizing me!" But the incident had taken on a momentum of its own.

Sister Sofia, the Latin teacher, lectured the class on the evils of unsupervised contact between the sexes and was quite certain no self-respecting young lady would make a spectacle of herself on a boy's handlebars. Rita blushed with angry embarrassment and bolted from the room in tears. Summarily, she transferred to the public high school. At the end of the term, Lansky did the same. He'd had his fill of the shaming, the little inquisitions, and the catholic guilt . . .

He had lost his faith in conventional religion but was gaining belief in his spiritual vision. His spirit saw the dragon when he needed it. The dragon provided for his spiritual needs. When he was frightened, the dragon was his warrior shield. Protected by the shield, Lansky felt confident about his survival. He could now hear a quiet voice from within repeating the phrase, "I will survive." Maybe it was the voice of God. He didn't know. Lansky only heard the voice when he saw the dragon. When he heard the voice, he felt protected. It comforted him and gave him rest. He knew he would find a way through, whatever the war presented.

Lansky couldn't explain it, even to himself, and certainly not to another human being. When he tried to reason it out, it sounded crazy.

Maybe someday he would be able to penetrate this mystery. But today wasn't that day. He had stopped trying to understand where the dragon had come from or if it was real.

The dragon demanded acceptance as it was, something beyond explanation, beyond understanding, a rare and special gift from the universe. He had faith in that.

Sipping some water, he lay back and closed his eyes.

CHAPTER 23

She tiptoed up to the table, tray in hand. Glossy black bangs nearly covered her eyes. "Chee I wan fissa?"

Lansky looked at the other men around the table in the enlisted men's club.

"Yeah, we want pizza, bring us two, and more beer." John Eberhardt held up two fingers to make sure she got the message.

A Korean band dressed in rumpled tuxedoes started up on the tiny bandstand. The first bars of the "Orange Blossom Special," made the men smile. Huddle let out his rebel yell, and they all began tapping their feet.

Something was in the air that night. High-energy vibrations bounced around the small room. They always did on the first night of stand-down.

Eberhardt looked at Lansky, raised his glass, and unleashed a goofy grin. He was like a match just struck, inflamed, released from the mud, bugs, rain, and fear—the cold paralyzing fear aroused by eerie jungle sounds in the black of night.

All that gone for a day, replaced by the simple pleasures of dry socks, cold beer, and a country beat.

Lansky felt liberated, celebrating his release from twenty-one days in the bush. Eberhardt's goofy grin usually annoyed him. It signaled a night of merciless agitation and practical jokes. But tonight his smile matched Eberhardt's as he said, "Two pizzas? Man, we just had chow. You're beau coup dinky dow, Big Husker!"

Looking out the window of the club, Lansky could see rice farmers herding their water buffalo along the narrow dikes between the paddies. A patchwork quilt of gray-green stretched off toward the mountains along the coast. At the foot of the mountains, a huge white Buddha favored the valley with his serene gaze. Motorbikes, buses, and trucks buzzed noisily along Highway 1, passing the monument.

Back inside, Lansky surveyed the collection of GIs sitting at various tables. Sweating and drinking, they tapped their feet to the music.

One group in the back, the militant blacks, were not tapping a foot to the beat. White culture was a target for their resentment. None of them spoke to whites unless it was mandatory. When in the rear, they had their own hooch known as the "Black Shack." They had angry discussions about fighting Whitey's war, read Black Power literature, and most definitely were not in the EM club for country and western. They came only for the beer.

Lansky noticed a black soldier enter, freshly tied cornrows bouncing, chin up, legs pumping a rhythmic strut. He focused on the Black Shack table, looking at no one else. As he approached, the black nearest him jumped up, scraping his plastic and metal chair on the cement. They exchanged a rapid series of handshakes, grasps, finger pops, and hand slaps. Each man around the table jumped up, with the same intense expression and gave precisely the same pattern of shakes, grasps, pops, and slaps. While doing the dap, their gaze remained rigidly fixed in space. This was more than a greeting, it represented mistrust of whites, symbolized their brotherhood and the idea that "you watch my back, and I'll watch yours." On completion of the circle, they broke into animated big city street corner conversation, physical in gesture and expression, their cynical laughter lingered long and loud over the table.

The bar girl delivered the pizza and another round of beers to Lansky's table. Eberhardt immediately shoveled a steaming piece into his mouth.

Lansky tried a piece and looked at Eberhardt. Swept up in the heady vibe, he decided to needle the needler. "This stuff tastes like cardboard. How come you ordered this shit?"

Eberhardt looked over the piece poised in front of his mouth, surprised by Lansky's aggression.

"A'll take y'ers," he said, barely getting the words through his mouth engorged with cheese and dough.

The band brought out a pretty Korean woman in a strapless blue sequined dress. Her first song was "Proud Mary." "Lef a good chob in a city. Workin' for a man every night and day."

Eberhardt partially cleared his mouth with a beer wash. Turning to the band, he yelled, "Hey, not bad, only about the nine thousandth time I heard that one."

"Thought you liked it here, Big Husker," jabbed Lansky.

"Quit callin' me that." Eberhardt looked bothered. "It's Mr. Eberhardt from the great state of Nebraska to you, buddy."

Two more blacks came into the club and followed the same ritual as the previous entrant.

"Them dudes sure do make it a point of doin' that dap." Eberhardt, along with the rest of the club, was noticing Black Shack's ceremony.

"Boa, I'll tell you what, it pisses me off." Huddle was speaking for the first time. He'd been quietly sipping beer and studying the Black Shack.

"Why's it piss you off?" asked Lansky.

"It's stupid, man! It's number ten!"

"Well, wadda' you care what they do?" Eberhardt said.

Lansky noticed the twinkling eye and toothy grin were back.

"Ah don't care about no Black Shack, man. They're nowhere!" Huddle was very agitated.

"Ya know yer right, Huddle. They're doin' that jus' ta piss us off," said Eberhardt.

"Ah know it."

Lansky looked over his shoulder at the dark militant faces staring at the singer. He didn't like the way this was developing.

"Ya know, Huddle, when they stand up there and do that dappin' all the time, it's like they're showin' off or sumpin'. Like they're sayin' they're better than us." Eberhardt continued his agitation.

"Ah know it."

Eberhardt ordered more beer and kept feeding Huddle inflammatory comments, building him up to a fighting rage, then laughing as the others tried to calm him down. The conversation got drunker and meaner as the night went on.

Eberhardt started yelling at the band.

"Hey, c'mon. Gimme the banana act. C'mon, gimme the banana act."

Lansky remembered the Filipino band they last saw featuring a guy who ate a banana and played harmonica at the same time.

The tiny Korean singer looked at Eberhardt as they were taking a break.

"Gimme the banana act. Huh, c'mon."

She walked backstage giving Eberhardt a confused look. Later the guitar player from the group came out with a hat in his hand.

"Two hundred MPC and she strip."

Huddle yanked a wad of orange and blue bills from his pocket and stuffed them in the hat.

"Better 'n bananas."

"I'll put some money on it. How 'bout you, Lansky?"

"I can see it, or should I say, I'd like to see it."

They all stuffed orange and blue MPC in the man's hat. The other tables did the same. He bowed to each as they stuffed it in.

The band assembled and swung into their version of "The Stripper." She came out with tiny, mincing steps, hands over her head, and started with the gloves she had just put on, taking them off inch-by-inch, bumping and grinding in time with the drummer's beat.

All the GIs at the back tables stood to improve their view. Even the "Black Shack" members were on their feet.

The group was easily excited. Every move she made brought excited cheers. The more she took off and bumped and wiggled, the more they whistled and yelled. Clapping and hooting began to build.

Slowly they began edging toward her. By the time she was unhooking her bra, a tight semi-circle had formed around the band.

Dropping out of her bra, she held her round brown breasts out for display. Some of the drunker ones attempted to grab her, but she was too quick.

Lansky stood in the second row, Eberhardt on a chair behind him.

Huddle was in the back, his view blocked. He kept poking Eberhardt. "Waas she dooin' now, man?"

"Woa, Woa, boy, she's wigglin' like crazy. You should see it!"

"Yas, sir, I know it!"

Hardly any of the Black Shack group had a view. Cautious about mixing with whites, they did not join the initial move forward. This was one of the rare instances where they had a common interest with whitey. Like the rest in the back, they were elbowing and pushing for a view.

One of the Black Shack members, Charles Laughton, or "Sir Charles" as he was known, started elbowing past Huddle. He was thrown back, and they exchanged hot words.

As the band built to a climax, the lovely Korean displayed the full beauty of her round little figure. Commotion in the back started sounding ugly.

She considered dancing a little longer, having done none of her acrobatic tricks that involved GIs placing money in various places.

But the NCO in charge was giving the hand-across-the-throat "cut it" signal. She looked at the drummer who understood, and the band chugged into a finale, as she made a hasty exit. All the lights came on.

Instead of shouting, "More, more, more," most of the men were distracted by the flaring tempers in the back.

The head NCO and his aides hustled around the crowd.

Sir Charles and Huddle had each other by the shirt. The NCO got between them just in time.

"Sumbitch poke me in a chest an bus' up my cigars, Sarge!" yelled Laughton.

"Ya, well, ya was shoving me, so I shoved back." Huddle's face was contorted in drunken anger, one eye squeezed shut in a ferocious expression, lips twisted. Beads of sweat dripped from the oily red curls.

The NCO was calm but firm. "I'm gonna suggest y'all drop it because if there's any fightin' in here, y'all gonna spend the night in the brig."

"Wadda 'bout my cigars, Sarge? Cost me fify cen' apiece."

"Sorry 'bout 'at, troop. Like I say, no fightin' in here." He was very sure of himself.

Slowly, they released their grips on one another and backed off.

"Now you dudes leave first." The sarge gestured Sir Charles and the Black Shack out the door. Their voices could be heard rising as they left.

"We'll get 'em in the company area. Gonna fix Mr. Honkey."

"Fifty cen' apiece da dude owe me. I had 'em all line up in my pocket real nice, and da dude smash 'em." Laughton was angry.

Looking at Huddle, the sarge said, "Now *you* go."

Broad green banana fronds scratched against each other in a humid wind as they slipped along toward the company area.

Lansky ran ahead of Eberhardt and Huddle, turned, and stiff-armed them at the shoulders. "Hey, I know Sir Charles. Let me talk to him. You don't need this."

"Fuck off, shit bird." They pushed his arms aside. Long, purposeful strides carried them on toward the low row of old French barracks that had become their new home when in the rear.

As they entered the company area, a group of six dark figures stood to one side of the cement volleyball court. Lansky caught up to Huddle and Eberhardt as they heard, "Hey, Huddle, wan' you to pay for my cigars, man!"

They stopped in the dust.

"Ain't givin' you nothin', *Sir* Charles." Huddle put extra mocking venom on "Sir Charles" as it rolled off his tongue.

"Yo shit is weak, Huddle. Guess I gonna hafta get my money one way or another."

The dark figures moved across the dusty courtyard. Huddle and Eberhardt stiffened. Lansky thought about running, but couldn't go.

"Wan' my money, man." Sir Charles swaggered a little, looming closer, head to one side.

"Hey, what ta fock goin' on here?"

The booming voice froze them all. They recognized it as the bark of First Sergeant Bulldog Rodriguez.

"At ease now, men! You start fightin', an' I bring smoke on jor ass!"

Standing in the dim light, they could see him approach, dressed in his fatigue cap, olive-drab underwear, and floppy untied boots. His giant belly added weight to his words. He stared them into submission.

Bulldog was about to ask them what the problem was, but stopped and listened.

A far-off chugging, steaming sound grew in volume. Three hot-orange smoke trails came jetting over the hills.

"Da fockin' VC shooting rockets at us, men! Dee to da trenches," yelled the first sergeant.

The locomotive roar of rockets increased as they sprinted for the trenches on the edge of the company area. A warning siren cranked up, adding an eerie, wavering wail to the scene.

They all ran together, unconcerned about who was black and who was white. Huddle had started ahead of the group but slowed because he was so very drunk. Sir Charles grabbed his arm, tugging him along. Huddle lurched behind, head bobbing.

The first rocket hit. A loud detonation threw a giant orange shadow across the whitewashed building. Lansky flew headfirst into the ditch. It seemed as if the ground jumped up and hit him in the chin.

The second rocket detonated in the middle of the company area, the third landed well beyond them, making a mucking, sucking, sizzle in the rice paddies.

A mortar company pumped flares into the air. The siren wailed.

Lansky's chin hurt, and he had a hard time focusing his eyes.

Eberhardt grabbed him by the collar. "Hey, Mr. Graceful, you okay?"

"Ya, guess so. Musta hit my head." He hunched up on his knees with Eberhardt's help. Huddle and Sir Charles had landed next to each other in the trench. As they crawled out, they exchanged furtive glances.

"Hey, Laughton, look at 'em stogies now." Eberhardt smiled.

They all looked at the contents of the chest pocket. What had been a row of cigars, was now a smashed flat mixture of tobacco and dirt sticking to his shirt.

"Heh, heh, my girlfriend don' like me smoking anyway." Sir Charles almost smiled. "Hey, what happened to First Sergeant?"

"He ran the other way when we took off," said Eberhardt.

"Les go see if he's okay."

"Yeah."

The group trotted back through the company area. A hole eight feet in diameter decorated the center of the volleyball court. Cement chunks and rocks were scattered all over the courtyard. Fresh pockmarks could be seen in the stucco around the courtyard.

As they approached the NCO hooch, the first sergeant came out the door with a Budweiser in his hand.

"Hey, First Sergeant, how come you didn't hit the trenches with us?"

"Well, I just got a fridge in my hoosh, and I had to protect it. Yeah, I got two cases of Bud in there an I'd hate to lose 'um. Hey, you wait here, I bring you a beer, and we form a patrol to report on the damage."

They laughed. Huddle and Laughton looked at each other. They stopped laughing, and tension crept back into the space between the two groups. Everyone looked away.

The first sergeant returned and handed out an armload of beer. They popped the tops and followed him in two separate groups.

CHAPTER 24

January 27, 1972

The morning sun threw a harsh yellow beam into the hung-over eyes of the ragged formation. First light packed enough heat to start little droplets of reprocessed Budweiser trickling under rumpled fatigues. They stared at the rocket crater in front of them.

A squat, broad-shouldered man with a basketball belly strode confidently to the front of the rank, his glossy boots blinked sunshine at the formation.

First Sergeant had just shaved, but his five o'clock shadow was indestructible, stretching from his chest to his ears. The brown eyes narrowed, showing displeasure. He possessed the intangible essence of leadership. Officers with much more rank never held sway over men like this charismatic character did. His voice and eyes had great power to show compassion or intimidation. Fractured Puerto Rican English never prevented him from communicating a firmness and fairness that all could accept. Today he would use his powers to condemn and then forgive.

"At ease, men. Da VC shoot rockets in last night an fock up da wally wall court. That's no sweat, but we have men fighting in da middle of da rocket attack! I hope you learn yer lesson about dat fighting!"

He paused briefly for effect, scanning the entire rank, then increasing the disgust and volume in his voice. "We won't have no more a that fighting! Da next man I catch fighting, I bring smoke on his ass! I make him wish he was never born."

He paused again, the squint loosening slightly. "You men should do like me. I go to my hoosh, I get drunk, I go to sleep. You should be like me!" The eyes opened and twinkled. "Hey, by the way, I need a volunteer."

Everyone relaxed and smiled. They knew he was easing off now with this introduction to his standard joke.

"I need a volunteer to come by my hoosh tonight."

No one answered. Everyone smiled.

"Hey, who gonna volunteer ta come by my hoosh tonight? I need a volunteer to suck my dick!"

They always laughed at this weird joke. Even the officers broke up. Only First Sergeant Bulldog could get away with that one.

"Hokay, you see me 'bout it later. Now for orders of da day: oh-seven-hundred, breakfast; oh-eight-hundred, clean company area; ten hundred, draw weapons, clean weapons; eleven-hundred, weapons testing; thirteen-hundred, clean weapons; fourteen-hundred, lunch."

As First Sergeant mentioned weapons cleaning and testing, Huddle and Lansky looked at each other. They hated weapons cleaning and testing, then cleaning them again.

"Less go on sick call, feel bad anyway," whispered Huddle.

"Yeah, me, too."

As the formation dispersed, most of the men went to the mess. Huddle and Lansky approached First Sergeant to request permission to go on sick call. Edging up nervously, they shifted uncomfortably waiting for him to conclude his conversation with the CO.

He turned to face them, looking up at their lanky figures, striking a bulldog pose. "So, a two-man detail volunteering to come to my hoosh tonight ta suck my dick?"

"No, no, First Sergeant, we injured ourselves jumping in the ditches las' night, and we wanted to go on sick call," Lansky said, wide-eyed.

"What's wrong? Lemme see."

"See, under my chin, gotta bruise."

"Uh, huh. What about you, Huddle?"

"Ya, wall tell ya, Top—"

"Ain't no top! A top spins on a ground."

"'Scuse me, First Sergeant! Ah, well my back's kind of pained."

Bulldog's eyes narrowed. "Men, hi been in da harmy tweny-seeks jeers an I only go on seek call two times, an' both times I was chot!"

Shrinking back, they decided not to press it. They had a right to go if they really insisted, but no one went against Bulldog.

"Well, ya, ah . . . I see where you're coming from . . . I guess we'll jus' go to the mess hall." Lansky felt ashamed.

As they walked up the hill, they smiled at each other.

"Haven' had me a real breakfast in weeks, Lansky."

"Nope, me neither."

"Guess we betta make the most of our las' day in a rear."

"Yup."

"Gonna go to the club tonight?"

"Wouldn't miss it."

CHAPTER 25

February 6, 1972

The heat of the day had passed, but the humidity lingered through the evening. Heat lightning danced noiselessly over the far mountains.

A C-130 Specter gunship hung in the heavy air over the far valley showering the ground thousands of meters below with sporadic bursts of red tracer fire.

Lansky viewed the scene from a trench on top of Hill 266. His company was on guard duty protecting the northern approach to the city of Da Nang.

A low-flying Huey growled along the side of the hill, its huge door-mounted spotlight cast a shaft of white light into the wire below the trenches. The wire was clean.

Lansky sat back on the ammo boxes in the trench, bracing his knees against the wall like a churchgoer tired of worship.

AK-47 fire chattered sporadically from the bottom of the ridge. Dogs barked.

The sound of an amplified guitar tuning-up rose from the village below. Tuning turned into a melody. A guitar riff cut the humid air, then another attempting flashy rock chords. Driving bass and drums kicked in, thumping out a passable bluesy beat. The guitarist chopped out a boogiewoogie lead, long on volume but short on rocker's élan.

Lansky guessed the distant guitarist was attempting "Johnny B. Goode."

A young man's voice tried the lyrics in English. "Go, go, go Chonny go, go, go," was understandable. But when he tried the first verse, it got garbled at "carry hi kitar an a cunny sack."

He switched to Vietnamese for the second verse. Lansky was entertained.

Huddle came out of the dark. They exchanged quizzical smiles while listening to the music.

"Boa, boa, never heard no one sing like 'at. Can't say ah even wanna hear someone sing like 'at," said Huddle. "Gawddamn, sounds so . . . so . . ."

"So foreign?" said Lansky.

"Yeah, foreign. 'At's right. Foreign. Dinks shouldn't be trying to sing our stuff. Why don't they sing their own music?"

"It is their music, it's everybody's," said Lansky. "It's revealing. You know some of the adults in that vil are VC, but when their kids put a band together, they play American rock."

Sergeant Tiny moved noiselessly along the trench. "Sounds like a party goin' on down in the vil."

"You could call it that," said Huddle, squinting through his starlight night-vision scope.

Looking over Huddle's right shoulder, Tiny said, "Lemme look through your scope, Huddle."

He saw grainy, green images of wire and bulldozed earth.

The village was beyond the starlight's range. Tiny licked his lips, scope at his side, listening, motionless. "Sounds different, huh, fellas?"

"Yeah, real different," said Huddle. "Number tan fer sure."

"Well, it is different, but kinda interesting," said Tiny, raising the scope again. Soon he lowered it, switched it off, and put it in its case.

"They're partying down in the vil tonight. Wonder what it'd be like to go to that party?"

"What? Party with a bunch o' dinks?" said Huddle. "You're crazy, can't party wit' no dinks."

"Aw, I've done it before. Last tour mostly."

"What about the VC that's probably at the party too?" said Lansky.

"Well, we'd have to watch out for them."

Lansky gulped, "We?"

"Yeah, I'm damn horny, Lansky, need me a boom-boom girl. We could go down, hire a few girls, and come back before anyone knows it."

"Wait a minute! Crawl through our own wire? Take a chance on getting shot? Risk an unauthorized trip to a vil that's probably got VC in it? Then sneak back through our own wire with women?"

"Can do, Lansky, takes some guts, though."

"Don't know if I have enough guts for that, Tiny."

"Well, I'm gonna try it. I can low-crawl down this hill and recon the vil. If it's safe, I'm gonna go in, get me a few girls, and bring 'em back. Cover my butt when I'm gone."

"You're nuts."

Ignoring Lansky, vaulting the trench, Tiny low-crawled rapidly down the hill through the wire and out of sight.

Lansky and Huddle looked at each other, astonished. It seemed out of character for Tiny to go AWOL, but his personality changed when he left the bush. Guard duty was babysitting to him. He needed action, even if he had to create it. Like many great field soldiers of history, he was not suited to garrison duty.

Sergeant Massey came out of the dark, stopping at their shoulder. "What's that noise?"

"That's rock and roll, Sarge," said Lansky, snapping out of his surprise.

"Sounds like a car accident to me. Hey, the lieutenant is sick, could be malaria, so I'm doin' the rounds tonight."

They stood listening to the guitarist chop up the final bars of "Johnny B. Goode."

"Glad that's over," said Huddle.

"Yeah, me, too," said the sergeant. "Looks like a quiet night, huh, fellas?"

"Sure thing, Sarge," said Lansky. "Quiet."

"You guys keep that scope on the wire. Never can tell what you'll find down there," said the sergeant over his shoulder as he continued his rounds.

"That's fer sure," said Huddle.

The distant musician and his band continued to play vaguely recognizable songs and melodies. Lansky listened, fascinated, to the crude rock crackling with static and microphone feedback.

Huddle continued to grumble about "them damn dinks fuckin' up our stuff."

To relieve his boredom, Lansky decided to tease Huddle with a song he made up to the melody of "Sweet Little Sixteen."

"Well, they're rockin' all over Veetnaam.
From Saigon to the DMZ,
All the cats gonna dance with Vern Huddle and me,"

He started shuffling his feet, bobbing his head and snapping his fingers.

"Well, they're rockin' in Phu Bai, Chu Lai,
All the way to Cam Ranh Bay,
All the dudes are groovin',
Ain't gonna be no war today."

Lansky was hoping to get a rise out of Huddle with his routine. Huddle tried to ignore him by looking through the starlight scope. "Hey, Lansky, knock it off. Think ah see some movement."

They both studied the dark, listening and looking.

"Ah guess it's nuttin'. Just wavin' bush," said Huddle.

"Let me see." Lansky raised the scope and scanned the edge of the hill. Green bulldozed rock, gravel, and crooked trees. No movement.

"I don't see anything, Huddle. You know, I can't figure out how Tiny expects to come back in through the wire. I'm not going to stay up all night waiting for him. Even if he crawls back right in front of us, someone from another position could fire him up."

"Yeah, an' he'll have some women with him."

"If he's smart, he'll stay there until morning."

"Yeah, if he's smart."

The next person on guard duty appeared. He offered no greeting, simply walked up to his post and rested his elbows on the top of the trench, staring off into the night.

"Hey, Chief," said Huddle, "we got ourselves a situation here for you ta handle."

Chief had yet to speak to anyone. His eyes were always straight ahead, face impassive. Knowing Chief would never acknowledge them, Huddle walked up to him. "Listen. Tiny is down in that vil outside the wire. No kiddin'. He's gonna be comin' back during your watch through the wire down front.

He's gonna have some mama-sans with him. Keep an eye out for him. Don't shoot him. Tiny is really out there! Got it?"

Chief stared off into the dark, inert.

"This ain't no joke now, Chief, wake me up, if you see something." They looked at him for a long time, then crawled into the bunker at the back of the trench and lay down on the dirty cots.

Lansky was awakened hours later by thick smoke boiling through the bunker. He fell off his bunk choking, blinded, groping for an exit. Disoriented, bumping his head on the back wall, then backing into Huddle who had just gotten off his cot.

Eventually, they found the opening, spilling out into the trench, coughing uncontrollably, eyes streaming, collapsing on the trench floor to the sound of laughter, Tiny's booming baritone, and the shrill cackle of young women.

As his vision cleared, he saw yellow smoke still rising from the bunker. Tiny stood in the trench with his arms around two small Vietnamese women. The tops of their heads were level with his navel. They were laughing at Huddle and Lansky.

"Sonovabitch, Tiny," yelled Huddle. "Why'd y'all go an' smoke us?"

"I didn't do it," said Tiny, still chuckling. "Chief did it." Tiny stood aside to show a drunken, swaying Chief with a sheepish grin on his face and a Budweiser in his hand.

"Yeah, sorry, fellas, we was just talkin' about wakin' you up for a little party action. I guess Chief decided to take care of it." Tiny's voice had a tinge of sympathy.

Chief reached into a cardboard box, pulled out two cans of beer, and brought them to Lansky and Huddle.

"Hey, yer sumthin', Chief," said Huddle, taking the beer.

The two men gathered themselves up and popped their beers open. Looking around wide-eyed, they continued deep breaths. It took several minutes of coughing and spitting to clear their airways.

Lansky looked at his beer, then at Tiny. "Where'd you guys get the beer?"

"Down in the vil," said Tiny. "Got these two lovelies and a case of warm Bud for fifty P. Coulda got three girls and no beer for fifty, but I thought two was enough."

One of the girls climbed nimbly up the side of the trench, sat cross-legged with a beer in her hand. A row of straight black bangs bordered the top of her smiling face, her manner, light and animated—the confident professional. "You gimme cig'rette? Hey, GI, you got Salem?"

"Got no cigarettes," said Tiny.

"Awa, Cheap Charlie." She jumped down into the trench and walked up to Huddle, patting his pockets for a cigarette. "Gimme Salem, hey, you got Salem?"

"Hey! Okay! Givya a cigarette." He shifted from side to side, embarrassed as he pulled out the pack. He attempted to give her one, but she snatched the pack from his hands and took three more.

"Gawddamn, yer a far ball, ain'tcha." As he lit the cigarette for her, she smiled up at him. Huddle smiled back. She blew smoke in his face and then said, "Oh, you beau coup numba' wan! You short timer? You take me USA? You take me USA, I be big honsho?"

"Naw, I'm not takin' you any farther than that bunk in there."

"You gimme money."

"Sure, les'see." He pulled his wallet out of his pocket and removed it from the plastic bag. "Here ya go. Ten P."

"Aw, no, cheap!"

"Got no more money, honey."

"Me see." She examined his wallet, searching it thoroughly, then started going through his pockets. Reaching into his front trouser pocket made Huddle smile. "Keep reachin' down there, honey," he said with a goofy grin.

"Haw, hokay," she said, curt and resigned. "We hurry." She pulled Huddle into the bunker.

Lansky finished his beer and walked toward Tiny. "How'd you get back without getting shot?"

"The girls know a way around the wire. We walked up the ridge next to the hill, and they found a way through to the service road. So we just walked up here on the service road. Hey, take a look at this one." Tiny squashed the plump young girl against his side. She was the first fat Vietnamese Lansky had seen. Large breasts pulled the buttons on her peasant blouse taut. Dark cleavage ascended to her neck. She was shy, with none of the self-assurance displayed by her partner.

"She's got some credentials, don't she? Gotta admire a girl with credentials."

The girl smiled nervously, unaware of what was being said about her.

"Yeah, she's got 'em all right. Can I have another beer?"

"Hep yerself."

Lansky walked toward the case, noticing Chief's thousand-yard stare. "Hey, pretty militant of you, Chief, old boy, to throw that smoke canister in our bunker."

Chief stared off, drained his can, and then smiled. This was the first time since Thanksgiving that Lansky got a reaction from Chief. "Pretty loose tonight, huh, Chief?" They passed several minutes drinking and gazing into the night.

The Huey with the searchlight made another pass over the wire.

The loud young girl that had pulled Huddle into the bunker was already out looking for her next mark. She walked up to

Chief and put her arm around him. "Hey, you gimme—" Before she could finish her sales pitch, Chief elbowed her to the ground. Turning his back, he walked off. The girl sat on her elbows and backside, watching Chief storm away. Turning her head to one side, she smiled, then looked up at Lansky. "Beau coup *dien cai dow.*" She got up, swayed lithely, and dusted herself off, looking at Lansky. "Hey, got cig'rette?"

"Nope." He wasn't in the mood.

"Hey, you want suck-fuck?"

"Got no money."

"Cheap Charlie! Lemme see!" She reached into Lansky's back pocket and pulled the wallet out of his pants searching for money.

"Aw, Numba' Tan, no take me USA. No money."

Lansky noticed a silhouette approaching in the trench. It was Marty. "Hey, LT is sick. Need an RTO to take night watch on the radio."

"Well, I'm busy."

"LT wants you up to the commo shack now. Needs someone who can use the cack wheels."

"I already had guard duty tonight."

"He's in no mood, you better go."

"Yeah, okay." Lansky put his wallet back in his pocket.

"I'll take guard duty down here," said Huddle as he emerged from the dark. He looked at the girl staring up at them. "Boy, Allen, she tightened me up, jus' right."

"Yeah." Marty was trying not to think about it. "C'mon, Lansky. Lieutenant's waitin'."

As they walked past the bunker, they heard Tiny and the plump little girl inside. Marty looked at Lansky.

"Where'd you get the girls?"

"Tiny went through the wire and got 'em down in the vil."

"Tiny went through our wire?"

"Yes, he did."

"He's nuts."

"I'm beginning to think so, myself."

"Yer gonna miss the party, huh?"

"That's affirmative."

"Yer pretty happy 'bout it, I see."

"No, I'm somewhat miffed about my current circumstance if you really want to know."

"I didn't really want to know that badly."

Two hours later, Lansky trudged back to the bunker as dawn crept out of the eastern sky.

One solitary figure stood in the trench watching him approach—Chief. He had his M-16 in one hand and a beer in the other. Crushed cans lay all over the trench. Chief rocked back and forth, humming a low private tone, unsteady, barely conscious.

Lansky heard several people snoring inside the bunker.

"So the party's over, huh, Chief?"

Drunken, deadened, bleary eyes stared into the distance.

"Sounds like they're all in there sleeping, huh?"

Chief stood mute.

"Well, guess I'll just lie down here and get some rest, long as you're on duty, Chief."

Lansky sat down and stretched out, getting ready for a nap on the trench floor. Reclining in the dust, he looked up at Chief. "Be kind of funny if we threw a smoke canister in there now, huh, Chief?"

Suddenly, Chief lurched stiffly toward the bunker.

Lansky sat up.

Chief's attention focused on the bunker opening. The safety on the side of his weapon was on semi.

"Hey, Chief, wadya' doin'?" said Lansky, rising to a kneeling position.

Chief swung the barrel into the opening.

"No!" Lansky lunged at Chief as a round went off.

He shouldered the drunken Native American hard against the sandbag wall, pressing the barrel against the bags as the second round fired.

Gripping the weapon with both hands and ripping it away, he threw the rifle over his head down into the wire. Tackling Chief, Lansky sat on him.

Shocked, incoherent, and unaware of what he had done, Chief's head rolled back and forth on the trench floor.

"What you doing, Chief?" yelled Lansky. "Hope you didn't hurt anyone."

Tiny and Huddle were stirring in the bunker. They crawled out with the two women, looking hung over and serious.

"You guys okay?" said Lansky.

"Who'se shootin' in the bunker?" Huddle looked at Lansky squinty-eyed.

"Chief was. You okay?"

Huddle patted his chest and looked down, examining himself. "Lak ta have another beer ta see if ah leak."

"Chief drank 'em all," Lansky said, letting Chief up.

Tiny grabbed him by the shirt. "I'm forgettin' this one, Chief. But next time you try a stunt like that, I'm putting you in a world of hurt. Got it?"

Chief's head swayed in pain and incoherence.

"Aw, you're wasted." Tiny let Chief go. "You don't even know what yer doin'. It's my fault fer getting this whole thing going. C'mon, girls, we gotta get off the hill before the lieutenant shows up."

Tiny led them away.

Lansky took Chief by the shoulder and led him toward the bunker. "I want you to go in and lie down, man. I'll retrieve your weapon later."

Chief stumbled into the bunker and dropped onto a cot.

Huddle and Lansky listened until they were sure that he had settled down. They turned to stare silently out at the far mountains.

The vil was silent except for an occasional dog barking.

Lansky studied the purple mountains in the distance. The rising sun colored them with ever-lighter hues.

Huddle snored peacefully on the bottom of the trench. It wasn't long before Lansky joined him.

CHAPTER 26

March 1, 1972

They swayed and bounced off one another in the crowded truck bed. Clutching the side rails, the men spread their feet for stability. It would be hard to relax until the deuce and a half had negotiated the last turn at the bottom of the foothill.

Now on a straight stretch of road, the exhaust note of the diesel changed from the fluttering rasp of deceleration to the roaring whine of acceleration. Each gear raised the crescendo in Lansky's ears.

As the truck bounced through a sequence of potholes, a flickering light drew his attention out across the rolling hills. Dust devils swept across the narrow hogbacks. Whirling columns of debris spun slowly over the baked terrain. The dragon rose above the folded ridges, flapping its wings powerfully past the dust devils then gliding in descent, down and away below the horizon.

Lansky stiffened, hoping to avoid an overt reaction that would require an explanation and the on-rush of confusing emotions that accompanied a dragon sighting.

The rich odor of spent diesel mixed with the acrid stench of raw sewage as they approached the last village before the air base. Hoping to blast through without trouble, the drivers of the convoy accelerated.

Lansky turned to see the low row of tin roofs approaching, glad that his secret was safe.

It was a busy market day with vendors arranging bits of merchandise on both sides of the dirt road. Festive awnings of brightly colored cloth waved in the breeze.

The shoppers noticed the trucks approaching. A singsong buzz of nervous clucking rose in warning over the crowd. They started grabbing children and pushing to clear a path. Some of the vendors were shoved back by the crowd beginning to panic. Precious bits of merchandise were trampled and broken.

As the trucks approached, only the village dogs and one elderly mama-san burdened with her purchases remained on the road. The bent, old woman was pulled aside as the trucks hit the market at fifty miles per hour. Yapping dogs scattered. Some made futile attempts at chasing the giant tires. Many in the crowd were yelling and gesturing at the convoy.

Lansky noticed an adolescent boy running out of the alley amid the blur of color and faces. He flung the contents of a canteen cup at the men on the truck. They felt the spray and immediately noticed the unpleasant odor of urine. Waving their arms, they tried to shake it off. Some grabbed their weapons. "Goddamn dinks." Lansky saw the boy-san standing in the convoy diesel wash, smiling and waving.

The village was shrinking and disappearing. A cloud of dust rose over the roofline, casting a yellow haze on the purple mountains in the background.

They all looked at one another squinty-eyed, with hair and shirts flapping in the breeze. Some of them continued to cuss out the whole country and "them damn dinks throwing piss water on us."

Now on a paved road, they approached the air base. Behind the concertina wire, C-130s waited on the airstrip.

Entering the heavily guarded compound, some of the GIs began checking their bulging rucksacks. They swung bandoliers across their chests, picked up claymore bags, checked grenades, and stuffed machine-gun ammo into every available opening in their packs.

The singing exhaust stacks finally quieted to a rhythmic pant as they stopped behind the C-130s.

A few men swung over the side, others jumped out the back. Packs and equipment were thrown and handed down. They lined up in loose formation, fully dressed for battle.

First Sergeant Bulldog Rodriguez stood in front of his men, clipboard at the side of his beach ball belly. "Now, men, when we get on the planes we gonna keep da muzzles of our weapons pointed down. We doan wanna shoot a hole in da roof of da plane. So keep 'em muzzles down, hokay? Hokay, Bravo Company, follow me."

Top led his men to the yawning cargo bay of the C-130. The men pushed together and shuffled up the ramp. They stopped halfway up. Body odors drifted through the group, along with a faint smell of urine.

It was slow going because the first sergeant was talking to the air force crew chief.

"Sorry, men. We got no seats so we just come all da way forward and set on da floor."

As Lansky walked into the cargo area, he noticed the slippery stainless steel floor. The air force didn't have time to install the aluminum frame jump seats on these no-nonsense transports. The men sat, then looked for something to hang on to.

Nothing was available.

One of the GIs told Lansky, "No seats, huh. Bet they don't serve breakfast either."

They sat cross-legged or sprawled on their packs with the butt plates of their weapons pointing up. It was so crowded, Lansky didn't have room to stretch his legs.

A row of bare bulbs cast a yellow light on the uncomfortable troops. The cargo bay motor whined loudly as it slowly shut the tail of the plane. Four engines squealed, then coughed roughly, revving to a roar. Conversation was impossible until the cargo door snipped off the last glimpse of the horizon.

They were moving now. After a short pause, the plane gained speed. It bounced lightly, wobbling the heads of the soldiers, like cheap ceramic cats in the back window of a car.

Lansky noticed the angle of the floor was tilting. As the plane took off, those in the front started a slow slide back. Surprised at first, not knowing what was going on, they swore at each other. The takeoff compressed them like a squeezed accordion. Falling into one another and losing balance, they pushed and kicked to avoid being crushed. Rifle butts fell and hit heads. Men toppled, poking barrels into eyes. Those in back crushed against the door yelled loudly.

"Get off my arm."

"Sonavabitch."

"Hey, ya poked me in my eye, shithead."

The angle of the floor increased. Not having anything to hold on to, Lansky strained against gravity. The stainless steel slid them back.

The air force crew chief sat stoically, watching the crowd drift away.

A screeching servo sound came from the walls as the landing gear retracted.

They were three-deep stacked on the cargo bay door before the plane leveled off.

Those in front were finally able to creep back, dragging packs and weapons across the floor.

Lansky turned to see the tangled mass of bodies slowly unstack itself, like football players after a pileup.

"Glad I didn't join the air force," said Huddle, rearranging his pack and sitting down again with his rifle butt in the air.

"Hokay, men, settle down, yer all right," barked First Sergeant over the grumbling men. "Gotta whole hour to go, so settle down and get some rest."

The flight felt much more stable, and the men did settle down. Their experience in the Asian Army had taught them to become accustomed to the unaccustomed. Another incomprehensible incident to be written off with the customary, "Fuck this Mickey Mouse shit."

Lansky lay back on his pack and did what most GIs do when they closed their eyes: he thought of home. He thought about where he'd rather be and trips he'd rather be taking.

Half asleep, the image of one trip, in particular, was dredged up as a dreamy escape from the unpleasantness surrounding him. He could see himself in the backseat of his father's jeep . . .

The fine dry chalk of gravel dust tickled his nose and made him sneeze. A squat gray-haired man in a red, plaid hunting outfit looked into the backseat.

"You guys okay? Should I close the window?"

"No, nope," came the young hunter's reply. "We'll be all right, Harry."

The stiff suspension of the green Willy's Overland bounced the four dusty occupants along the old road. This would be their last partridge-hunting trip of that fall.

Lansky studied the harvested cornfield stubble. It reminded him of his father's five-day-old beard. Someday he'd have one just like it.

"Can ya get the Wisconsin game on, Dad?" Lansky yelled over the roar.

The radio sat above the four-wheel-drive shift levers between the two men. The front-seat rider turned on the radio. He was attempting to tune in the Wisconsin-Minnesota football game. Hearing anything over the rumble of snow tires on gravel would be remarkable. Harry knew this, but he tried his best to please the boy.

"Let's forget it, Harry. We're almost there," said Lansky's father.

"Okay, Doc, this son-of-a-bitch ain't gonna work with the antenna knocked off anyway."

"Thought you told me that coat hanger would do the trick."

The jeep slowed along a row of pines and turned off the gravel onto a logging road. Shuddering into a lower gear, it tossed the hunters' heads up to the ceiling while negotiating the uneven ground at the head of the trail.

They stopped.

"Should we let the boys go first, Doc?"

"Yeah, you guys go first, okay?"

Lansky and his friend Larry looked at each other.

"Okay, we'll go first."

Getting out of the jeep, the two fathers shared a smile over the unusually quiet mood of their fourteen-year-old sons. Carefully, the two boys negotiated the climb from the backseat over the corner of the square front seat.

As they walked around to the back of the jeep, they clapped dust off their bulky pants and coats, costumes that made them look the part. Being dressed like a hunter helped some, but they still felt awkward.

They uncased their sixteen-gauge shotguns. Dads gave sons red shotgun shells, then pulled down the tailgate. The shells were shoved home.

Climbing the high gate brought some relief as they rested their guns on the roof of the jeep. The two boys stood on the tailgate looking over the roof at the line of trees along the forest road.

After the hour's ride in the back of the jeep, it was good to be in the woods. The insecurities that had been building were released as they looked down the wall of pine and aspen bordering the road. Funny how going up north always made people feel better.

As they lurched forward, the two extended their arms across the roof to hold on. They looked at each other and cracked the first smiles of the trip.

The trees seemed to absorb the sound of the jeep. Only the unsteady whine of the transmission could be heard as they crept along. The wind in the pines replaced the rattle of gravel.

They were swaying along now, having an excellent view of it all from their elevated perch. The higher drier ground held oak and maple. The lower wetter areas showed viburnum, ironwood, cherry, and alder. Stands of aspen and evergreen were scattered throughout the Chequamegon Forest.

The moment was good. It temporarily overcame their teenage aversion to family life. Instinct was leading them away. Even when they did spend time with their families, they wouldn't show any pleasure. Being sullen and looking off was their usual habit when confronted with a family outing.

But there were some things in the family realm that couldn't be resisted. Partridge hunting was right up there with cars and food. They surveyed opposite sides of the road, looking for the flutter of brown wings.

Inside, the two men tossed back a shot of whiskey from Harry's flask. They enjoyed this even more than cars and food.

The tall, slab-sided vehicle lumbered up and down the hills, then into a bog, plowing through the muck with all four wheels throwing mud.

Coming out of the bog, the jeep stopped at the bottom of the hill crowned by a stand of poplars. An understory of hazel sat in the shadows. Each bush bore hundreds of catkins that partridge would feed on for the coming winter.

Harry whispered, "See 'em up there, boys?"

"No." They squinted at the woods.

"At the top of the hill."

"I see 'em," said Larry, too loudly.

"Shh, not so loud."

"Go gettum, Larry. You're ready," Lansky encouraged his friend, because he didn't feel ready.

Larry slowly stepped down from the rear of the jeep and released the safety on his pump-action sixteen-gauge. Stopping by his dad at the window, he seemed to need reassurance.

"Just go slow and easy. Lead him when he takes off."

"Okay."

Lansky could see three brown and white heads jerking along in the brush at the top of the ridge. They were eating gravel and hadn't noticed the hunters yet.

Larry took three careful steps in front of the jeep and sighted a line above the unwary birds. The men watched him edge forward with a stiff sideways shuffle. He held the gun against his shoulder. The men smiled.

A rapid whirr of wings beat the air. Larry fired. One of the three birds fell, leaving several tufts of feather down suspended in the air.

He raised the gun over his head and jumped a stiff-legged semicircle.

"I got one! I got one!"

"Go get him, son. He might limp away. And put that thing on safety before you hurt someone," said Harry.

Running up the hill, Larry's boots clomped a quiet, rapid beat. He almost fell over them before he got to the bird.

"Ya-hoo!" He jerked the tiny carcass from the bush for all to see.

They drove the jeep up the hill to look at his treasure. Larry held the still warm carcass in the palm of his hand. Lansky examined the delicate brown and white mottled feather pattern. Its head hung incongruously off to the side of Larry's hand, and smelled of blood.

"Let's get going. You guys stay up there awhile," said Lansky's dad.

"Okay, Dad." They smiled, one of the few pleasant exchanges of recent memory.

As they remounted the tailgate, Lansky listened as Larry began to retell the story, swollen with pride. They were quieted by the "Knock it off" from inside the jeep.

The shadows lengthened as they swayed along. The evergreens turned darker as the sun dived toward the horizon. The wind carried a little more bite that nipped at the boys' noses, making them sniffle.

They passed a creek. Tamarack along its bank had turned golden. Under them, viburnum still held some deep purple berries. Closer to the road, wood thrushes flitted among the bushes seeking fuel for their southerly migration. Fresh buck scrapes had shaved the bark from some of the trees.

The jeep stopped.

Lansky saw two partridges crossing the road and stepped off

the back. Hunching over slightly, he attempted to take advantage of the cover between him and the birds. They were off the road now, but he had marked the spot where they crossed. When he got there, he turned to look under the branches. They were scooting away on the bed of birch leaves covering the forest floor. The notch and bead of his barrel swung over the head of the first one. He released the trigger, driving the butt into his shoulder. His head snapped back. The blast of his weapon faded. Both birds nosed into the ground, rolling among the leaves.

Later in the tavern, the boys played pool while the two dads told everyone about "two birds with one shot." Lansky beamed as he leaned quietly over the green table. He scratched the cue ball, sending it into the wrong pocket on an easy shot. The other hunters in the bar kidded him about how he must be a helluva better shot with a gun than he is with a pool cue.

He walked over to his barstool and sat down staring at his cola. It occurred to him that shooting the birds on the ground wasn't quite the feat that his dad and Harry had made it out to be. They had described it as a shot on the wing. He decided he wouldn't tell them the truth. Sitting back, he rested his shoulders on the hardwood bar rail . . .

The sweetness of this distant memory was disturbed as his shoulders slipped off the pack resting on the stainless steel floor. A rude reminder of the present found him falling forward across his pack as the plane began its descent. He felt a boot slide into his butt. Lansky propped himself up stiff-armed and turned to align his pack for balance during the plane's down-glide. Kneeling now, he felt his toes and knees slide toward the forward bulkhead as he lifted his pack into position. The rest of the company was drifting in an eerie effortless slide toward him. Soon they would be on top of him. It would have been nice to ask Harry what to do about it.

CHAPTER 27

March 10, 1972

Clunking his spoon around the bottom of the can allowed him to trap the last meatball and shovel it into his mouth before finishing off the sauce. The oven-like heat dulled his appetite. Eating had become a tiresome ritual.

Standing, he stretched and took a long swig from his canteen.

The white-hot sun seared the sky, bleaching the blue from it. Only anemic shades of azure were seen near the horizon.

Lansky surveyed the scene from the top of a sandbagged bunker at Firebase Longbow. He looked at the South Vietnamese firebase across the barbed wire from his position. Being so close to the Laotian border, the allies had constructed firebases next to each other for mutual support. ARVN's bunkers were built into the scorched soil and around large boulders, making a formidable defensive position.

An entire regiment of the Army of the Republic of South Vietnam stood in formation on the landing pad in full field dress. The back row carried disassembled mortars. A single rank of men stood in front of the regiment, holding the yellow and red South Vietnamese flag and their regimental colors.

A low-flying Huey droned in for a landing on the huge

corrugated metal landing pad, which was met by a contingent of crisply dressed ARVN officers who saluted the first man off the chopper. Artillery batteries behind the regimental formation began putting out a twenty-one-gun salute.

The arriving officer turned with his huge field glasses to look at the terrain in the target area.

Lansky sat on the high ground and could see several kilometers out into the bush. He was curious about what the ARVN were looking at. Fetching his own binoculars from his rucksack, Lansky glassed the pockmarked terrain on the far side of the nearby village.

Impacting rounds began erupting on one of the broad hills, detonating in a pattern that seemed to be spelling out letters.

The first letter was an "N." The next letter was difficult to make out because of the smoke and flying debris.

As he put his glasses down, Lieutenant Halverson appeared at his shoulder. "What the hell they shooting at?"

"Don't know, LT. Looks like some artillery salute. I think they blasted the ARVN commanding officers' initials into the hillside about half a klick on the other side of the vil."

"Really? Let me see."

Lansky handed LT his binoculars. "At your four o'clock. Looks like two initials: 'N'. . . and is that a 'D'?"

"Could be, Lansky."

"Hey, LT, look over there!"

Halverson lowered his binoculars to see ARVN dragging several men between ranks up to the commander. The prisoners' hands were bound with poles behind their backs. Three terrified men were held rigidly at attention while the commander gestured vehemently and shouted in their faces.

"They're going to execute those three ARVN today for

desertion. They invited our CO and the other officers in the company to come and watch."

"You mean you're not going to go? Seems like your style, LT."

"The CO said he respectfully declined for all of us. Too bad, would have been a nice outing. Helleva thing to shoot them right in front of their own formation just before they go to the field. Guess they do things differently."

The ARVN commander concluded his tirade by repeatedly slapping each of the prisoners. He threw them down on the hot, corrugated metal.

"Oh, that must hurt on a day like today, huh, LT?"

"Their pain will soon end."

The man in charge took a split bamboo stick from one of his aides and beat on the prone men. He forced them to crawl across the hot metal for a painful minute, then gestured that they be taken away.

As they were picked up and dragged away, Lansky saw stripes of red ulcerated skin on the necks and faces of the terrorized men.

The commander walked to the front of the formation and began a speech with grand, aggressive gestures. He pointed out across the sun-blasted hills toward the Laotian border.

Lansky couldn't hear what was said, but the example the commander had just set seemed to say, "Deserters will be punished." Three sharp bursts of automatic rifle fire erupted behind the formation.

The far horizon filled with a string of helicopters, chugging toward the pad, nose up. They landed in front of the formation, driving dust over the regiment.

Lansky counted eight birds on the pad at once. One of the ARVN companies began filing toward them. Each Huey loaded itself, then took off slowly over the vil and out into the boonies. Others hung in the air behind the pad, waiting for room to land.

LT and Lansky silently watched the large lift-out. It lasted almost an hour.

When they were gone, Halverson said, "Boy, those ARVN fly a Huey like it was a truck. Our guys fly them like they're Indy Five Hundred Cars."

"That's true, LT, but their choppers look pretty old and shabby. They don't seem to be able to keep up with the maintenance."

"They're flying our used birds. Must be a little scary."

Eberhardt and Huddle ambled up. Huddle squinted through one eye in the bright sun. Eberhardt smiled his long toothy grin. He looked confidently at his commanding officer. "Hey, LT, can we go swimming today?"

"Well, as long as the guard is posted, those off duty can go."

"Great," said Huddle. "Gonna go down to that swimming hole today and get me a mama-san to go skinny dipping! Almost got one to come in yesterday, but she got scared."

LT's face became serious. "You got a lot of dink civilians over there?"

"Yeah, lots," said Huddle. "It's a regular circus!"

"You got weapons security when you go in the water?"

"Yes, sir. One guy is always on weapons security when we go in."

"Sure that's enough?"

"No sweat, LT, just a bunch of mama-sans selling trinkets and headbands."

"Oh, yeah. The other day I heard someone had a clip stolen out of their weapon when it was in the stack."

"Yeah," Huddle said seriously. "Guess we did have a clip stolen."

"We'll watch it," said Eberhardt.

"You'll have to watch it. The guy on weapons security has to have the stack under control."

"We'll watch it, LT," said Huddle. "Damn! It's hard to have fun over here."

"Let's go, Lansky," said Eberhardt.

"Okay."

The three of them walked down to the concertina wire and carefully stepped through it.

Out on the road, Huddle started a conversation. "Hey, Lansky, what was you doin' down in the wire last night? We almost shot you! Thought you was a dink."

"Well, I was up at the arty party. Got pretty loaded. Heading down toward my hooch I got lost. I couldn't see a thing. Felt myself along the wire and knew I was in trouble. When I heard the bolt go back on that sixty, I knew I better say something."

"Yup, lucky you yelled or you'da been one crispy critter this morning."

"Scared me. Should have known better."

"Yeah, you shoulda. Lucky we recognized your voice. Everyone was pretty jumpy last night after that dink drove by on his scooter and threw that grenade in the wire."

"My luck still holds."

A large diesel truck lumbered by, sucking up a fine cloud of chalky dust.

Through the white haze, Lansky saw black uniformed local militia sitting in the truck bed. Fifteen heavily armed men on patrol in an open deuce and a half. Each of them wore a black baseball cap and had an M-16 with bandoliers strung across their chests. These ruthless cops regarded all with suspicion. Suspects never saw a court or jail, their street justice was sudden and immediate.

The truck stopped next to a mama-san laden with packages strung on a pole. She broke into tears and fell to her knees. The militia roughly searched her meager possessions as she knelt sobbing uncontrollably. They found nothing and left.

She lay face down in the road crying convulsively, unable to regain her composure.

Huddle and Eberhardt collected her bags and packages. Lansky walked over to help her up, placing his hands on her shoulders and lifting.

When she turned to see who it was, she burst into hysterical fits and threw herself to the ground.

They watched her briefly. Then, not knowing what to do, they moved on.

"Helluva neighborhood, huh, Huddle?" said Lansky.

"Yeah, cain't even go to market without trouble."

The heat and dust made them anxious for a swim. They climbed off the road and up a low sunburnt hill.

Their mood lifted as they surveyed the scene around the large pond, a popular place on a hot day.

To their right, a collection of noisy women did laundry. Wading into the water, they doused their clothes with liquid soap, rinsed them in the water, beat them on rocks, wrung them dry, and neatly piled them on top of higher rocks.

Young children frolicked and splashed around their mothers. Smiling little faces with happy eyes, nut-brown skin, and glossy black hair, making an unrestrained free-spirited racket.

On the far bank, farmers tended their water buffaloes drinking from the pond.

To the left, young women and girls crowded the shore with boxes of goods for sale. The object of their attention was the five smiling Americans bobbing in the water twenty feet from them. They grinned at the shrill voices beckoning them to come to the shore.

Brian Hazuka stood naked, M-16 on his hip, guarding the

stacked weapons of the swimmers. He nervously watched the crowd pushing around him and the weapons.

Each time one of the swimmers moved toward shore, the sales ladies waded out into the water, voices rising, singing their sales pitch. They held up their bars of soap, candy, gum, and offered cans of soda, film, peace medallions, and plastic Buddhas, jostling each other for the front row.

Lansky and the others walked down the shore.

"Hey, grunt!" said Hazuka.

"Hey, grunt," replied Eberhardt. "How'd you get stuck with weapons security, ya big geek?"

Hazuka looked at him. "I've already been in. I guess it's my turn. I'll watch your weapons for a little while, if one of you guys will take the next guard duty."

The girls were now pushing up against Lansky and the new arrivals, holding up their wares, shoving each other, hoping for attention.

Lansky stood on one foot, attempting to remove a boot. The girls crowded so close and yelled so loud, he stumbled over.

"Hey, Number Ten. Dee dee! No way!" He gestured them away, creating enough space to take off his boots and pants.

"Yo, Hazu! I'll take security for you in fifteen minutes," said Lansky, now nude, as he stacked his weapon with the others. "Just let me get in for a swim."

"Okay, it's a deal."

"'Atta boy, Lansky, you take over," said Eberhardt.

"And Neverhard will take over for me after I've done fifteen minutes, right, Neverhard?"

"I thought you was gonna do it."

"C'mon, Big Husker, you can handle it."

The women watched the three naked men stack their boots and pants next to the weapons.

Huddle attempted to pull one of the girls out into the water with him. "C'mon, Mama. Let's go skinny dippin'!" He undid imaginary buttons on his imaginary shirt, then gestured that she should take off her clothes and come in. She ran away from him, embarrassed, and the other women laughed.

"C'mon out here with ol' Vern, Mama, c'mon." He gestured to her as the three GIs waded out in the water.

She shrunk back behind the group, hiding her face.

Soon they were waist deep and plunging in.

Lansky crawled along the top of the warm, placid water until he reached the others bobbing in the middle.

The water reflected the women's chattering voices.

Lansky dove under into a quiet and peaceful world. He enjoyed the few seconds of serenity. Surfacing again, he took a deep breath, dove straight down to the lower, cooler layers, and held himself there. Out of breath, going limp, he floated to the surface, following his bubbles.

On top of the water, Lansky took a few overhand strokes toward the women doing laundry, stopping to tread water while watching the children at play.

A bugle call split the air, a staccato sequence of warning notes bounced across the water, then reverberated through the low hills.

The dragon swung a broad arc over the low hills behind the children, black in shadow, profiled by the sun. Diving down, flapping once gracefully, gaining speed, it leveled twenty feet above the water, coming right at Lansky, red eyes locked on the busy scene behind him.

"La-a-a-a-n-s-kee! H-e-e-e-y, L-a-a-a-n-s-keeee!"

Someone was calling his name. He turned to see Hazuka waving at him.

"He-e-e-y, L-a-a-an-skeee! Ca-mo-n, in!" Hazuka had

ROBERT GOSWITZ

waded several feet out into the water, turning his back on the women and weapons.

Lansky noticed one of the women behind him drop her box of trinkets, pull an M-16 from the stack, and raise it to her hip.

Lansky yelled, "Hey, Hazu—" Before he could finish the man's name, the weapon cracked, and Hazuka fell hard into the water.

The other women seemed surprised and ran off shrieking.

Mama-sans at Lansky's end of the pool looked up, then began yelling, grabbing their children, and wading out, running past their laundry, dragging their kids over the hill.

The collection of GIs in the water could see the young girl swing the barrel in their direction. They all dove underwater. A burst of automatic fire flashed from the muzzle. It ripped high, thin geysers in the water where the men's heads had been.

Lansky was away from the group and knew he was next.

She looked at him, took several steps into the water, and raised the weapon to her shoulder.

Ducking under the water, Lansky pushed himself down with furious paddling motions. Down, deeper, darker. Looking up, he saw the bottom side of a splash on the surface. The bullets squeaked as they burrowed into the water above his head.

He decided to stay low and swung his arms up repeatedly. Lansky wanted to maximize the time he was able to stay under. The thought went through his head that she may be aiming at the spot he had submerged. It seemed like a good idea to come up in a different place for a quick breath and get under again. Using his last few seconds of breath, Lansky struggled against the pressure in his chest, swimming underwater as far away from her as he could. Breaking the surface, he exhaled loudly.

Gulping air, he dove under again, short of breath. It would

be difficult to stay under now. He surfaced again, panting hard and blinking his eyes. Initially, he saw nothing, but hearing no firing, stayed on the surface.

Then he spotted the girl down in the water. Hazuka had his knee on her back, raising the butt of the rifle over his head with his left arm and bashing her head repeatedly. A golfball-sized hole in his right shoulder was bleeding profusely.

The bullet had entered the back of his right shoulder and exited below the collarbone. His right arm swung limply as his left continued to raise and lower the rifle butt. With a deep gasp, he collapsed, falling on her.

The men swam toward shore and dragged Hazuka out of the water, placing him on the bank. They placed a fatigue shirt under his right shoulder and had another one pressed against his upper chest.

The girl floated limply in scarlet water. "How is he?" asked Lansky.

"Missed the lungs, but he's bleeding bad. Lansky, run back to the firebase and get a dust-off up."

Lansky started up the hill, then stopped.

A row of black uniformed militiamen came over the hill on line, weapons pointed at him. They stopped in front of Lansky. One of the militiamen, with a gold bar on his collar, gestured over the hill. "GI! Dee-dee, a twuck!"

Lansky looked at him. "Yeah, right! Dee-dee a truck! Hey, you guys get him up here! The militia will take him back to the base in their truck!"

They quickly made a stretcher for the semiconscious Hazuka from several shirts, carefully lifting him on it. Flinging weapons over shoulders and stuffing clothes and boots under arms, Hazuka was hustled up the hill and down toward the truck. One of the men ran beside the stretcher, keeping pressure on the wound. Lansky, Huddle, and several others followed with armloads of weapons, boots, and clothing.

Hazuka flinched in pain as he was bounced along.

The militia officer ran ahead, yelling orders to the truck driver. The men eased Hazuka onto the truck bed and climbed aboard. The truck made a rapid U-turn, diesel pipes blasting soot, and headed for the American base.

Lansky sat next to the hard-looking little officer, who looked at him with angry eyes. "You beau coup dien cai dau GI! Namber tan! Many VC here. No go!"

"Okay, don't worry, we won't do it again."

The truck bounced roughly along the road. The men in the back tumbled into each other. Hazuka cried out as his shoulder slammed against the truck bed.

"Hey, tell 'em to slow it down," yelled Eberhardt. He held the compress on the wounded man's chest.

The officer crawled forward and hammered on the cab window. He gave the driver the thumbs-down sign. The truck slowed.

Soon they stopped at the gate of the American firebase.

Eberhardt stood up, still nude, and yelled at the two gate guards. "Got a seriously wounded GI here. Get a corpsman and a dust-off. ASAP!"

One of the guards picked up his radio receiver and started talking into it.

"Hey, you guys got any bandages?" yelled one of the other men. "This man is bleeding bad."

Within a minute, a company corpsmen was on the truck cleaning up Hazuka and bandaging his wounds. Another man held a plastic IV bag. The medic inserted the needle into Hazuka's arm.

"How's he doin', Doc?" asked Lansky.

The medic continued his labors with great intensity, not

answering. Then he said, "Lost a lot of blood, shoulder's tore up, clavicle is broken. Guess he's gonna live, though."

They carefully lowered Hazuka off the truck and laid him on the road.

A growling helicopter approached at high speed. It landed in the road before they could get their clothes on. Hot sand whipped their bodies as they loaded Hazuka onto the chopper.

Huddle, Lansky, Eberhardt, and the others stood naked in the road, watching the chopper hum away. They were covered with white dust.

"Looks like you boys had a good time." They knew it was the lieutenant. "Don't even try to explain this mess. You look pitiful! Put your fucking pants on and get up to the platoon AO."

They started pulling on their clothes, wiping bloodied hands on their pants.

"Is Hazuka gonna make it?" said LT, a little more calmly.

"Yeah, LT, I think so. His shoulder is torn up, but he'll live," said Lansky.

"You're lucky. You're damn lucky. You let your security down and got someone greased. You know better! No excuse! There's no excuse for this!"

He turned and left.

Lansky, Huddle, and Eberhardt walked slowly up the hill to the platoon area. Dust on their skin chafed against their fatigue pants. It hurt. They walked with their legs wide apart to decrease the rub.

Massey stood shaking his head as they entered the platoon area. He spit tobacco juice at their feet as they walked by. "Sorry lookin' sons-of-bitches here, boa, sorry lookin' al tell ya. Hey, LT, look at them cowboys."

They walked past, eyes ahead.

Lansky turned to Huddle. "Ya know, Huddle, we gotta change the way we're living. And you know what else?"

"Huh?"

"I don't like this neighborhood."

"Me neither, Lansky, we gotta get out of this place. Nuttin' but Mickey Mouse crap goin' on around here."

"Time for arty party?" said Lansky.

"Past time," answered Huddle.

"Getting to be a habit."

"Wudya 'spect in this neighborhood?"

CHAPTER 28

March 10, 1972

Lansky and Huddle headed for a low hill facing away from the main camp at Firebase Longbow, the secluded location for "arty party."

The 175-millimeter artillery crewmen reclined on the side of the hill. Eyes glazed from that white powder tamped into the top of those Kool cigarettes. Dirty fingers slowly twisted cigarette tops shut, flipped Zippos open, igniting the flame.

Wump! Long deep drags swelled their bare chests. Glowing Kools kept coming around.

Huddle and Lansky had been going to the arty party each night.

Lansky worried about getting hooked. A line of poetry from one of his college literature classes kept coming to mind: "I am a thread too slender to support all this reality." This simple line summed things up. Heroin was the false mirror that fogged his view of brutal reality. It saved him pain and allowed him pleasure.

Some mornings, Lansky tried to tell himself he was done with it, but the impact of most days drove him back most nights.

This day had hit particularly hard. They continued to discuss it.

"Ya know, Lansky, the thing ah can't git over is why that dumb girl thought she could fire us up and git away with it. Hope Hazuka's okay."

"Me, too. Don't think she was thinking, Huddle. She saw an opportunity and was in the mood to do it."

"Ooh, ya. Some mood! Hate to have her for a girlfriend."

"Musta been so full of hate she didn't care. Probably lost some of her family to the big green machine and was looking for a payback."

Huddle took a glowing Kool from one of the arty crewmembers. "D'jue see what a good shot she was? Them rounds was close."

"Sure were. She put a bullet right on me at sixty meters. Lucky I was underwater."

Huddle exhaled. "Phaa wooohaaa, ya! Ha. She was trained. Must'a been hardcore. Here, smoke some of this, rounds off the edges."

"Gotta few sharp ones sticking up. Lemme take a look at this." Lansky inhaled deeply. His head spun, his stomach jumped. He gagged. His heart raced, sweat broke out on his forehead. Incoherent for a moment as his system absorbed the narcotic shock, then everything smoothed out into that quiet, peaceful, underwater, slow-motion glide.

"Where was I . . . ahh. Was I saying something, Huddle?"

"Naw, you wasn't, but your jaw was flappin'."

"Purdy fuckin' funny, asshole."

"Cool off, Lansky, don't let this snow overheat you. Being a Yankee, you should be able to handle the snow." Huddle pulled on the next cigarette coming around and handed it to Lansky.

"I can handle it." Lansky filled his lungs with the mentholated tobacco and then exhaled.

Looking at one of the artillery crewmembers sitting at his right elbow he asked, "So you guys smoke this stuff, then go up there and fire artillery missions all night?"

"Yup, arty has a party, then we go fire up Charlie."

"That almost rhymes."

"Don't care. Smoke this." He produced a pre-rolled Kool. "Yeah, we get higher-na-mudder-fucker. Then we go on up an' shoot them fire missions all night."

"Do you ever miss?"

"Hell no!"

"C'mon. That big gun can fire a round twenty miles, right?"

"Twenty-one, but all our misses are outside fifteen."

"I'll remember that next time I'm out in the bush calling in arty support."

"All these fire missions are aimed at Uncle Ho's trail. Interdiction and attrition, accuracy don't count."

The sun was going down as Lansky noticed two black men walking up the hill, one with a pronounced limp.

"Hey, Sir Charles," said Lansky nonchalantly. "You're back. How's the foot?"

"It's okay, I guess. Hey, Lansky, meet the new blood in our platoon: Cliff Smiff."

"It ain't Smiff, Laughton!" said the new man. "It's Smith."

"Sorry, kinda hard to talk wid new choppers. See." He leaned over and smiled. A row of gleaming white dentures lay where gray stubs had been. "They fixed ma teef when they fixed ma foot."

"You were lucky," said Huddle, staring up at Laughton. There was a sharp quality in Huddle's voice.

"Ya, I was lucky. Got to stay in the hospital for four weeks."

"No, I mean, you was lucky ya' didn't blow your foot off. I

cain't figure how ya' shot yourself in the foot with a grenade launcher and the round didn't go off."

"Yer even more lucky now, Laughton. Here! Smoke some of this," said Lansky. He offered Charles one of the cigarettes. Sir Charles took a long drag and exhaled loudly. "Oowoo, some good shit. Did some in a hospital. Brought ma own little stash along. Here, Smiff."

"Smith! Thanks!" The new man took a drag.

"C'mon down to my hooch tonight, Lansky. We party. Got guard duty now." Laughton and Smith started down the hill.

"Yeah, see you later. Hey, where are you staying?"

"They gimme a bunker down on a wire, close to the ARVN base. I'm right by the one-seventy-five they got sitting out in the open."

"Okay, later dude."

"Okay?" said Huddle. "You gonna party with them guys?"

"Yes, I am."

"Can't see it, Lansky. Them guys in Black Shack'll turn on ya in a minute."

Lansky tried to calm his friend down. "Well, some of them would, some wouldn't. I trust Sir Charles. Hooks is okay, and Smith hasn't been here long enough to get angry."

"No way, man! Black Shack is numba' fuckin' ten!"

"I think you're overreacting, Huddle. Besides, I'm not risking anything."

"They gonna set you up and rip you off!"

"Rip what? I got nothing of value."

"You wait, you'll get burnt." Huddle stood up, kicked some dirt, and walked down the hill.

Lansky reclined on the hill and silently studied the horizon. Shades of pink, red, purple, then black blended as the sun set. Colors on the platoon horizon didn't blend as well.

Black of night followed Lansky to Laughton's bunker. Smith and Chief sat on the sandbagged entrance next to Sir Charles watching a giant mechanized artillery piece maneuver into its night firing position.

The 175-millimeter, self-propelled gun, had a thirty-five-foot barrel, it fired a 150-pound projectile. The crewmembers stood nearby waiting for the driver to finish orienting the gun.

With a diesel roar and steel track clatter, the machine pivoted back and forth until it was in the right position. The exhaust note died to an idle pant.

The four men slid inside the bunker.

Laughton lit a candle and put it in the middle of the floor, then tuned his tiny radio to the armed forces station.

"Waz happ'nin', Lansky?" said Laughton as he lit a twisted Kool with his Zippo.

"Nuttin."

As Laughton passed the cigarette to Chief, the 175 fired its first round. *Kaaawooomsssssssss*. A powerful compression wave swept into the bunker, raising dust, and blowing out the candle.

Laughton fumbled for the candle in the dark. *Wump*. His Zippo found the wick and the light flickered weakly.

Kaaaaawooooomssssssssss. It went out again.

The noise was deafening.

"Sombitch," said Laughton, lighting the candle and moving it to the farthest corner of the bunker.

Smith hung a towel over the entrance to baffle the compression waves. After the candle went out again, they hung a second towel. Finally, they had adjusted the setting enough so that the candle remained lit and the dust was suppressed.

Kaaaaawoooomssssssssss.

The sound of each outbound round reminded Lansky of

hitchhiking on a rainy day and listening to a station wagon sizzle by on the wet pavement.

"Them rounds sure are something," said Laughton.

"Ya, sure are. So how's your foot?"

"Ah, it's stiff, but I can walk on it."

"Man, yer lucky. Shootin' yourself in the foot with a grenade launcher and living to tell about it. How'd it happen?" Lansky sounded sympathetic.

"I was slip slidin' up this muddy bank, an' my weapon got tangled in them wait-a-minute vines. So I pulls on it, and *pop* she goes off. Crushed a buncha bones, man. Hurt like hell. The live round bounced off ma foot an fell down by Hooks. He looked at it, then threw it out in the bush."

"Man, you're lucky."

"Yeah. The round don't arm itself till it's ten meters downrange."

They whiled away the evening listening to top forty songs on the radio.

Chief sat passively in the back of the bunker, taking his turn on the Kools but saying nothing.

All four 175s were firing. Compression waves kept the towels fluttering in the doorway.

"So where's Huddle?" said Laughton.

"Huddle still got a problem with you, Charles, ever since that square-off you had."

"Well, I got over it. I give up on all that hating when I was in da hospital."

"Don't want that no more. Don't want it."

In between outgoing artillery rounds, Lansky heard the armed forces radio announcer say, "Here's an oldie for all you folkies out there: Peter, Paul, and Mary singing, 'Puff the Magic Dragon.'"

During the song, Lansky looked at Laughton and said, "Sir

Charles, you know what this song is about?" Lansky sucked on a twisted Kool.

"Huh? Na, never listen to this stuff."

"Puff!" Lansky exhaled, filling the air with smoke. "Puff, get it? It's about puffing on magic dragon powder."

"Fer real?"

"That's the way some people see it."

Laughton looked surprised. "I didn't know that."

"Since I been in country, I've developed an interest in dragons. Did you know the dragon is a symbol of Vietnam just like the eagle is a symbol of America?"

Laughton looked confused. "You sayin' these people believe in dragons?"

"Many do. I've had my own eyes opened to the possibility as well."

These words snapped Chief out of his daze, he seemed curious about what Lansky was saying.

A sly smile crept over Laughton's face. "S, S, S, heh, heh, man, you playin' me now."

"I used to think like you, but I've had experiences that expanded my mind. Sir Charles, are you experienced?"

Smith leaned into the conversation. "Dudes trippin', man. Talkin' shit to you, Laughton. Dudes terrriiiippin'."

Chief continued to stare intently at Lansky.

All conversation stopped. A new sound joined the walloping bang of artillery. In between the heavy report of big guns, a smaller, quicker *wump* and *crump* could be heard. Small weapons fire crackled, gaining intensity.

"What's going on out there?" said Laughton.

"Better take a look-see," said Smith.

Crawling out of the bunker, weapons in hand, they could see an assault developing on the ARVN base perimeter. Mortars flashed from distant paddies with a dull *thump*. Impacting mortar rounds walked toward the ARVN perimeter. Green tracers from multiple sources in the paddies scampered through the wire.

Red tracers from the ARVN base answered. Howitzers, lowered to point-blank range, fired into the paddies. The green tracers advanced, following right behind the mortar rounds, walking toward the wire.

The 175 in front of them roared to life. Its tracks clattered as it pivoted toward the ARVN perimeter. A servo whine issued from its bowels, lowering the barrel. The engine roar dropped, and the servo stopped, then started briefly, making small adjustments. Then silence.

KAA-A-WOOOM. The gun carriage recoiled violently, and an orange gaseous flash erupted from the barrel. It made small whining adjustments and fired every forty seconds. Dust on the chassis decking jumped in the air each time the gun fired.

Lansky plugged his ears. Each round made his shirt collar flutter. The impacting rounds moved tons of earth on the ARVN perimeter.

It was too late.

Heavy spasms of small-arms fire filled their ears, M-16 fire answered by AK-47 chatter. Red tracers out, green tracers in. Invisible explosions shook the ground and red tracers arced wildly into the sky. The explosions continued, moving across the firebase, all artillery stopped, small-arms fire dropped off.

Silence.

"ARVN caught lunch, huh, Lansky?"

"Looks like it. The VC waited for the ARVN regiment to leave, and then hit their lightly defended base."

CHAPTER 29

May 17, 1972

An economy of effort ruled Huddle's manner of speaking. Words seemed to slide out easy. The lips hardly moved. Thoughts flowed naturally. Unaffected. Huddle, a son of southern Alabama, reclined on his pack in the twilight of the Asian evening, content to wait for the right moment to speak. He took a long pull off the fifth of bourbon clenched in his hand, porcine skin glowing under the avalanche of oily red curls. Ten months of torrid, equatorial sun couldn't tan this white boy. He'd just get red, then peel down to another layer of pure ivory.

Lansky, the easygoing Midwesterner, sat next to his redheaded friend studying the flakes of skin on the side of his face as the lips opened but hardly moved.

"Ya know, Lansky, this is my secon' favorite position."

"Your second?"

"Yup, lyin' down's my first favorite position."

Night sounds began to amplify. The whirr of crickets drifted across the platoon perimeter. Frogs croaked.

The two men surveyed the dimly lit swamp and trees, passing the bottle back and forth. Huddle tipped the fifth up to his pale lips. Bubbles bounced up the neck of the bottle. He took it away with a small popping sound. A drop of Old Crow ran down his chin. Huddle smiled a narrow, squinty, lizard smile. "Soun's lak home." The words oozed out.

The wind rose, heaving clouds away from the shimmering moon. Translucent beams cut the crooked trees, casting fractured shadows across their faces. The long narrow leaves carpeting the forest floor had an iridescent quality that reflected the moonlight. Low-power neon glimmered across the foreground.

Footsteps behind them made Huddle stash the bottle under his rucksack. They turned to see the camo-green face of Sergeant Massey leading Second Squad toward the perimeter.

Lansky stood, shouldering his radio, pulling the bolt back on his M-16, releasing it, pushing a round out of the magazine into the chamber.

He got into line behind Massey and followed him out across the glimmering leaves. They walked slowly for ten minutes through the Lien Chieu Forest.

Stopping on the trail, the sergeant used hand signals to direct most of his squad into position. Massey and the two remaining men then walked twenty yards down-trail, placing the claymore mine off-trail and stringing tripwire from a peg on the other side. Using needle-nosed pliers, he cautiously attached the wire to the firing mechanism of the claymore.

The group slowly backtracked up-trail to the squad position, now twenty yards off-trail, weapons pointed into the killing zone. They began the night's wait.

Broken cloud patterns blotted the moonlight. Larger, darker clouds rolled across the face of the moon, shutting off its light for longer periods.

Lansky squinted at the darkened trail. His eyes didn't adjust to the darkness for several minutes. He stayed up with the first watch. An anxious hour passed.

Clouds streamed across the sky, blocking moonlight, revealing moonlight, carving it into irregular patterns.

His eyes grew weary from continual adjustment to the ever-changing light. The moon climbed, shining brightly between the clouds. A gentle wind hissed through the treetops. Twisted trees broke the moonlight into angular patterns. Shadows shifted as the trees waved in the night breeze.

Moving shadow patterns began playing tricks on the weary soldier. Lansky nudged the man on watch, pointing the barrel of his weapon at any movement.

"Nothing," was the whispered response.

Closing his eyes, Lansky lay on the leaves, relaxing into sleep.

Several hours later, the roar of the claymore jerked his head upright. He saw the wall of orange flame finish its sweep across the trail in front of him.

Lansky joined the squad in a ferocious volley. Weapons emptied on full auto followed by silence.

He keyed the handset on his radio receiver twice to let the platoon know they were okay, then lay on the cool ground, staring into the dark, listening.

The explosion and heavy volley disturbed the forest.

Lansky put his ear to the ground. He sensed movement.

A shadow, propelled by the blast, scenting death, abandoning stealth, closed on his position.

Low moaning stirred the ambush patrol. Far away at first, then moving closer, circling their position, the moaning intensified, interspersed with hissing and spitting. Something was stalking them.

Lansky shuddered, the back of his neck felt prickly.

Each man trained the muzzle of his weapon on the sound.

Tossing a grenade into the blackness risked hitting a tree and rebounding the explosive back at them.

Sergeant Massey decided to take the chance. Pulling the pin, he made a stiff-armed throw toward the menacing growl.

A loud, aggressive snarl answered the exploding *whump* and flash of the grenade. The moaning resumed, moved off, and faded.

Too jittery to sleep, the men whispered quietly. Some suggested bolting for the night logger. But the night logger would fire on any movement, so they sat nervously, waiting out the night.

First light of day revealed nothing. Massey duck-walked forward, weapon pointed at the trail. He knelt before it, looking up and down the path, listening. Massey's trigger finger switched off the safety.

The claymore had incinerated a triangular pattern of foliage across the trail.

Massey stood, pointing his weapon at the opposite side of the trail. Edging along, searching the spent shrubbery, he froze, shouldering his weapon, lowering it. Leaning forward, Massey poked something with the muzzle.

He straightened and muttered, "Shee-iitt." Looking back toward the patrol, he called, "C'mere!"

Lansky and the others came out of the brush, forming around Massey.

"It's a goddamned tiger!" said one of the men.

"A *god*damned tiger!" said another.

"Get on the radio, Lansky, and tell them we're coming in."

"Roger that."

"This is really something," said Massey, shaking his head slowly. "This takes the fuckin' cake, I tell ya."

They walked down the trail toward the platoon position.

* * *

LT Halverson and Huddle joined a group standing on the platoon perimeter waiting for the ambush patrol to return.

"Ambush comin' in. Boy, that was a ferocious sounding animal out there last night," said Huddle.

"Yeah, sure was," said the lieutenant. He rocked on his heels, arms folded. "I wonder what set off that claymore?"

The question was answered as Massey and the rest of the ambush patrol came through the woods.

"We got a tiger!" said the point man.

"A big son-of-a-bitch!" said the man behind him.

"He's lyin' back there off the trail by our ambush!" said Massey, now face-to-face with the lieutenant. Massey's eyes flashed with excitement. He huffed and puffed in the lieutenant's face. "You gotta see this, LT! A big cat! We blew him away. This one takes the cake. It takes the fuckin' cake, LT!"

LT waved Massey's bad breath away from his face. "Yeah, well, if you blew one away, what the hell was it that made all that racket after the claymore went off?"

Massey shifted his weight, and then wiped a dirty sleeve across his mouth, pointing his weapon toward the woods. "Musta been another one. Tell you, scared the shee-itt out of us! He was no more'n forty meters away from us."

"You threw a grenade?" said the lieutenant, now standing a safe distance from Massey's mouth.

"Yup."

"Missed him?"

"Couldn't tell, couldn't see a thing."

"Well, I better look," said LT.

A large crowd gathered. Most of the men wanted to go along. Some started walking down the trail.

"Get back here!" LT barked. "We don't want a mob out there making noise. I'll let you all go, but we'll go in shifts. Keep the perimeter secure. Take me back there, Massey."

Lansky didn't feel like going back. The sight of the carcass disturbed him. He walked toward their squad position with Huddle.

"After hearing that cat last night, I was purdy sure I was done drinkin'," said Huddle. "But when I woke up this mornin', and started thinking about it, I started lookin' roun' for another bottle."

"Bothered me, too," said Lansky, slumping to the ground. "Bothers me more now."

"You okay, Lansky?"

"No, not really."

"You didn't get hurt, didja?" Huddle stood over Lansky, looking concerned.

"Not physically. Something got to me when I looked at that dead cat. When you can walk right up to it and take a close look at its . . . its stunning symmetry. There's something wrong when an animal like that gets killed." Lansky had covered this emotional ground before. On his first and only deer hunt near his home in northern Wisconsin, he had the sights of his deer rifle on a ten-point buck as it crested a glacial ridge. When he lowered his weapon without taking a shot, his father became angry. Lansky told his dad that killing such a magnificent animal was not his idea of sport.

"You know that cat was stalking your ass. Lucky the claymore got him first."

"Yeah, I suppose." Lansky's eyes were closed, his face twisted in a sour expression. He had a bad taste in his mouth. "If I hadn't seen him, I wouldn't feel like this. There was something about it, when I saw the body, something turned in me. Something turned in me right away. It felt bad. You'd think I was looking at my mother or something." He sat up, restless.

"I don't know, Lansky. Too bad you feel that way," said Huddle. "Hey! When I got up this mornin', everyone was talkin' about the scratch marks on the tree by Fourth Squad's perimeter. Something gouged two-inch-deep scratch marks into that tree, eight feet off the ground!"

"Really?"

"Big scratch marks, musta been the cat claimin' territory. C'mon, Ah'll show ya."

They walked across the perimeter. Huddle pointed at the clawed tree with the barrel of his weapon.

"Big cat, huh, Lansky? Big fuckin' cat, I tell ya! Let's see if the lieutenant is back yet," said Huddle.

"Okay," Lansky agreed, not caring what happened.

They got to the perimeter as LT returned. Shaking his head, the officer said, "Never seen anything like it. Gonna radio the rear and let them know. Coupla more of you guys can go out there now. Be careful! You lead 'em, Massey."

"I'm gonna look," said Huddle. "Comin'?"

Lansky didn't want to go at first, but he couldn't get the cat's image off his mind. He needed to confront his problem if he was ever going to get over it. After some hesitation, he fell in with the group in hopes of staring down his problem. Several of the others brought cameras.

A sudden reverence came over them when they saw the tiger.

Shredded vines and flakes of green foliage lay across the silky black stripes on orange fur. White spots flecked the regal head, neck, and chest. A row of large teeth lay along the curled lips. Massive shoulders and forelegs exuded power. White paws were the size of baseball gloves.

Lansky's despair increased. He knelt and rubbed his hand across the smooth fur. No holes disturbed the velvet coat. Rubbing his fingers against the nap of the coat was more revealing. His fingers found broken skin and large shot holes. He rose in disgust.

Huddle stood next to him now, understanding. "I see what you mean, Lansky. This shouldn't happen."

Chief walked into the clearing, standing motionless, eyes closed for a minute. A man of few words, the Native American radiated a spiritual light, a palpable but unspoken presence so powerful it spooked some of the men. Kneeling, he removed items from his rucksack: bamboo sticks bound tightly in wild grape vines with palmetto fronds attached to the end, and loose dry twigs arranged in a circle on the ground. He doused the pile with lighter fluid and put a match to it. Flames erupted. He added green leaves, and white smoke plumed the still air.

Next, came bound dry branches. Placing the tip of the branches in the fire, he rose. Stripping off his shirt, standing in the smoke, palms up, and eyes closed.

The GIs in the clearing stopped taking pictures.

Silence, all eyes now on Chief. His hands lifted slowly over his head. Palms clasped. Arms arced wide, slowly, down at his side.

He knelt, placing the bamboo in his left hand and smoking stick bundle in his right. Standing slowly, he walked to the north side of the tiger, raising the bamboo and stick bundles over his head, silently holding his pose.

Pivoting gently, he passed the smoking bundle over the tiger. Smoke rolled over fur. He repeated the same on the west and south side of the cat.

Smoke lingered. Men shifted out of Chief's way. Returning to the east, now facing the jungle, raising the bamboo and stick bundles over his head, he froze. Something startled him. Chief stared out into the bush.

Lansky looked along the Native American's sight line to see the dragon-head sticking out of the shrubbery.

Chief turned to look at the group, all eyes downcast except Lansky's, who nodded his head, as if to say, "I see it, too."

Chief looked surprised, shocked by his unexpected vision and the fact that someone else saw it. He stared at Lansky for a long minute. Lansky stared back. They now knew each other in a new way.

Eventually, Chief gathered himself and focused on the group standing in a circle. He returned to his fire, placing the two bundles on it. The palmetto flamed, creating a sweet smoke that filled the circle. They linked hands. The fire crackled and sputtered.

Several minutes passed. Dropping hands, they stood silently. Soon they filed out of the clearing back to the night logger.

CHAPTER 30

May 18, 1972

In the afternoon, a helicopter with a large net took the tiger to the rear.

"S'pose that skin's gonna wind up on some REMF officer's wall," Huddle said sarcastically.

"Yeah, probably. And when he takes it home, he'll have a story to tell about big game hunting in Asia," Lansky answered in the same tone.

That evening the lieutenant decided to skip the ambush. Lansky listened as he instructed the squad leaders. "If it was dinks out there, we'd put out an ambush. But that cat's too sneaky. We'll all stay in the perimeter tonight. Tell you what, though, I want each squad to put out three claymores on each quadrant of our position."

At sunset, Lansky watched bent forms sneak through the trees, stringing wire. Huddle placed his claymore and came up the hill.

"You hear what Massey said about them tigers?"

"No, I didn't."

"He said, on his last tour, tigers were dragging away wounded and dead guys after a big battle. Couldn't even find their dog tags by the time it was safe to look for 'em."

"C'mon, that's hard to believe."

"No, that's what he said. Swear to God. He said it happened in 'sixty-seven."

"I don't believe it. I'm tired of this crap. Got any more of that whiskey?"

"Wish I did, kinda dry now. Could go fer a swaller er two. How about you takin' first watch tonight, Lansky?"

"Okay. I'm too pumped up to sleep."

Huddle took a few steps toward his sleeping position then stopped. Turning toward Lansky, he said, "Hey, can I ask you a question?"

"Sure you can."

"When we was standing 'round the tiger, what was it you and Chief were looking at?"

Lansky tensed. "Nothing really."

"Well, Chief thought he saw something, it surprised him. Whatever it was, you saw it, too. But when I looked, nothing was there. What did y'all see that I din't?"

"It was just a shadow. We overreacted."

"Whole lot a hoodoo going on round you, man. You're seeing things."

"No, just this tiger business has made me a little goofy. I think it bothered Chief, too."

Huddle stared at Lansky a long time, then looked at the ground, smiled, and shook his head as he walked toward his sleeping position.

The evening was dark and overcast, darker than any in the last few weeks. Time dragged as Lansky stood at the guard position. He checked his watch, expecting to find an hour had passed, yet only ten minutes had gone by.

Chief's startled response to whatever he saw out in the bush, while standing over the tiger, confused Lansky.

Huddle's questions added an extra layer of complexity to the situation.

Lansky fought himself back to conscious awareness of the moment, this dangerous moment. The three-hour stand was a struggle. Lansky could not fix his mind on the present. It seemed like six hours by the time it was over.

Lansky gently kicked Huddle's boot sticking out of the rolled poncho.

"Time already, Lansky?"

"Yup, it's twenty-three hundred."

"Yeah, I guess it is. Okay, I'm gettin' up. Y'all hear anything?"

"Quiet so far."

"Good, hope that cat just moves away."

"Me, too." Lansky saw a book open on Huddle's pack. Too jacked up to sleep, Lansky walked back to the perimeter with Huddle. "So, what book was that sitting on top of your pack?"

"That's The Book."

"The Bible?"

"Yes, sir, a Bible given to me by my granny's hoodoo conjurer friend the night before I left."

"What's a conjurer?"

"Well, this ol' black lady claimed the Bible has magic that can be used to influence the spirits around us."

"You see spirits around you?"

"No, but my granny and this ol' conjurer saw 'em all the time. I thought they were wacky. Tried to give the Bible back, but my granny started shrieking. The conjurer pushed the Bible into my belly and said, 'Son, when you're at the crossroads, read the thirty-seventh Psalm, then leave the book open for three days with its head pointed east. It will get you through.' So, I humped it roun' wrapped in plastic for ten months. After watching you today, I knew it was time to get it out."

"You think we're at the crossroads?"

"Maybe not just yet, but were gettin' closer."

Lansky didn't know what to say, he felt confused. "This is wearing me out. I need time to think, need some rest." He turned away from Huddle and headed for his sleeping position.

Lansky lay on half his poncho with his weapon at his side. Reaching under his pack, he pulled out a sweat-soaked, sour-smelling towel and shook off the dirt. Wadding it up, he laid it at the top of his poncho and put his head on it, then pulled the other half of the poncho over him.

Sleep didn't come, but he lay there with his eyes closed, trying to help it along.

The scene in the clearing next to the dead tiger kept coming back to him. *Did Chief see the dragon?* His reaction showed he saw something unusual. The only unusual thing Lansky saw out there was the dragon.

This bewildered Lansky. He had grown comfortable with his dragon as a delusion—a stress induced hallucination. When the stress went away, so would the delusion.

A second witness allowed the dragon to escape the realm of hallucination and crash through the window, separating reality from the imagined. Shards of psychic glass would be everywhere.

But, if the dragon is real, how come only two people saw it?

Lansky's disorientation grew.

If the dragon is a delusion suffered independently by two separate people, how could our reaction be so strikingly similar? Shared madness?

His mind spiraled. He began to panic. *Could this shared madness be something beyond delusion? Something worse? Has a new gate opened to yet another level of consciousness? Can I trust Chief if I encounter him again at this new level? Should I attempt to talk to Chief about it?* his mind raged.

Chief still stood mute within the platoon. It would look weird if Lansky tried to talk to him about a dragon. He was not ready to talk about this.

And now Huddle was beginning to notice what was going on. He'd asked a serious question, and it deserved an answer. His secret wouldn't last forever. Yet, finding a place to start explaining the dragon was beyond him.

It would have to wait. The matter was beyond his resources. He did not know what to do. Whoever had sent this dragon would have to work this out.

For the first time, he felt a burden had been placed on his warrior shield. His gift from the universe, that powerful presence, seemed to be testing the depth of his faith. *Is there room for two or three under my warrior shield? Yes. There's room under the shield.*

Lansky tried to slow his breathing, to calm himself. He wanted to quiet his mind enough to hear the voice. As his heart rate decreased, Lansky focused on waiting patiently.

A low moaning made him sit up. It was faintly audible across the darkness, closing.

Picking up his weapon, Lansky shook his head, attempting to clear it, then walked to the edge of the perimeter.

Huddle stood guard.

"Where is she?" Lansky whispered.

"Can't tell, Lansky, but I think she's near last night's ambush."

The bawling continued. Moving through the brush. Restless energy. Angry yowling.

Lansky said, "Do you think it's the dead tiger's mate?"

"Could be."

The groaning stopped, loud hissing, an angry roar pierced the night.

No one was asleep now.

The hair on the back of Lansky's neck stood up.

On all sides of the perimeter, bolts were engaged, rounds entered chambers. Safeties off, grenades were lined up, claymore detonators were brought to hand.

Moaning continued in a circle outside the claymore perimeter. Hissing.

Huddle whispered, "That cat knows where the claymores are located. She's staying away from them."

"Too cunning to test the perimeter, but she's not letting us off the hook either," said Lansky.

The tigress circled for an hour. Threatening. Lethal. Invisible. Then, hissing and howling, she faded away into the night.

CHAPTER 31

June 15, 1972

Lansky felt dispirited, seized by a debilitating lethargy. Constantly on patrol, always afoot with no end in sight. His fatigue wasn't entirely physical. It included a burden of iniquity that accumulated as he walked.

He stood at rest now, looking down at his blackened boots, wondering how much farther he could go. With a shrug of his shoulders, he scanned the burnt prairie grass that covered the foothills in which he waited. His eyes settled on ground his platoon had just patrolled.

The back-trail brought his entire ten-month tour to mind. Memory took him over the prairies, into the hot flat paddy land, down into the rain forest, then climbing through storms into the fog-shrouded mountains. The faces and places were blurred by the speed of the walk. Exhausting. He needed rest *now*.

"Hey, Lansky, c'mon, I want to check out our positions and make sure everyone is covered. Need the radio in case it comes in early." Lieutenant Halvorsen's order got Lansky moving again.

Sergeant Tiny joined Lansky and the lieutenant ambling along the top of the blackened ridge behind the platoon position.

"Think we're far enough back, Tiny?" LT stopped to glass a tree line three thousand meters away.

"Yeah, we're far enough away. Don't worry. No short rounds with these guys."

"Okay."

They continued their walk. The platoon was spread across the charred ground in groups of two. As Lansky passed Huddle's position, he noticed an open Bible on the ground. Lansky knelt quickly and whispered, "Are we at the crossroads?"

"Not yet, I'm just keepin' my Bible open to the thirty-seventh Psalm whenever I can."

Lansky was not a Bible reader, though now he felt like becoming one. He hurried to catch up with LT, even though it took all his strength.

"Few minutes to go," yelled LT. "Don't forget, keep your head down." He started walking back toward his own position. "Five minutes! C'mon, let's get back up to our spot. Five minutes, everyone!"

The men lay prone, helmets on, as LT, Tiny, and Lansky joined them, positioning himself as low as possible on the defoliated hill, his arm turning darker each time he moved it across the charred earth. This area had been torched to deny cover to the enemy. With Agent Orange banned, igniting diesel-soaked vegetation with M-60 fire became the new defoliant. An accelerant doubled the flames advantage in the dry season. Once lit, nothing stopped it for miles.

Lansky tried to tell himself it didn't matter. There was a point months ago when he might have felt angry about the destruction, but that day had passed. It was more than he could handle at this point.

He waited.

"One minute," yelled LT. "One minute to go."

It was quiet.

Lansky checked the second hand on his watch. He wondered if something might happen, if this might be it, the final rest, the end.

The minute passed. Then another. The men stared at the tree line. Some of them began to whisper, wondering what had happened.

Lansky didn't share their concern. He just watched the target with his ear resting on his ink-colored forearm.

Something, a fresh presence rustled in the stubble behind him, salt-brine scents overrode the burnt prairie grass atmosphere so familiar in recent days.

He would not look to see if it was the dragon, he couldn't risk the disappointment, the possibility that he might be alone, unaccompanied by his warrior shield at this moment of dissipation. The suggestion of the dragon's presence quieted him, even if it was only a chimera.

A piercing white light arced over the western edge of the woods, violently expanding a massive shroud of concussion, collapsing, gone.

Ejections of brown soil began covering the trees. The ground erupted silently. White light and brown soil billowed across the target.

The earth trembled. A distant rumble became a heavy vibration, the sound of thick fabric tearing. Not on the surface, but deep within the ground. The hill on which Lansky lay shook with growing intensity.

Soil rose continuously over the target, roiling the air, climbing, forming clouds. The scale of the eruptions dwarfed the countryside.

It was over in a few seconds.

The B-52s had dropped forty 2,000-pound bombs through

the middle of the tree line. Each bomb placed in a precise pattern of alternating rows.

Soon the earth became still. The rumble faded.

LT sat up. "Ain't nothing alive in those woods anymore."

"Not much alive up here," said Lansky under his breath.

"Whad ya' say, Lansky?"

"Nuthin'."

"Anything from the CO?"

"Nope."

"What's the matter with you, Lansky? You look tired."

"I *am* tired."

The radio handset crackled.

"Hey, LT, it's the CO." Lansky handed the receiver to his officer and stood up, uniform the color of coal.

Brown clouds formed an irregular smudge drifting across the horizon. The woods remained obscured.

LT put down the receiver and yelled at Tiny, "Mount up, let's get on the line and move out. The CO and the other platoons are going to block for us. We'll drive toward the trees. A LOACH will work out ahead of us."

The men stood and shouldered their packs. They formed on line, blackened by the scorched earth, arms and faces smeared with charcoal-colored sweat.

As they slipped off the ridge, a small helicopter flew swiftly overhead, then down between the foothills. It flew below their position, leading the way for the platoon, carving nimble patterns above the ground. A gunner sat in each hatch, wearing the brown aviator's coverall, helmet, and black face shield with M-60s in their hands. The pilot flew sideways or banked steeply to keep his shooters at advantageous angles. The LOACH hopped in and out of sight as it covered each of the broad, boulder-strewn hills. Its gunners sat impassively in the doorway until a possible target was overflown. Then, they leaned into their harnesses and pointed the M-60s into the boulders or trees.

Lansky didn't watch the LOACH for long. Being on the move locked his attention on the next hundred meters. His head pivoted slowly 180 degrees. It always did when he walked.

His boots stirred up the dusky ash of the burnt prairie, adding another layer of soot to his face. His eyes watered. The earth smelled of sulfur. Sweat broke out after several hundred meters. Stygian water beaded his arms, catching light like a string of ebony pearls.

Men blackened from boots to helmets marched along, souls of the lost, faces shadowed, inky rings formed around crusty eyes.

This used to be the best time for Lansky. Walking into the unknown, never knowing what was next, his need for survival kept his mind focused on the present. The next hundred meters was the only thing that existed—every faculty occupied, sensing what might lie ahead.

Fatigue had dulled him. Perception lost its edge. Distractions grew. He walked with less focus, but pressed on.

Days were losing their identity. Artificial boundaries of time were broken and blurred. The months that had passed seemed like a long walk. When something happened, he remembered it as where and when he'd been walking.

The M-60 gunners in the LOACH brought Lansky back to the present. Long bursts of machine-gun fire pummeled a rock formation.

The small helicopter banked and turned above the rocks, allowing the gunners to fire straight down as they passed over. Tracers howled off the rocks, bouncing in all directions.

The grunts lay on their stomachs, weapons pointed at the rocks, and watched the LOACH work. The gunners ceased fire.

"Black Dog, this is Gooney-Bird, over."

"Go, Bird," Lansky spoke into his handset.

"Rodg, Dog. Had some movement in them rocks. We'll hang around until you take a closer look, over."

"Roger, copy, Gooney-Bird, over. Hey! LT! The LOACH driver saw movement in the rocks, he's gonna wait for *us* to check it out."

"Yeah, easy for him to say."

LT was about to request volunteers. Sergeant Tiny made that unnecessary. "I'm on my way, LT." Several men followed. Most of the grunts sat up or assumed a kneeling position. Lansky remained prone. LT looked at him, sensing something was wrong.

Lansky responded to the commo-check from the RTO in Tiny's patrol. He was behaving oddly but still functioning, cool and professional, so LT let it pass.

Tiny returned after a complete inspection of the rocky area, finding nothing.

On the move again, LT became distracted by the look on Lansky's face. Fatigue and depression were obvious.

Secretly, LT felt the same. He'd had his bouts with moral fatigue, not as deep as Lansky's, yet there were days when LT questioned his ability to walk another step.

He looked down at his feet breaking through the burnt stubs of grass and noticed Lansky's doing the same.

They approached the target area.

Flames billowed over the bombed-out woods.

LT was not a religious man, but he said a short prayer for the day when their walk would end.

CHAPTER 32

June 27, 1972

Tiny dumped his blackened field pack on his bunk and declared himself on a mission to capture some hot water.

Lansky joined the group that followed.

The men moved through the hooch shadows beyond the Bravo Company area.

With a running leap, Tiny kicked the lock off the headquarter company's shower door. Looking inside, his expression was that of an Egyptologist opening an ancient tomb.

They entered as one, be-slimed in black. The hot water soon rinsed their skin tones down to shades of pink, tan, and brown.

Hot water ran down Lansky's arms, its warmth lifted his spirits. No longer shadowed by the blackness of the last mission, he stood clean, released, breathing in the luxurious steam, soaping his infected saw grass cuts until they stung. The pain made him feel alive again.

Laughter and animated banter echoed in the cinder block building. Towel snapping matches started.

It wasn't long before they were discovered. "You're not authorized to shower in my AO. Turn off the water and gedout! Now!"

Lansky looked past the row of naked GIs in the hot steam.

First Sergeant Milton, top NCO in the regiment, had given an order and he expected a response.

No one in the shower moved.

"Hear me? Ged da' fuck out!" He noticed the door. "Hey! Who ripped the lock off the door?"

They ignored him, lost in the pleasure of the water.

Sergeant Tiny's massive freckled back cut off Lansky's view of the first sergeant. The rumble of his voice gained a sharp edge as it echoed off the cement shower walls.

"With all due respect, First Sergeant, we feel that we deserve a hot shower after twenty-one days in the bush. This ain't no great inconvenience for you REMFs to have us take one shower every twenty-one days. Give us a break." Tiny's voice had a cheerful quality to it, the sarcasm of false happiness.

First Sergeant stared bullets at Tiny. "This is not your area of operation, troop! You take your shower in your own company AO!"

Tiny returned the first sergeant's enmity with a grin as he slowly toweled off his arms and legs. No hurry. The happy look of derision grew a little.

"But First Sergeant, isn't it your job to support us?" Tiny toweled his crotch standing bow-legged in the middle of the shower. "Regimental HQ supports troops in the field. Letting us shower here once a month for stand-down would be real supportive. It'd really boost morale."

Tiny toweled his crotch contentedly.

First Sergeant blinked, Tiny's grin was unexpected, time to regroup. A subtle response was called for here. Rather than pull rank he'd outwit the big oaf, beat Tiny at his own game. Making Tiny look bad in front of his men would end this game.

It would have worked, too, if First Sergeant could have kept his eyes off that grin. The towel continued to work on Tiny's crotch. The grin continued to grow eroding First Sergeant's hopes for subtlety.

"Every time we let some grunt company in our AO, something gets wrecked. Like this lock, who's gonna fix it? Look at the slime on the floor! This place reeks after you guys use it." First Sergeant's grip was slipping.

Tiny smiled and worked the towel.

First Sergeant couldn't stop himself. "Now I'll have to assign a three-man detail to this shower to make it fit for human usage!"

Tiny dropped the towel, didn't need it anymore. He pulled on some clean fatigue pants and gathered his toilet articles. "But, Sarge, you got the only hot water in the regiment! We need a hot shower after being in the bush."

"You'll have to manage with a cold shower in your own company area." A look of deep weariness came across First Sergeant's face. "You grunts make my ass tired!"

All the men in the shower looked at First Sergeant with sudden interest.

Tiny's smile narrowed.

"You come in here like a buncha outlaws." First Sergeant was frustrated. "You raise hell, all day and all night.

You pick fights with the men in HQ Company. You tear up the regimental AO, you get so fucked-up you shit and puke all over. You're a buncha animals! I've had it! You're in the army. You live by the rules. You follow orders! Your orders state that this shower is off limits to you!"

Tiny was on his way out by this time. He stopped in the busted doorframe and stared down at the first sergeant. His words were less careful. "First Sergeant, you got it backward, your half-assed rules get in the way of our hygienic maintenance."

"Half-assed! Half-assed! You're the one who's gonna be half-assed pretty soon if you don't watch your mouth, Buck Sergeant. I think you been in the bush too long, Tiny. You're a bad influence. You stir up trouble, and I don't need it. Stay out of the regimental HQ area. I don't want you draggin' my men down to your level."

Tiny was walking away, but the last phrase stopped him.

First Sergeant's turn to smile, he'd found a way past Tiny's armor.

Lansky watched Tiny stiffen. He turned to face First Sergeant. "Aw, Sarge. You sayin' the guys in HQ is superior to grunts?"

"All I know is, things run smooth back here and my men are exemplary soldiers until you guys show up. Your one day in the rear for stand-down fucks up things for a week! You drag 'em down!" He pointed emphatically at Tiny.

Lansky could see Tiny searching for a comeback.

The corners of Tiny's mouth turned up as he said, "I could say a lotta things right now, First Sergeant, but I ain't gonna. But ya know what? I bet you can't prove what you're sayin'."

"Whadya mean?" First Sergeant Milton was surprised. "Prove what?"

"I bet you can't prove REMFs is superior to grunts, man for man."

"We have enough fights already, Tiny. I'm not gonna give you an excuse to pound on my men."

"I don't mean a fight." His smile was coming back. "I was thinkin' along the lines of a sportin' proposition. A contest with a little wager attached to it."

The sarge hesitated, suspicious. "Like what?"

"When I flew in today, I could see you guys got a little ball diamond set up on the flats inside the wire. How 'bout a ball game?"

"A ball game?"

"Yeah, a ball game to decide who's better."

Tiny's smile blossomed. "We win, we get to shower in your AO every twenty-one days. If you win, well, we never bother you or your men again."

Sarge didn't like that smile. He wasn't going to put up with it anymore. "I don't need a game to keep ya away. I already told you to stay away. That's enough. That's all you need to know." Sarge thought this would bring Tiny back to reality. He thought this would knock that smile off his face. There wasn't anything to smile about. After all, he'd lost.

Tiny responded, "Okay, First Sergeant, you're right." His voice, flat and defeated, but his expression, an ironic smirk. His head thrown back, arms folded massively, everything about him said, "I knew he'd back down."

All the men were out of the shower now. Taking Tiny's cue they all posed, mimicking his erect stance.

Milton knew this was a farce. Yet it rankled him. He could have turned around, walked away, and forgotten about it. Pride made him stay. He stared back at Tiny and the rest, trying a grin, but Sarge wasn't the grinning kind. So he glared into the silence.

It was work for him, play for them. Finally, he got fed up and said, "That's enough!" and walked away.

They mumbled just loud enough for him to hear. "He's afraid. He's afraid to lose."

"We'd whip 'em REMFs."

"He's afraid we'd kick their ass."

"We got Tiny."

"Yeah."

First Sergeant stopped, a move he would regret. Several seconds passed. He turned with a controlled look on his face.

"Okay, assholes. Tonight, eighteen-hundred hours. Be at the diamond. I'll take your terms. Just to wipe them shit-eatin' grins off your faces. Hope you enjoyed your last hot shower in Vietnam."

Then he was gone.

CHAPTER 33

June 27, 1972

Tiny led his grunt patrol down the barracks path onto the ball diamond. The REMF team was practicing on the field.

First Sergeant Milton stood at home plate with a bat in hand. He threw a ball into the air and hit it toward a collection of REMF outfielders. The first man in line began to dance under the high fly ball, pounding his glove then raising it for the catch.

Just before it dropped into his glove, a long freckled arm snared the ball barehanded. Taking a hop and a long stride, Tiny hurled the ball on a line to the catcher standing next to home plate. The ball made a loud cracking sound as it sizzled into the glove.

Practice stopped to watch the massive fiery-eyed man do his John Wayne walk across the diamond.

Tiny told his men to sit on the side and then ambled over to First Sergeant.

"We gonna play softball?" The big man showed contempt.

"Yeah, what did you expect?"

"I'm a hardball player myself, Sarge, pitched in the Adirondack League for a year." Tiny stood over First Sergeant, hands on hips.

"We haven't got any hardballs. I had to scrounge around a long time just to get this softball stuff." First Sergeant was offended by Tiny's lack of appreciation.

"Well, okay," said Tiny. "You'll let us use your gloves and bats, right?"

"Yup. We'll give you a coupla minutes to warm up."

"Don't need a warmup. You're the home team, so we'll take the field."

"Roger that."

"You got an ump?"

"No."

"Good, let's play ball."

Tiny swaggered over to the grunt bench, his men gathered around. "We got 'em all set up, men. I'll get 'em so mad they won't be able to play their game, you just relax." Tiny looked satisfied. "We're gonna borrow their gloves. So, that starting group that I mentioned before, let's get out there."

Lansky stood in left field watching Tiny pitch to the first batter. The ball arced twenty meters into the air then fell through the strike zone. It bounced sharply off the board used as home plate. The batter did not attempt to swing at the pitch. He looked at First Sergeant with a surprised expression.

Sarge came off the bench yelling, "That's too high, Tiny. You can't throw the ball that high."

"Why not?" said Tiny, as he delivered another, it fell like a mortar round on home plate. "Looks like strike two," he bellowed.

"It's against the rules to throw that high. You can't do it."

"We're playin' Asian rules here, Sarge. Anything goes in Asian rules," said Tiny with a blithe grin. The third pitch plummeted almost straight down through the strike zone. "Looks like strike three to me."

"You can't do this! You're cheatin' and ya know it." Discontent stirred on the REMF bench.

Unaffected, Tiny continued dropping mortar shots on home plate.

The batter had not swung yet.

The giant took a few menacing steps toward him. "Hey, you gotta swing at these pitches, they're strikes!"

The batter looked intimidated.

First Sergeant fumed and paced in front of his bench.

Tiny continued to demand that the batter swing.

"Time out! Time out!" Sarge walked toward Tiny. "Now listen, you *gotta* decrease the arc on those pitches. This isn't right!"

Tiny sneered, put his glove on his hip and looked at First Sergeant. "Don't tell me you're goin' to try and change the rules after the game starts, Sarge. That's bush league."

"I didn't know you was gonna cheat."

"Show me where it says I gotta pitch a certain way. This is Asian ball, Sarge, it's like everything else, ya gotta adapt to the situation, Sarge. Ya gotta adapt!"

"Okay, Tiny, if you're gonna throw those high bombs, my pitcher is gonna do the same." The REMF pitcher on the bench gave the first sergeant a doubtful look.

"Fine," said Tiny. "Long as he throws strikes, he can throw it as high as he wants."

"Two can play at that game!" First Sergeant walked away frustrated. His men grumbled about Tiny getting away with one.

Eventually the batter took some half-hearted swings. The pitches were around the strike zone, but they fell straight down, picking up speed. Contact would take great timing.

Tiny struck out the side.

The REMFs were talking revenge and looking angry as the two sides exchanged gloves.

The grunts gathered around Tiny, gleaning courage from his swagger. "Try to hit ground balls, guys. Just get the ball in play, make 'em throw you out. If any of you can get on, I'll drive you in. Here's the batting order: Marty, Huddle, Laughton, myself, Eberhardt, Lansky, Massey, Arocha, and Chief. Get out there, Allen, and swing eeeezy."

The REMF pitcher tried to throw pitches with a high arc. They were not close to the plate.

When one went over the catcher's head, Tiny yelled, "Hey, ya better adjust for windage!"

The pitcher was upset by his inability to get the ball near home plate.

The grunts gave him a hard time.

After seven wild pitches, the arc on his throw decreased enough for Marty to swing at it. He missed.

"Slow down," yelled Tiny. "Swing eeeezy."

He made contact with the next pitch, sending it at the third baseman. The ball bounced high off the hard dirt. The infielder charged the ball then froze. He leaped, catching half the ball in his webbing. The ball spun out, falling behind him.

Marty closed on first as the third baseman scrambled for the ball. A high, desperate throw sailed over the first baseman's glove. Marty was on third base by the time the ball was back in play.

First Sergeant was off the bench berating his players. Some of the REMFs yelled at the third baseman who was mad and embarrassed.

Tiny smiled and the grunt bench laughed and cheered.

Huddle hit a grounder to the shortstop who threw him out. The pitcher settled down. He got Laughton to pop up to the catcher. Marty was still on third.

Tiny stepped up to the plate, bat looking small in his hands.

Lansky could hear the *whooshing* sound it made, cutting the air, on several vicious practice swings.

Tiny coiled into his ready position with the bat waving slightly. He took the first pitch, and then stepped out. When he stepped back in, he cocked the bat over his head, fingers twitching the handle. He took another pitch.

Lansky could see the glare in his eye as he stepped in before the third delivery. Tiny took several slow deliberate practice swings before going into his coil, exaggerating the follow-through, pointing the bat up and out.

The outfielders backed up to the concertina wire serving as an outfield fence. They didn't back up far enough.

Tiny swung smoothly at the next pitch. The ball accelerated off the bat, following a high trajectory toward centerfield.

As it slowed and began its descent, all eyes focused on the centerfielder. He shuffled back as far as he could. It looked like he might have a play. But then he turned to watch the ball bounce off the ground, fifteen feet into the wire. Tiny was crossing second base by the time the ball landed.

The early innings followed the same course. Tiny kept throwing his twenty-meter pitches, which the REMFs had trouble hitting. Some did connect for weak grounders. Tiny dashed around the infield snagging the balls and throwing base runners out.

In his next at bat, Tiny took the pitcher's glove off with a line drive, but was stranded at first because no one could drive him in. In the fourth inning, he hit another long home run with a man on to make the score 4-0.

The REMFs improved their timing during the bottom of the fifth.

A high fly ball came out to leftfield. Lansky took a step forward then turned and ran hard. The ball was over his head curving right. He picked up its flight, stopped, then backpedaled, the ball smacked into his glove.

Huddle yelled from centerfield, "Had that one surrounded, hey, L-a-a-n-s-k-e-e-e!"

He threw the ball back into the infield with a smile on his face.

The REMFs scored a run on several ground ball singles. A confident tone rose in their chatter as they took the field for the last inning.

In the grunt half of the sixth inning, Lansky smacked a ground rule double into the wire.

It was the last ball they had so play was stopped for ten minutes while one of the outfielders picked his way through the wire to retrieve the ball.

The wait cooled the grunts down. Massey flew out to left. Arocha grounded out, and Chief struck out.

Tiny tried to cross up the REMFs in the bottom of the sixth by lowering the trajectory on his pitch. The batter hit it well over Lansky's head for a home run.

Play was stopped again to retrieve the ball.

A pop fly gave the grunts one out, but then two REMFs singled. This brought the tying run to the plate with the score 4–2.

A cheer arose from the home team bench. First Sergeant became animated, jeering at his opponents.

Tiny went back to the high arcing pitch. The grunts slipped into tactical mode, single-minded, one with common purpose. A cohesive force welded together by the heat of battle.

The next pitch fell out of the sky toward home plate.

A hard ground ball skipped by Tiny, headed for Laughton at shortstop. He gloved it gracefully in a sliding motion to his left. Laughton shoveled the ball toward Marty whose right foot dropped on the second base board. He threw sidearm toward first, a low throw, forcing the base runner down, letting the ball breeze overhead, thumping into Massey's outstretched glove at first, and beating the runner by two steps.

The grunts erupted, jumping on Tiny and shouting in each other's faces. Some of them turned and started pelting the REMFs with their own gloves.

An angry exchange of words started until Tiny stepped in. "Knock it off!"

They did.

"We'll show respect and remain disciplined."

Lansky saw a look of admiration on First Sergeant's face. He stood waiting to talk to Tiny.

The grunts passed him on the way back to the barracks, loud and happy.

Tiny walked toward First Sergeant. "Hey, Sarge, we played fuck-around-with-ya today. How come you're not mad?"

"Oh, I was mad as hell, you son-of-a-bitch. I know you got over on me. But then . . . how do I say it?"

"I don't know. How do you say what?"

"Well, something happened today to change my opinion of you guys. I was impressed with how you hung together."

"We hang together in a fight, Sarge."

"Yeah, you really do."

"But check those same guys out tonight after they've had a bunch a beer. Someone will say something, and the other guy will take a swing at him. It's helter-skelter after that."

"Wish my group could function at a high level when they needed to. I was bullshittin' you before. Things aren't always so great with these men in the rear. They whine a lot, and they're selfish. Sometimes they're not the best soldiers. I was hopin' softball would build teamwork. So far it hasn't."

"Maybe you should send them to the bush for a few missions." Tiny smiled.

First Sergeant laughed. "That thought has occurred to me." They walked toward the noisy barracks. "But then I wouldn't have anyone back here to take showers, or play softball."

Tiny chuckled.

"Beers on me at the NCO club tonight, Tiny."

"See you there."

CHAPTER 34

August 9, 1972

Dawn glowed gray against the stark trees.

Lansky woke in a fevered sweat to stand the last watch on the last night his platoon would spend in the bush.

Five companies of 3rd Battalion, 20th Infantry, 195th Brigade would be lifting out for the final time.

They were going home.

Lansky felt the melancholy of change. This life must die so a new one could be born.

Scanning the land, Lansky tried to discover the source of his dysphoria. This harsh strange place, so unforgiving. His emotions surprised him.

Sunlight brought the terrain into focus. Well-worn footpaths curled off through the trees. He'd walked trails like those so long they seemed like home. *What will I do after the last walk?*

Lansky, the prisoner, was acclimated to his confinement and not anxious to leave his jail. A whole new life in a whole new world loomed along the horizon. It was this beginning that made him cling to the end.

A distant dull explosion jolted him from his pensive mood.

Down on one knee slowly scanning the foreground, comfortable, weapon in hand, his trigger finger pushed safety to semi, feeling ready, grateful for this return to the familiar. His attention locked on the hundred meters in front of him.

Tiny and LT walked up behind Lansky. He answered the question they were about to ask. "Wasn't one of our claymores, too far out, it sounded like a frag."

"Any movement?" asked LT.

"Nothing."

"This makes things complicated, don't it, Tiny?"

"You mean because we're going to have to send out another patrol?"

LT nodded. He dreaded asking men to go out on patrol, on this the last day. It was a day he had hoped would involve no risk. Looking at Tiny, he wondered if he should forget the request he was about to make.

"Gotta get out there and poke around, LT, don't want Charlie sneaking up on us when we're lifting out," said Tiny.

Lansky could see the conflict on LT's face, a moment of hesitation.

"You're right." LT looked at Tiny, no conviction in his words. "I'll make this voluntary. See who you can find."

"I'll go!"

"Gung-ho on the last day, Lansky?"

"Yeah, I'm ready. I'm finally ready to be in the army."

LT and Tiny disappeared through the bush back toward the platoon area. Lansky decided to wait at the guard position for the patrol to assemble. Tiny and LT soon returned with a few men.

Pulling the bolt back on his weapon, Lansky checked the round in the chamber and made a visual inspection of the grenades on his web gear.

Marty broke through the brush with his radio. "Why you goin', Lansky?" he whispered. "I'm RTO today."

"I'm gung-ho."

LT smiled at Lansky, the ironist.

Huddle emerged with bandoliers across his chest and around his waist. He stood silently, reading his Bible.

Eberhardt came from behind and poked his rifle barrel into the back of Huddle's knee, causing it to collapse.

After regaining his balance, Huddle swatted his tormentor with The Book. It flew out of his hand and landed open on the trail.

"You hit me with a Bible?" Eberhardt laughed. "You can't smack nobody with the Bible."

Huddle ignored him, fixing his eye on the page the Bible had opened to.

"Uh-huh, okay, The Book opened itself to the thirty-seventh Psalm. That tears it. Mr. Neverhard, you are at the crossroads! Get ready, 'cause you goin' to get pitched a wang dang doodle 'fore this day is done!"

He snatched his Bible off the trail with unusual energy, dusted it off, and slid it into the cargo pocket of his fatigue pants. Pulling the charging handle back on his M-16, he released a round into the chamber. Standing tall, he announced, "I am ready for the last patrol."

Tiny turned on the distraction. "Knock it off. Noise discipline from now on."

They were both quiet.

Laughton pushed through the bush to the trail. He exchanged a surprised look with Lansky, then smiled a bright white, perfect denture grin.

Lansky looked at LT. This would be their last patrol together. LT dropped his officer's stony façade. They stood silently in mutual respect.

"What ta hell ya gonna do, kiss each other?" said Tiny. "Let's get this one over with."

The shrubbery parted again, Chief formed the end of the line. All eyes were on the trail now.

Tiny began the patrol at a brisk pace. After a few minutes, he resumed his cautious, quiet movement. They walked for over an hour along the forest path.

The woods thinned, palm trees came into view.

A familiar rhythm developed as Lansky walked along the worn, brown trail. He heard an internal melody at the edge of consciousness, keeping time with his boot strides.

LT stopped so suddenly Marty bumped into him. They knelt, looking at a body lying across the trail. Tiny turned to look at LT. "I'm goin'. Cover me."

The lieutenant nodded. Crawling off the trail, Tiny started a long circle around the body. They dispersed to the sparse cover on either side of the path watching for Tiny. The giant man was invisible. Even in this relatively open land, he moved undetected.

After ten minutes, he low-crawled out from behind a tree, stood, pointed his weapon at the body then edged in, poking it several times, satisfied, waving everyone up.

A teenage boy had tripped a wire, flies buzzed angrily at the raw meat of his wounds, the body bloated turning gray, yet the boy's face was peaceful and content.

"What'd the kid walk into?" asked Huddle.

"He tripped a wire attached to a baseball frag over here," said Tiny, indicating the side of the trail from which the explosion had come. His rifle barrel swung across the path, pointing at the small wooden peg with wire coiled around it. "Kid walked right into what was meant for us."

"Action is picking up around here," said the lieutenant to no one. "Can't Charlie wait one more day?"

"He probably knows we're leaving, LT," said Tiny. "He'll get bolder now."

"Yeah," the lieutenant agreed. "Heavy fighting going on up north. Three NVA divisions with armor and artillery crossed the DMZ last week. That will stir up the local VC. They say there's a couple hundred thousand refugees in Da Nang."

"Three divisions of the North Vietnamese Army, thirty-five miles to our north?" Tiny was surprised.

"Yeah, last I heard ARVN has them held up in front of Hue. The B-52s are chewing up the NVA."

"That's going to piss off Charlie," Tiny responded.

LT nodded his head thoughtfully.

"What we gonna do with this kid, LT?"

"Nothing. His people will be along soon. Let's move on."

Tiny stepped out at point, his pace slow and cautious.

They passed through groves of banana and tamarind trees. At one time this land had been highly cultivated, but now underbrush had begun its reclamation.

After another hour, they came to a rice paddy. The men moved off-trail to the nearest cover while LT and Tiny conferred.

Tiny smiled at LT. "Gonna cross the paddy, Lootenaant?"

The LT looked at the men waiting on his decision. The burden of command weighed more heavily on him today than any other in recent memory. He got out his map and looked at it for a long time.

"Well . . ." He checked his watch. "If we cross this paddy, we've completed a circle around the night logger. Lift-out is in two hours. Looks like the shortest distance." LT looked to Tiny for advice.

Tiny turned away from LT and looked out into the paddy. He sensed danger. His gut gave him a solid warning to avoid it. Yet, he knew this was the last day, the last patrol, and the last paddy. The last shot of adrenaline combat always released in him, his last chance at the experience, which he considered semi-orgasmic, the last opportunity in his life to be in *his* element.

He needed it one more time. "Hate to be late for the lift-out, Lootenaant. Let's just get across this paddy and head home." Tiny only referred to him as "Lootenaant" when he was being sarcastic.

This mixed message confounded LT's ability to make a decision. The men were forming on the trail, anxious to finish. LT looked at his watch then at Tiny's smile. "Kick us off, Tiny. Let's go."

Lansky waited near the end of the column, ready to go.

"Hey, Lansky," whispered Chief.

"Huh?" Lansky was surprised that Chief was talking.

"You got any toilet paper?"

"You're *talking* to *me*?"

"I gotta take a crap. You got ass wipe?"

"Yeah, here." Lansky pulled a small roll of toilet paper from the hip pocket of his fatigue pants.

"Watch the trail for me, will ya?"

"Okay, I'm gonna tell the lieutenant to hold up."

"No! Don't tell no one." Chief was embarrassed. "Just take a minute." He hustled several yards off the trail.

Lansky looked down the trail anxiously, as the patrol headed out into the paddy. They didn't know he and Chief were left behind. This broke the unit pattern of communication and support.

Chief was true to his word and took only a minute. He walked out of the banana shrubs, smiling shyly.

"Thanks, Lansky, for covering my butt." His eyes glimmered.

Lansky was intent on catching up with the others, but Chief's comment stopped him. "Chief! You're joking?"

The Native American smiled, eyes intent on the paddy, wanting to catch up with the patrol.

Lansky watched the smile pinch off Chief's face as the firing started.

A powerful weapon pounded the paddy.

The patrol dove behind the paddy dike, splashing into the fetid water as the unseen gunner found their range.

Chief and Lansky watched helplessly as the high-caliber automatic weapon carved up the dike and paddy water. Violent geysers shot into the air. Huge clods of moist soil exploded all around the patrol.

The men crept to the top of the dike to return fire, but heavy spasms of machine-gun rounds drove them down repeatedly.

Chief pointed through the palm and banana trees bordering the paddy. They couldn't see the gun, but the loud report identified its general location.

Chief ran bent over, to the first palm tree off the trail. Lansky followed. There was room for both of them to kneel behind the tree and scan the next hundred meters.

Lansky surprised himself by taking off for the next patch of cover. He fell behind a clump of banana plants. Chief soon hit the ground next to him.

"You ready for this, Lansky?"

"I'm not sure. I was hoping to avoid this situation, actually."

"Don't worry, Lansky. I'm a Salt River Pima Warrior. My ancestors fought the Apache. We've defended our land for two thousand years. I can take care of this."

"Okay."

"I'm going to ask two things of you."

"What things?"

"First of all, don't call me Chief. My name is Nuñez, Israel Nuñez."

"Sorry. Can comply."

"Forget it, Lansky. When I saw your spirit at the tiger purification ceremony, I knew we were drawn together for a purpose."

"You saw my dragon?"

"Your spirit revealed itself to me as a dragon. It has guided us to this place to get that machine gun. Also, I owe you a favor."

"How's that?"

"You saved me from doing something terrible up on Hill Two-Sixty-Six. So, I'm going to give you the easy part."

"What's that?"

"We're going to crawl up to the next line of trees. The gun is right on the other side. You're going to stay there. I'm crawling behind them. Two minutes later you'll do something distracting. I'll take them out."

They crawled silently up behind the banana trees. Nuñez pointed at Lansky's watch, held up two fingers then crawled away along the tree line, curving out of sight.

Lansky was close enough to hear the heavy brass shell casings *ping* on the ground each time the gun fired.

He felt his body harden with paralyzing fear. Pressure was choking off the flow of blood to his brain. Consciousness was fading. His vision dimmed. The sound of the gun receded. His head, suddenly too heavy to hold up, turned toward the paddy just before it welded itself to his forearm. Barely conscious, eyes on the dike protecting the patrol, he watched tracers fly.

Suddenly there was movement in the paddy. Tiny ran across a dike perpendicular to the one where the patrol had walked.

Seeing Tiny broke the weld. Lansky's head jerked up. Stiffness in his neck made it a major effort.

Tracers arced toward Tiny but arrived too late. He disappeared behind the dike.

A long angry burst blasted the dike uselessly. The gun jammed with a loud *clang*.

Lansky heard excited voices jabbering on the other side of the banana plants. The gunner wrenched the bolt forward and back to clear the jam.

Huddle flopped out of the far paddy and joined Tiny by leaping across the dike.

The bolt banged forward as Laughton jumped out of the water, trying to follow Tiny and Huddle.

A short but accurate burst bracketed Laughton's legs. One of the rounds made contact, taking his legs from under him. He spiraled head over heels onto the broad paddy dike. His weapon turned in the air, landing in the water.

Small waves disturbed the paddy water in front of Laughton.

As the gunner fired a long burst at Laughton, a shimmering mirage rose in front of the dike.

The dragon spread his wings to protect Laughton. Hot rounds sparked on the armored scales of the dragon's body and neck.

Huddle leapt from the paddy and began dragging Laughton toward the water.

Another burst from the gun arced toward Huddle.

The rounds flashed on the dragon's right wing. A nimbus of golden light pulsed from the dragon's head. Then the beast faded, becoming hazy, sinking into the water, disappearing as quickly as it had risen.

Huddle had Laughton safely behind the dike.

Green tracers ripped the paddy wall and the water behind it.

The dragon's appearance startled Lansky. The scene brightened. The sound of the gun returned to full intensity. White light exploded in his brain.

Lansky crept into the clump of banana plants. He saw an arm feeding an ammo belt into the gun.

On his feet, Lansky shouted. "You assholes! You shot my dragon!" Finger flipped safety to semi. A three-shot burst. Lansky's loose rounds flew over the heads of the gun crew.

The gun stopped chugging. Shocked expressions. They couldn't believe their eyes, confused by the sight of Lansky standing fifteen yards away.

Another three rounds. They ducked beneath the rim of the gun pit.

"You bastards! You shot Laughton! You shot my dragon! Now, what am I supposed to do?" Lansky screamed.

He sprinted back toward the main trail firing three-shot bursts at the gun pit over his shoulder.

The rattle of AK-47s being picked up came to his ear.

Lansky's weapon emptied with a click as he dove behind a ylang-ylang tree. AK rounds zipped through the leaves above his head, releasing a sweet perfume.

Nuñez was forty yards behind the VC, kneeling in a comfortable firing position.

The three gunners stood to shoot at Lansky.

This gave Nuñez a perfect sight picture: dead, solid, perfect. He would take them left to right. Safety off, finger on trigger, a gentle squeeze.

The gunner closest to Lansky went down hard. The other two froze. Blood and brain matter splattered their left side. The man in the middle dropped, shot through the neck. The third dove for the bottom of the pit.

Nuñez came out of the banana trees, firing a short burst. Dirt danced on the gun-pit rim. He dashed to easy grenade range. Fired again. Snapping a grenade from his web gear, pulling the pin, releasing the spoon, waiting a second before lobbing the grenade into the pit. Shouldering his weapon. Firing to empty. Reloading as the grenade went off. *Wump!* Sprinting up the rim of the gun pit, weapon on auto, finger pressuring the trigger ready to empty his weapon in one burst, he jumped to a stop on the edge.

The mangled remains made him shudder.

He flipped his weapon to safety.

In the sudden silence, he took a moment to say a small prayer of gratitude to his ancestors.

Nuñez dropped into the gun pit touching each enemy with his rifle barrel.

Down in the paddy, Huddle was taking care of Laughton who had been hit in the same foot he'd crushed with the grenade launcher. Huddle wrapped a bandage over the top of Laughton's mangled boot. Laughton was writhing in pain, unable to hold his head out of the water. Huddle knelt in the water, bracing an arm and knee under him. "Take it easy now, Laughton, ol' boy . . . uh, I mean, man."

Laughton looked at him with a painful expression. "It's okay, Huddle."

When the big gun stopped firing at them, Tiny started peeking over the top of the dike. He noticed AK and M-16 fire.

Huddle yelled at Tiny. "Hey, call down to the lieutenant for a dust-off. We need to get Laughton to the doctor."

"Yeah." Tiny straightened, "Yo! Hey! E-L-L-L-T-E-E-E! Need a dust-off for Laughton! Foot's tore up!"

The lieutenant waved a positive response, then yelled back, "What they shooting at?"

"They switched to a target near them."

Their attention returned to the gun position. A grenade exploded with a quiet *shuuu*. A GI ran up on the lip of the gun pit, stood in the silence, and then jumped down into the pit.

Tiny stood. "Hey, Huddle, did you see that?"

Huddle stared ahead silently as he continued to hold Laughton. He did not respond. A tear rolled down his cheek.

"Kee-fuckin'-risst, it's Chief." Tiny was incredulous. "You stay with Laughton. I'm gonna dee-dee up there and help Chief." Tiny stepped out of the water, ran along the dike, then up through the palms, walking through the banana trees quietly and cautiously, closing on the gun position.

Lansky and Nuñez sat on the front of the gun pit, weapons in the dirt.

"How'd you do it, Chief?" Tiny stood before them.

"It's Nuñez," said Lansky. "His name is Israel Nuñez."

"Okay." Tiny walked up on the gun pit rim. Coppery saline odors of fresh blood made him wince. The big gun ticked and smoked. "Our shit was weak. They had high ground. We were outgunned. How'd you guys do it?"

Lansky said, "Nuñez took over and led the way. He got it done. But we had some spiritual help, didn't we, Nuñez?"

The Native American nodded in the affirmative.

"We all owe you our lives," said Tiny. "You saved our ass."

After the medevac bird took Laughton away, the whole patrol came up to the gun pit.

Lansky sat in the dirt, thunderstruck. Eberhardt pulled him up and slapped him on the back.

Everyone demanded a retelling of the story.

Lansky was able to recount the events in a shaky voice.

As Tiny listened, he put Nunez in an affectionate headlock. "So you stopped to take a crap. It put you in perfect position to flank the VC, classic infantry tactics there, Nunez. It's a classic, I tell ya! You saved our ass by taking a crap!"

LT looked relieved. "There's a silver star recommendation in this for you, Nunez. This was heroic beyond the call. Even Lansky is probably going to get a cluster on his bronze star."

Tiny said, "What about Huddle?"

"I'm putting Huddle in for a silver star, too. By the way, where is Huddle?"

At that moment, Huddle walked through the banana grove, covered in paddy mud, tears in his eyes, looking at Lansky.

Everyone stopped talking.

Lansky wasn't sure what was going on, so he walked toward his friend.

Huddle grabbed Lansky by the collar and began shaking him. "How come I'm alive, Lansky? How come?" His voice quivered with emotion.

"I don't have the words to explain it. I don't know what to tell you." Lansky could hardly speak.

"You fucking know, Lansky! You fucking know! I think you know what's going on. Tell me why I ain't dead!"

Lansky reached his arms around Huddle and embraced him. Huddle dropped his hands, and they hugged. Both men cried.

Huddle continued, "I saw those rounds inbound. That gunner had me zeroed. I knew I was dead. How come I'm standin' here, Lansky?"

"My mind is gone, Huddle. I'm fried. We will talk sometime. It's going to take a while, but we will talk."

CHAPTER 35

August 3, 1973

In August of 1972, the 195th Brigade left Vietnam one week after the last patrol.

Lansky spent three weeks in the army hospital at Fort Hood, Texas, being treated for saw grass infections.

He had long hours alone in the sterile, quiet hospital environment to reflect on the last patrol. Visceral images from the intense little battle kept coming at him, the smell of blood, his part in the kill shots, and the grisly remains.

Hot rounds had hit his dragon hard. *How will I go on without my warrior shield? Is my gate to the spiritual world now closed?*

Whoever had sent this dragon would have to answer these questions. He began the process of learning how to face life without his dragon.

Lansky was discharged from the army in January of 1973. He returned to Wisconsin and enrolled in the graduate school of education at the university. Sitting in the library stacks, attempting to focus on educational research, the last patrol lurked on the periphery, ambushing his ability to stay on task.

Huddle wrote him a letter, repeating his question about the last patrol: "What stopped those heavy rounds from hitting me and Laughton? That gunner had us zeroed. I could hear the impact in front of us. But when I looked up, nothing was there. How could nothing stop high caliber rounds?"

Lansky remembered the promise he had made to his buddy. They needed to talk about the last patrol.

He convinced Huddle to vacation with him in southern Mexico. About a year after the last patrol, they landed in Puerto Angel, Oaxaca. It was a relief to see Huddle. Lansky enjoyed his droll sensibility. Sitting in the open-air, thatched-roof restaurant, bare feet in warm sand, Lansky smiled at his old friend.

"Ya know, Lansky, don't think I ever told you 'bout my third favorite position."

"Vernon!" Huddle's new wife seemed embarrassed.

"Don't pay no never mind, Dorabelle. It's not about that."

"Can't believe I know this guy better than you do, Dorey." Lansky leaned forward in his cabana chair. "Let me review Vernon Huddle's Hierarchy of Favorite Positions. Number one is lying down. Number two is sitting up after lying down, and now we observe position number three, sitting up to eat after lying down."

"'At's right." Huddle smiled as he forked red snapper into his mouth, and washed it down with a long draft of beer. "Sounds kina scientific when Lansky says it."

"Lately, that's his first favorite position," said his slender, red-haired wife sliding an arm around his neck, smiling affectionately. Her other hand found the paunch hanging over his swimsuit. Shaking the bulge gently, she nibbled on his ear.

"Cut that out now, Dorabelle. Ah don't like that stuff in public." He looked down at his belly. "Ever since ah got out of the army and married you, that thing keeps on growin."

"Honey, that ain't the only thing you got growing down there." Covering her mouth, she snickered, turning a soft pink.

Sheila, the leggy brunette with indigo eyes, shared Dorabelle's laugh. "Well, this one hasn't put on much weight. Look at him."

"You are too skinny," said Dorabelle.

Lansky looked defensively at Sheila and Dorabelle. "I've put on twelve pounds since I got out of the army."

"Ya, and I know where he puts it," said Shelia.

The women broke out in a tipsy giggle then slapped hands.

"Boa, boa, boa, give you women a few margaritas and it's circus time." Huddle laughed at the two women. "C'mon, Lansky. Let's head for the water."

Dorabelle became serious. "But, Vernon, honey, are you sure you should go in the water after eating?"

"Ah'm okay. I made it through Vietnam. Ah can make it out ta that little old bay and do some snorklin'. Right, Lansky?"

"Can do, Señora! Dos Tecate, por favor."

"Sí, dos." The teenage girl lingering by their table hurried off to get more beer.

Lansky dropped several blue bills on the table.

"Dorabelle and I are going to have another margarita."

"That's right, Shelia! Vernon, gimme some more of that funny money, honey."

The women chuckled.

"Let's get outta here, Lansky. Too goofy for me." Huddle put money on the table.

They gathered their snorkeling gear and walked toward the beach. "Lansky, when you called me up and told me 'bout this deal, I thought you was nuts. But I've enjoyed it, really, man, gimme five." They slapped hands. "How'd you find this place?" Huddle seemed curious.

"Used to come down here when I was an undergrad, before I was in the army."

"Only thing that bothered me was that flight from Oaxaca." Huddle took a long drink of beer.

"Better than an eight-hour bus ride down the mountains, with a chicken in your lap."

Huddle smiled. "Well, wasn't the flight that bothered me so much, it was the pilot not looking at the runway when he was landing. He was eyein' Sheila's dress instead of the airstrip."

"That dress got a lot of attention." Lansky grinned. "The pigs on the runway bothered me more. What if a pig ran in front of the plane when we were landing?"

Huddle laughed. "Guess there would be a barbecue."

On the beach now, they dropped their gear and scanned the tiny bay. Desert rock and scrub surrounded the blue water. Gentle waves crashed.

"Lansky, that was one hell of a story you told me when we walked down the beach this morning." Huddle was unusually emphatic.

"Wouldn't blame you for calling me crazy." Lansky looked down at the sand.

"Blows my mind, takes me round a sharp corner on two wheels." Huddle seemed confused. "I been looking for the faith to believe it . . . but . . . like I say . . . blows my mind."

"I can remember feeling the same when I first saw it." Lansky was abashed. "But I have no reason to lie. I'm telling you what I saw."

"You're sure you wasn't seeing things? C'mon, it's a lot to swallow. A dragon rises out of the rice paddy to take hot rounds intended for me." Huddle kicked the sand, doubtful.

Lansky moved closer to Huddle. "I've spent countless hours wrestling with the presence of a dragon during my tour. It showed up at the beginning and was there on the last patrol. I've never had an experience like it. Thinking about it burned me out. I gave up." Lansky looked hopeful. "Eventually, I let my faith in the dragon rest right next to my doubts about it. I quit trying to control it and stopped passing judgment on myself. I just let it flow wherever it wanted to go—my gift and a burden from the universe. Mostly, it was good. The dragon was my warrior shield. On that day, it protected you also. Might have sacrificed itself to save you."

Hesitating here, Lansky, looked out to sea, then went on. "Once I was able to accept my doubt and faith as normal, I found contentment and gave up trying to think my way through to perfect knowledge on the existence or nonexistence of the dragon. It always made me feel better. It relieved my burden. Even if it was a delusion, it helped me. I didn't want to mess that up."

"Well, I don't know. I'm not there yet. My brain is still fighting it." Huddle stood hands on hips, deep in thought.

"A reasonable person would doubt my dragon story," said Lansky. "But I've found that faith tells us what our senses can't see. Faith is above and beyond the senses, not contrary to them. So anyone believing in my dragon has to take that leap of faith, but I'm not going to try to make you jump."

"Uh-huh, reminds me of a dream I had a while back when I fell asleep early one morning after spending the whole night drinking and thinking about the last patrol." Huddle's voice rose. "In my dream, I was wandering lost and drunk down some highway late at night. Suddenly a huge semi went by me at high speed with its lights off. It wailed down the road making that highway sound. Came so close it ruffled my clothes. Never saw it but I sure felt it. Brought me bolt upright from a dead sleep." Huddle seemed frightened. "Took me a couple days to figure out it was just a dream, yet it seemed so real, spooked me good."

Lansky nodded his head. "It might take you a while to figure out what's going on inside. But until then, look around, man, you're standing on a beautiful beach sipping a cool one. Your cute wife is yucking it up over margaritas in the cabana behind us. It's not a dream. You're alive! Thank God or angels or fate. Write it off as a strange episode in your soul's mysterious journey. Or you could do what I did."

"What's that?" Huddle squinted into the sun.

"Admit it's beyond you and leave it there."

"I'll have to think on it. Talking to you helps even when you sound crazy. It's going to take a while. My mind gets so full with it." Huddle plunged on. "When I think about the last patrol, I feel like a quail sitting up in a mossy oak just before dawn on a winter morning, wondering if that sun is ever going to come up."

"It will come up, but not because you control it. Let it be. It's okay to not have it all figured out. Wait on your faith to grow and guide you." This thought gave Lansky a peaceful look.

"Yeah, guess I gotta wait. No choice. Like you say, it's beyond me."

"There you go."

"Still sounds crazy. Not ready to talk about the last patrol or dragons out loud. Don't want Dorey to think I'm goofy."

"Now, why would she ever think that?" Lansky laughed.

"Hey, I'm not the one that claims ta see dragons."

"That would be crazy me. I'm not ready to talk to outsiders about it either."

A thoughtful silence followed. A small sense of relief came over both men. Wading into the water, they began putting on their gear. Lansky spit into his mask and smushed it around.

"We're lucky, Huddle."

"We are, Lansky."

Fins on, masks on foreheads, they started paddle footing toward the deep.

Head up, Lansky looked out into the tiny bay on the Pacific Coast near the Honduran border. Aqua wavelets danced in the narrow inlet, rising and falling against the rocks. Small rollers washed the shore rhythmically.

"Midy purdy, pardner." Huddle seemed relieved.

"Yes, it is."

"Let's do it," said Huddle.

Masks down and snorkels in mouths, both men slid along the surface. The sun warmed their backs.

Lansky crawled along, the sea lifting then dropping him, now in deeper water the ocean floor falling away. It provided a yellow-white background for the multicolored fish darting in and out of the coral. Tiny rainbows moved along casually and alone. Others, in schools, marched lockstep, darting left and right in synchronized movement, fluorescent in the refracted light.

He dove at them. They scattered.

Lansky bobbed around the bay until the water began to darken with the passing of the sun.

Raising his head, he located Huddle and swam to him.

They treaded water watching coral divers load their boats.

"Let's head in, Lansky."

"Okay, I'm tired."

They were soon on the beach approaching the two women lying face down on a blanket. Heavy oil glossed their backs. Their bikini straps were undone. It seemed they were asleep.

The two men smiled at each other. Slowly, Huddle reached down and attempted to yank Dorabelle's top from under her. She clamped the strap down.

"Vernon, you thing, you!" she said.

A Mexican family nearby began to titter.

"Haw'd ja figer it was me, Dorabelle?"

"I know you, Vernon."

"Guess you do. Hey, les go, time for el siesta."

The women seemed sleepy and subdued as they gathered their things, then linked up arm-in-arm as they left the beach.

"Where you wanna go for dinner, Lansky?" Huddle looked at his buddy. "Wanna go back to that cantina where all them surfers hang out?"

"Nope, I'm tired of hearing those California jerks make jokes about the Midwest."

Huddle smiled. "S'pose we could go to that hotel where the French stay."

"Dorey and I want to go back there," said Sheila. "We wanted to watch the girl and two guys who are always there."

"They are funny, aren't they?" agreed Dorey.

"Yes, a real ménage á trois! They have the juiciest arguments. Wish I understood French a little better," said Sheila.

"Another thing we'd like to understand is what you guys are talking about when you're down on the beach. How about letting us in on your story?" Dorabelle asked this question quietly.

"Huh," said Huddle. "We ain't had no trouble findin' time ta talk so far."

"Well, we talk, but you guys never tell us anything." Dorabelle was curious. "We want to know how you became so close."

"You really don't tell us anything. We'd like to hear the story," said Sheila.

Dorabelle was less diplomatic. "Vernon, what happened in Vietnam?"

"Not now, Dorabelle. Hush up!"

"Don't hush me!"

"When we're ready to talk, we will," said Lansky.

Huddle's face twisted in mild anger. "It's not fit conversation for mixed company."

Sheila was vexed. "Why not?"

"It's too . . . too . . ." Huddle stalled.

"It's too complicated," Lansky finished his thought.

"'At's right. Thank you, too complicated."

Lansky spoke, "For some things, there are no words that can be said out loud. No words to share. We aren't ready."

They'd reached an impasse. The women felt they deserved to be told the story, but the men would not permit them inside their Vietnam discussion.

It was a silent walk back to the hotel. Their eyes were downcast, the elevated mood was gone, and it would be some time before it returned.

Later in the hotel room, Lansky and Sheila lay on the bed staring at the ceiling. Another siesta was passing like the rest. Physical intimacy came easy. Yet on this afternoon, something essential seemed lost. Its absence diminished the satisfaction of the act for both.

Sheila rolled onto Lansky's chest, wiggled against him, and smiled playfully. Her hand stroked his scalp.

"You're different, Ed."

"Yes."

"I knew you'd change. I thought it would be good. I hoped it would bring you out."

Lansky sighed. He made a clicking noise of frustration with his tongue.

"You're hurting, Ed." She looked sympathetic. "You're in pain, if you let it go, you'll feel better." She continued to softly stroke his scalp and forehead.

"Talking just isn't going to work out now, Sheila. It's too much to drag out." A hint of fear tinged his last word.

Lansky checked the clock. "It's almost time to meet Huddle for dinner. Let's get ready." Gently pushing Sheila aside, Lansky got off the bed and headed for the shower.

He paused before the door and looked back, the graceful curve of her body stretched across the bed, a soldier's dream. Her beauty beguiled him. When in her arms, he smelled spring rain, tasted her tender tears, and, at the ultimate moment, gained a fleeting glimpse of the everlasting light.

She offered unconditional love, a heart that ached for him. Her gentle femininity warmed the wintery shadow over his soul. If he accepted her devotion, he would never feel alone again. Sheila only asked that he share his thoughts and feelings with her.

But something deep inside refused to release its grip. Talking did not seem safe. He was not able to share his secret.

"Hey, you're wonderful, but I'm just not ready."

"When will you tell me, Ed? When can we talk?"

"It's going to take a while."

CHAPTER 36

June 14, 1975

A tornado had cut the land. Tall pines lay on their sides, tops in the water, roots in the air, wind-twisted evergreens tipped at odd angles. Debris marked a path of destruction along the lake.

Lansky wasn't prepared for this. During the long drive up, he'd pictured this Canadian canoe trip as an escape from that which stalked him.

Lansky hoped the sweat produced by his body pulling itself across the water would help him forget.

It felt good to stretch, pull, and release, like a machine, gaining a moment's peace. The gurgle and swish of the paddle added a melody to the rhythm of each stroke. His labor produced a comfortable, consuming hypnosis.

A cool breeze whipped across the twisted lake, Lansky shivered, his sweat suddenly dry, his hopes of escape gone.

Darkness approaching magnified the gnarled landscape.

A yellow-tailed hawk cleared the near tree line. Crows followed, cawing and squawking as they dived on the trespasser, pecking at him from above and below.

Lansky admired the hawk's courage, flying straight and steady while under attack. He would need the hawk's courage to face the abyss within. His repressed memories were flashing back at him. They came at odd times making it difficult to remain present.

Presently, life was good. Lansky enjoyed being a teacher of cognitively disabled students. He worked with a staff of attractive young women in a suburban school district. On weekends, he still saw a lot of his college friends. The farmhouse he lived in was set in a rolling section of wooded countryside.

But in his quiet moments alone, his secrets had become an abrasive irritant. There were moments when his heart became so full that if it were shaken by a careless word, he felt it might split open, its privacies spilled to the ground for all to examine.

Anxious, unable to sleep, he drank alone.

When the school semester ended in June, Lansky loaded his car with camping gear and secured his canoe on top. In the heat of the day, he headed north seeking the cooling shadows of the woods.

Now Lansky sat in that very canoe eyeing the north end of the twisted lake.

He'd decided to follow a compass heading rather than the conventional portage-and-lake zigzag, straight north. Since childhood, going north was a release from the difficulties of the day. Everyone was in a better mood up north, problems seemed to solve themselves. He needed that northerly solution now.

Lansky paddled to the shore and splashed into the icy water, numbing his legs. The canoe clunked and scraped against the surface of the Canadian Shield as he dragged it out of the water and walked slowly up the glacial boulder shore with his map and compass bag. Water ran down his pant legs and oozed from his shoes.

Studying, the map showed another lake to the north. He looked up, searching. Straight north was tamarack bogs and mosquitoes. To his right was a path through balsam and spruce. Lansky decided to compromise. Not straight north. Northerly.

Back at his canoe, he shouldered both packs, grabbed his paddles and humped up the path. His canvas tennis shoes squished across the golden pine needles through the Norway spruce and underbrush. Filling his lungs with the scent of pine renewed him. A gentle breeze sang in the tops of the trees, an aural sedative.

There was an hour of sunlight left.

Sweat broke out on his chest again. He felt better.

His dry shoes found the boulders emerging from the next lake.

He'd been lucky because the maps were often inaccurate. Sometimes his sense of orienteering was unreliable. But today he'd gone farther north, crossing four lakes traveling over fourteen miles.

Lansky dropped his packs and turned to retrieve his canoe and tent.

It was dark when his fire crackled to life, the flame silhouetting his tiny camp. Lonely loons on the lake were quiet now.

He'd put on socks, a sweatshirt, and an old windbreaker that smelled of last night's fire.

Lansky felt peaceful, reattached to the land. His fatigue was complete and good. He'd survived the troubling memories of the twisted lake. Pouring a second cup of whiskey from its plastic container, savoring the strong spirits odor, taking a sip, the bite and warmth satisfied.

He waited for the fire to burn down to coals. Even though he'd been hungry for hours, he was determined to go slow and take it easy.

Picking up a stick, Lansky stirred the coals, pushing them into a mound and smoothed off the top.

Reaching into his pack, he pulled out a nested stack of aluminum pots, several packages of ramen noodles, a crushed loaf of bread, and some cashews. Lansky poured water into the pot and set it on the mound of coals.

Waiting for the water to boil, he pulled a piece of flattened bread from the bag and ate it.

When the water boiled, he tore open the noodle bags and dumped their contents in his old camp pot. On his knees, he ripped the spice packets open, pouring the powder into the foaming water. He stirred patiently until the hard noodles softened.

His hunger grew. The aroma made the juices in his mouth flow. It was too hot. He would wait.

Lying back, he nibbled cashews and sipped whiskey. Cashews went well with whiskey.

He held a spoonful of broth in front of his mouth, then slurped it slowly. The pot cooled. Lifting it in his hands, he drank the broth and spooned the noodles. Lansky dipped bread in the remaining broth savoring the salty flavor.

Standing, he picked up his canteen and took a long drink of water.

His back and legs felt sore, the pain adding satisfaction to the meal. Lansky felt a sense of accomplishment in how far he'd come and the goodness of the day.

The vast wilderness had swallowed him. He had flowed with it—outside himself, detached—until he'd come to the twisted lake.

That was behind him for the moment. The whiskey made it seem distant.

Lansky gathered the old camp pot and his utensils then walked down the rock and began washing his dishes.

He looked up at the night sky, as his hands worked in the chilly water. Stars crowded the heavens, a white blur.

Finishing his dishes, Lansky stood, scanning constellations on the horizon. His eye stopped on the Big Dipper, tracing it up the handle, around the last two stars of the cup. The edge of the cup pointed at the North Star. Polaris.

It sure is bright. Polaris sure is bright.

He'd been watching it the last few evenings. Polaris standing motionless over the celestial pole. All the stars in the northern sky rotate around Polaris, a navigation guide since antiquity, always visible, steadfast, drawing Lansky ever north.

He needed a guiding star, a natural connection, something to replace the dragon, which had been his transcendent bridge. Facing life without it left Lansky in a spiritual void. There were times when he looked for the dragon, something to give him courage, something to nourish a sense of hope. But he saw no dragons in Wisconsin.

Back in Nam, the dragon would eventually show up and relieve his burden. Lansky vibrated with a positive spiritual energy at the sight of the dragon. But now it just seemed to be a useless memory.

Stripped of his warrior shield, cut off from the spiritual, denied access to knowledge of the ancients, the menace of his unresolved Vietnam memory grew. He was lost and confused.

Lansky decided to do what he had always done: admit it was beyond him and go on. Whoever had sent the dragon would decide what came next. He would wait for the next thing to happen. Whatever it was, he would accept it.

He continued his observation of Polaris. So bright, so comforting in its constancy, its beauty brought a moment's relief. Instinct had guided him to this position, standing under the boreal star.

Eventually, a vague sense of vertigo made him look away.

He turned to look at the dying embers. Walking toward the fire, he grabbed various lengths of wood from the pile he'd gleaned from the underbrush just before sunset. There was a lot of dead wood around. No one had camped here recently.

Cracking the dry wood over his knee made a loud report. It echoed off the rocky bank across the blackness. In the still of the wilderness, this sound seemed too loud. Lansky snapped a few more pieces, anxious to build the fire. The night was chilly.

He felt disoriented after looking at the North Star. A sense of isolation came over him, a twinge of fear.

Feeding the fire made it glow and crackle again. The logs popped and whistled as the moisture boiled from their veins.

Lansky built the fire up chasing the shadows back. The yellow perimeter crept out into the underbrush and up the tree trunks. It continued along the underside of the branches, outlining the pine needles.

He felt less isolated now and poured another drink.

Picking up his packs, Lansky walked toward the perimeter of the firelight. He eyed one of the thicker balsam branches. It was his custom to hang his packs in a tree away from camp.

As Lansky waded through the first layer of underbrush, something at his feet sprang up and scurried away. He jumped back. The creature rattled the brush far off into the void, probably a muskrat or some little varmint attracted by the fire. It startled him. This was the first night visitor on the seven days of his trip.

Lansky stepped toward the tree and used a short length of rope to hoist the packs up over his head.

The fear faded. Lansky smiled.

Turning toward the fire, another sound made him hesitate. A

sound from deep in the woods came to his ears. The sound of a branch breaking lasted a few seconds. He wondered about it as he walked back toward camp.

The fire was friendly, inviting him to stay up for a while.

Lansky's hatchet made short work of the longer pieces of wood now stacked by the fire. He had enough for another hour. That would be plenty of time.

Getting comfortable, Lansky studied the flames and reviewed the day. He'd come a long way, but not far enough. The twisted lake had been there waiting. He was having second thoughts about the trip now that the phantom had found him. No matter how far he'd traveled or how much he had sweated, it was there.

This was not going away. It was time to face his issues. They seemed so out of place, half a world away from their origin.

He felt himself penetrating layers of awareness he'd not experienced since his army days. Ahead, he sensed a scary trail of emotion. Some of his experiences in Vietnam had been so shocking that his mind had snapped shut to protect the soft underbelly of his consciousness. Once shut, the vicious stimuli bounced off. At least he had thought they bounced off. His subconscious had recorded it all and continued to play it back.

The dragon couldn't be expected to carry it all away.

He'd spent a lot of time turning the volume down on these recordings. It seemed a necessary defense mechanism for the time.

Yet, times were changing. He wasn't there anymore; he was here. Being here included being in touch with his feelings.

Talking to Huddle helped, but he was way down South.

Sheila tried to help him find his way, but he never gave her a chance. So it left him alone to face it all, to accept what had happened.

When Lansky first got home, people always asked, "What did you see over there?" or "Were you in the fighting?" Those questions made him mute. He'd look off.

People thought him odd. Any answer brought a painful release of emotion. He'd stumble and stutter for an answer. "Ah . . . no, not really."

Tactful types would change the subject. Others pressed on.

It hurt. For a while, he wouldn't admit he was a Vietnam veteran. That didn't work.

Lansky had retreated as far as he could go. It was time to face up to what happened and start talking about it, get the energy flowing to the positive. He was taking his stand.

The sound Lansky heard at that point seemed to be coming from deep within his mind, but he soon realized something was galloping through the trees.

He wasn't expecting it this suddenly. It was surprising to hear the form it had assumed—galloping hooves. Snapping branches brought him back to the conscious level. Lansky looked around now, suddenly alert. This was not his imagination. Heavy hooves pounded the ground out in the timber. He heard the *crack* and *whoosh* of branches being thrown back. A large and powerful beast moved carelessly through the undergrowth smashing all obstructions.

First, it approached then moved away.

On some of the closer passes, Lansky heard deep and earthy snorts. The sound was primitive and aroused. Stopping briefly, a guttural grunt, then tearing off blindly, walloping the brush and splashing water, on a distant loop away from the fire.

By this time, Lansky was on his feet. More confused than frightened, he put the rest of the stacked wood in the fire and grabbed the hatchet. Growing flames brightened the scene. He stood now, arms at his sides, facing the darkness.

The sound turned toward him. Lansky shifted his weight. *Not long now*, he thought. The gallop slowed just outside the perimeter of light. Lansky stared into the dark.

A long massive head penetrated the light, suspended in the air higher than his packs.

As it emerged, Lansky said, "I was hoping you'd show up. I didn't know you'd be here so soon. I see you're no longer a dragon."

The head moved closer, revealing a broad shelf of antlers, a massive chest, and stilt-like legs. Large eyes reflected the campfire.

Lansky noticed a row of dimpled perforations stitching the moose's chest. The bullet wounds had healed but left the hide and fur irregular and bumpy.

"Looks like you've recovered. I'm so glad you survived." Lansky smiled. "Seeing you here makes me feel a lot better."

The moose lowered his head then raised it, snorting mightily. Lansky watched the nostrils quiver and flare. The front right leg scraped the rock with a heavy hoof.

They stared at each other for a long time.

"You've come a long way for this visit. Hope it wasn't too much trouble. Your presence is my deliverance. It makes me feel good to see that you are there, not here." Lansky pointed to his head. "What a relief."

Lansky pounded his fist gently over his heart, saluting the moose. "You are also here, forever, where you belong." Lansky held the salute.

A throaty bass vibration pulsed from deep within the moose's being. Eventually, he turned and galloped away breaking brush out into the woods.

Heart pounding, Lansky chuckled, and then laughed, louder and louder, until the sound filled the lake with reverberation. The laughter was sustained for a long time. He laughed until his sides ached.

His laugh became a cry. Lansky cried until he was spent. It had been a long time since he had cried like that, a sweet release. He tasted his tears.

Breathing easier, his burden released, he was deeply grateful for the moose's intervention.

At water's edge now, with a feeling of well-being, he gazed skyward. The sweep of galaxies unfolded in a new light across the vast moonless ebony. Embraced by the celestial ether, he felt a halo of ancient cosmic dust wrap around his shoulders.

Polaris burned bright overhead. Stella Polaris, luminous, always visible, fixed forever in perfect position to guide him.

Serenity.

Mind in radiant repose. Fearless. Open to the spirit of the universe. The spirit that he now knew had protected him all along. This was his home. Lansky felt like he belonged here.

GLOSSARY

Ao dai: Traditional Vietnamese long dress.

Actual: Radio term used to identify the speaker, usually the officer in charge. "This is Lonely Boy Actual," means the officer in charge is speaking.

AO: Area of operation, originally a map grid in which a military unit operated. Adapted by GIs to mean "my personal space."

Article 15: A non-judicial military punishment for minor rule infractions.

Big Honcho: Authority figure.

Blivet: A ten-gallon plastic bag with a spout.

Boonie cap: Circular soft cap that covered ears and forehead.

Cs or C-rats: C-Rations. Canned food.

Cack wheel: Code device that would scramble letters. Used to transmit sensitive information.

CONEX: Heavy metal shipping container used to transport heavy items. Then reused for many purposes in country.

Civvies: Civilian clothes.

Dap: Black power salute.

D-D: Department of Defense.

Dee dee mau: Vietnamese for "Get out of here."

DEROS: Date of return from overseas.

Dien cai dow: Means "very crazy."

Dinky dow: American pronunciation of the above term.

Draftee: A soldier who had been ordered by law into military service.

Deuce and a half: Large army truck with a load capacity of two and a half tons.

Dust-off: Medical evacuation.

11B10/Eleven Bravo Ten: Army MOS (Military Occupation Specialty) occupation code describing an infantry soldier.

EM Club: A social club for enlisted men.

FNG: Fucking new guy. Term of derision identifying a fresh replacement.

FO: Artillery forward observer. Artillery officer with an infantry unit who calls in fire missions.

Grunt: Infantry soldier.

HQ: Headquarters.

Huey: UH-1 helicopter.

KIA: Killed in action.

Klick: Kilometer.

KP: Kitchen police. A temporary kitchen helper.

LOACH: Light observation and command helicopter.

LBJ: Long Bin Jail. Prison for GIs in Saigon.

Lifer: Career soldier.

Lima Charlie: Radio term meaning "Loud and clear."

LRP: Long-range patrol packet. A freeze-dried meal.

LSA: Weapons lubricant.

LT: Most enlisted men addressed a lieutenant by using the abbreviation of his title.

MP: Military policeman.

Night logger: Night defensive position.

P (or MPC): GI slang for military pay certificates, money used in the war zone.

PRC-25: Army field radio.

RTO: Radio and telephone operator.

Sand patrol: Make work to keep new replacements busy by raking sand.

Shamming: Faking a disability to escape the bush.

Short: A short amount of time left in Vietnam.

Short round: An artillery shell that doesn't make it to its target, falling on friendly forces instead.

Stand-down: Time of rest and relaxation, in the rear area.

Sit rep: Radio term. Abbreviation for "situation report."

Spectre: C-130 gunship.

Ti ti: A small amount.

Two-oh-three: Grenade launcher.

Uncle Ho: North Vietnamese leader, Ho Chi Minh. Namesake for enemy forces resupply trail.

Willy Pete: White phosphorous.

ACKNOWLEDGMENTS

I got back from Vietnam, knowing that I had a story worth telling. Many people helped me learn how to write it, pitch it to an agent, and sell it to a publisher. I'd like to mention the names of those who went out of their way to help this book wind up in your hands.

Todd Hoffmeister took an interest in my writing early on. A patient teacher, my first editor, and a man possessed by a passion for the arts.

Kathleen Rodgers, this Texas sweetheart took me under her wing at one of my first Military Writers Society Conventions and opened doors for me that I would not have found on my own.

Jeanie Loiacono of The Loiacono Literary Agency put in countless hours on my manuscript. She guided my story toward a publishing contract in ways I didn't understand until after it happened.

Reverend Bill McDonald, founder of The Military Writers Society, was also a gracious early reader of my story. He was a Vietnam helicopter crew chief, and I respected his insight and found his review encouraging.

Joyce Gilmour, my hawk-eyed editor, infinitely patient and polite no matter how outrageously tangled the sentences that

I presented her were. I learned a lot from our dialogue. She nudged me toward credibility.

Jennifer Rude Klett, a gracious early reader who has become a friend, a fellow author willing to share her time and insight. Went out of her way as a newspaper reporter to tell the world about me, and my story.

Laurie Yingling, my sister, gifted with enough patience to set up my website twice, and guided me through the creation of my newsletter and blog. Did it all without spraining her eyerolling muscles too badly.

Andrea Greina, my precious daughter and graphic designer who enhanced old photos, created images that expressed important story content, and an actor in my book trailer. Rob, my first born son has been a patient traveling companion.

Also, I owe the stars to my parents and extended family. My mom and dad, my aunts and uncles have always been there for me. My brother-in-law Paul, also an early reader was willing to discuss my story.

And, I owe my life to my 196th Brigade brothers, who served with me.

Many more have made contributions to this book along the way, but my memory fails me at times, so let me conclude by saying thank you to all those who have taken time to help.

ABOUT THE AUTHOR

Robert Goswitz was born and raised in Chippewa Falls, Wisconsin, graduated from Milton College, and holds an MA in Education from the University of Wisconsin–Whitewater. He was drafted into the US Army in 1971 and served in Vietnam until 1972 on the 196th Brigade, the last American Army infantry unit deployed during that war. Goswitz was awarded the Combat Infantry Badge and the Bronze Star for his service. After the military, he was a special education teacher from 1975 until his retirement in 2007. Goswitz lives on the banks of the Bark River in Hartland, Wisconsin, with his wife, Jody.

INTEGRATED MEDIA

Find a full list of our authors and
titles at www.openroadmedia.com

FOLLOW US
@OpenRoadMedia

Made in the USA
Monee, IL
12 February 2024

53414560R00177